BLOODY
ARIA

Lorraine Ulrich

DREAMSPINNER
PRESS

Published by
DREAMSPINNER PRESS

5032 Capital Circle SW, Suite 2, PMB# 279, Tallahassee, FL 32305-7886 USA
http://www.dreamspinnerpress.com/

This is a work of fiction. Names, characters, places, and incidents either are the product of author imagination or are used fictitiously, and any resemblance to actual persons, living or dead, business establishments, events, or locales is entirely coincidental.

ISBN: 978-1-63216-486-5
Digital ISBN: 978-1-63216-487-2
Library of Congress Control Number: 2014952122
First Edition February 2015

Printed in the United States of America
∞
This paper meets the requirements of
ANSI/NISO Z39.48-1992 (Permanence of Paper).

To Maria, for being the first person all those years ago outside of my family to say they would read something I published. To Meg for always reminding me that I needed to get writing. For Mom and Dad for all of their support through the years.

CHAPTER ONE

ANTOINE SUVALESE stood at the railing of the aero, watching as inky black smoke billowed from the rapidly descending coal transport he had been on. Behind him, he could hear the raucous laughter of the air pirates celebrating a successful raid. Antoine heard it, but it seemed far away, his entire focus on the sinking ship they were pulling away from. He watched until the murky clouds from the still burning coal were all that was visible.

"Alright, you lousy pigeons, back to your stations!" The voice was loud and commanding, rumbling over the entire top deck. "The loot will be divided up as always, but first we need to finish securing our getaway! Everyone get moving!" Antoine turned slowly at the shouted orders, watching as the pirates that had taken him hostage began to disperse. Everything felt dull and distant to him, almost as if he were in a dream. Part of him wished it was a horrible nightmare that had overtaken him. Soon he would wake to the coarse sounds of the sailors on the coal transport shouting at each other on the upper deck.

It was a useless wish. He knew there was no way he could dream something like this. All Antoine could do now was wonder how he had ended up in such a situation. If it had been any other set of pirates, any other set of bandits, the situation may not have seemed as dire. Instead, he was at the mercy of the most infamous, and ruthless, air pirate known to haunt the skies over Titaneous: Rivas the Ramshot and the crew of the *Bloody Aria*. Someone grabbed Antoine's bicep, roughly pulling him away from the railing and up to his feet. His gaze slid down to the metal decking, and a pair of scuffed boots entered his vision. He didn't look up, not wanting to see the owner or where they were leading him. It was pointless to struggle, since his hands had been securely bound behind his back with a thick length of rope. The shock had left him pleasantly numb to everything around him, and he had no desire to change that yet. He heard a distant voice buzzing in his ears, the meaning of the words completely lost.

Antoine stumbled as he was led below the deck, the hand gripping his arm tightening to the point of pain. No doubt he would have bruises later. The change in the level of noise around him finally began to pull Antoine from his dazed state. The rushing sound of wind and shouting voices faded, replaced by the more rhythmic sound of machinery and the slight echoing sound of boots on metal plating. But even this change was not enough to completely break the comfortably numb shock that cocooned Antoine. It wasn't until he was roughly pushed and fell to the hard decking that his mind finally started to take note of his surroundings.

Blinking, he focused on the ornately patterned rug that he was now lying on. Slowly Antoine turned his head to take in more of the room he found himself in. It was nicely appointed and comfortable, yet it managed to avoid appearing lavish or ostentatious. The furniture was sturdy, mostly made of metal, and he thought he saw a desk bolted to the very floor. Several circular portholes covered two walls, the largest being on the rear wall, providing a view of the rushing clouds.

Antoine struggled to sit up, reflexively attempting to use his hands to steady himself only to be reminded of his bound state when the ropes bit into his skin. Compulsively he tested the rope binding him, and then let out a groan when it gave not an inch at his efforts.

"Those ropes are strong. You'll not break them. Even if you struggled all night, you would do naught but bring harm to yourself." Antoine turned toward the voice, trying to see who was speaking. His movement was too quick for his precarious balance, causing him to fall over. This time he landed on his back, his gaze resting on the ceiling rather than the floor. He heard a snort and the tread of boots approaching him. The electric lights that dangled from the ceiling were just bright enough to hide the features of the person who was now leaning over him. All Antoine could make out was blond hair that caught the light, creating a golden halo. However,

Antoine would never be foolish enough to think the person in front of him was any kind of angel.

Now that the shock had faded from his system, it was quickly being replaced by fear. Antoine was on board an aero full of ruthless pirates, completely at their mercy. There was nowhere to escape to, unless he wished to end his life by jumping over the deck rails. Antoine was not desperate enough yet to consider suicide as an escape—not if there was still a chance he might survive this. They had taken pains to take him alive and relatively unharmed, so he didn't think the captain planned to kill him yet—which was more than could be said for the rest of the crew that had been with him on the coal transport.

Strong hands came down, grabbing his arms and pulling him up until he was settled on his feet. Antoine attempted to move away, his movements clumsy due to the restraints. Thankfully the hands did not let him go until he was perfectly steady with no danger of falling over. Looking up, he found himself faced with a small mountain of a man. The hair that had looked like a halo was less bright when viewed directly, a dark blond with streaks where it had been bleached even lighter by exposure to the sun. It fell in thick waves around a strongly featured face, the most striking part being a scar that ran from his left ear over his jaw before ending at the chin. Eyes the bright green of summer leaves peered intently at Antoine, making his insides squirm strangely.

Antoine forced his eyes away, taking in the long dark red frock coat trimmed in leather that reached his knees. The coat was unbuttoned, revealing a simple white shirt tucked into a pair of tight leather breeches, which in turn were tucked into a pair of knee-high leather boots. Inanely Antoine thought all the man was missing was a tricorn hat to complete the popular image of a pirate.

"I do hope you will forgive my delay in introducing myself, Mr. Suvalese." Antoine blinked at the sound of the rumbling voice, refocusing his attention on the man's face. He was smirking now, the scar pulling slightly at the movement. "I am Captain Rivas Ramshot, and I welcome you aboard the *Bloody Aria*, Antoine Suvalese." Still smirking, he gave a mocking courtly bow, left arm coming around his front as he bent over it, eyes never leaving Antoine. Antoine swallowed around his dry throat as the words and their meaning registered in his mind.

Antoine tried to straighten up, desperately hoping that his fear didn't show, even though he had a feeling it was a hopeless cause. His father had always lamented how Antoine's face showed too much of his thoughts. He felt Rivas's eyes rake over him and compulsively swallowed again as he worked to find his voice. "Why have you kidnapped me? What is it you want?"

Rivas gave a low chuckle as he paced away from Antoine, clasping his hands behind his back. The movement made him seem even more intimidating, his coat falling open to reveal a long cutlass and a rather large wood-handled pistol, both of which rested in leather sheaths on each of his hips. "I would think it rather obvious. You are our hostage, and we will ransom you back to your father for a tidy sum."

Antoine's stomach plummeted all the way to the very distant soil. "What... what makes you think that my father could afford to pay anything for my release? Or that he would even bother to do so?"

CHAPTER TWO

ANOTHER QUIET chuckle, Rivas's green eyes twinkling with mirth and something Antoine didn't wish to identify. "Oh, but I think Adrian Suvalese, the owner of the great Suva Coal Company, will be willing to pay quite handsomely for the return of his favorite son."

Antoine had not thought it was possible for his stomach to sink any lower, but at those words he felt it begin to curdle as the full meaning of the words hit him. "I'm only the second son from the second wife—not worth very much in the end. I'm merely the spare. You would hardly get a single ducat of ransom for me."

"You underestimate yourself, Antoine." His name came out almost like a caress in that deep voice, forcing Antoine to fight back a shiver. "You may be the second son, but good rumor has it you are your father's favorite. The son of his second and more beloved wife who shows a greater work ethic than his other son. You are the one Adrian is grooming to take over the company."

Antoine swallowed, averting his eyes from the pirate. "You shouldn't trust rumors so easily. Even if it were remotely possible that what you heard were true, he would not pay an extravagant ransom and give any truth to the rumors. So your entire endeavor is completely pointless. Release me and I will not mention this to anyone." He managed to put much more confidence into the words than he felt. Antoine kept his face down, desperately hoping that by doing so he could hide how frightened he was.

"I know, which is why I shall not ask too high a price for you. It will be a fitting amount, though, for what Mr. Suvalese can afford. I have no doubt that he'll pay it." The hollow clicking of boots on metal plating alerted Antoine to the movement of his captor. A warm, calloused hand gripped Antoine's chin, tilting it upward with surprising gentleness until he was staring into that rugged face. "It would be a very cold man that would not ransom a handsome son like you."

Antoine blinked in surprise at the compliment even as he felt his face heat up. He had never thought of himself as particularly handsome. There was nothing unique about his features. Ordinary brown hair that currently fell in a thick tangle around his face, framing wide eyes that matched it in color. Perhaps his skin was a bit darker than others from Laitha, his mother's legacy, but he couldn't imagine what would make Rivas think he was handsome. "I doubt my looks have anything to do with it."

He watched as Rivas gave him a speculative look, a slight smile crossing his face. "You would be surprised." It was said quietly, those green eyes regarding him with unnerving intensity. Antoine looked down to avoid the too-intimate gaze. At the edge of his vision, Antoine saw a small dagger flash silver in the light as the pirate moved behind him. Reflexively Antoine tensed in preparation, expecting to feel the knife sinking into his flesh. Instead of pain, there was a sharp tug as the binding ropes were cut away.

Another smirk split Rivas's scarred face, the knife disappearing back into the top of his boot. "Since you are to be our guest for a while, there's no reason to keep you bound." Rivas moved back, once again looking Antoine over. "As long as you behave yourself, there should be no reason to bind you further."

Antoine flexed his fingers as painful tingles shot through his hands from the renewed blood flow. "What's to keep me from trying to escape now?" His emotionally wrecked mind let the question slip before he could stop it. Immediately he was cursing his rogue tongue, hoping the words had not just earned him a punishment.

Instead of getting angry, though, Rivas seemed amused by the question. "You are an intelligent man, Antoine. There is nowhere for you to go on this ship where we couldn't find you. The only way off the ship is over the deck railing. If you had wanted that escape, you would have done so earlier. Your best hope for surviving this unharmed is to cooperate with us while you are our guest."

Antoine did not want to admit it, but he knew the pirate spoke the truth. He would need to cooperate to ensure he lived through this, no matter what that cooperation might entail. Rivas did not seem inclined to hurt him, which seemed at odds with his reputation as bloodthirsty and ruthless. Of course, that might just be because Rivas couldn't ransom a corpse. "Am I free to move about the ship?" Antoine hoped to be allowed at least that much freedom.

Rivas smiled, the gesture much softer than the previous smirks. "You may wander around below decks, but you cannot go to the top decks. Also, I would recommend that you avoid the mess hall entirely tonight. If you are hungry, go directly to the kitchen. When you get tired, you may come back here." He gestured to a door to the right of the desk. "Through there is the captain's cabin." Antoine cast a nervous glance at the door, causing Rivas to smirk again. "There is a hammock that you can avail yourself of, unless you wish to sleep with me. If that is the case, you are most welcome in my bed."

Antoine flushed at the suggestive words and looked down at his feet. "I'll be fine in the hammock," he said, telling himself that the pirate was just trying to get a reaction out of him. Antoine refused to think about why exactly his stomach gave a twist at what Rivas had been implying.

"A pity, then." The words were quiet, and the rumble of Rivas's voice filled the room. "I have to take my leave now. If you decide to wander the ship tonight, be cautious. The men like to celebrate after a successful raid." Antoine didn't look up until he heard the thud of heavy boots moving over the deck behind him. Rivas stepped out of the room without glancing back, the door closing firmly behind him.

CHAPTER THREE

WITHOUT RIVAS'S rather intimidating presence, the terror slowly began to fade. The adrenaline remained, though, leaving Antoine full of restless energy. In an effort to settle himself, Antoine paced over to one of the windows, staring out at the clouds that streamed behind the aero. He tried to see if he could make out any trace of the ground far below, hoping that perhaps there would be some clue as to where he was now. Nothing was visible, though. The aero was too high in the clouds to allow a view of the ground.

Even without that, geography had never been Antoine's strongest subject. In fact, he had hardly left the Archduchy of Laitha in his previous twenty-three years of life. He wouldn't have even been on the coal transport if his father had not sent Antoine to take care of some business at the mine for him. Antoine wondered if his father would regret that decision when the news reached him.

Pushing that uncharitable thought aside, Antoine turned away from the windows. Still feeling restless, he decided to go and explore the areas of the ship that were open to him. With that in mind, Antoine walked down the first corridor he came to. It was only after going for several minutes with only the sound of distant machinery to guide him that Antoine realized he had no idea of the ship's layout.

Deciding to keep going despite this, Antoine walked on until he reached a set of metal stairs. Going down, he started to hear something besides the steady thrum of the distant machinery. Following that sound, Antoine entered a large space made of two decks. Antoine stood on the upper deck, which formed a walkway that circled the room. Spread out below him along the edge of the room were several long tables and benches securely bolted to the deck.

It was obvious that this was the mess deck. The *Aria*'s crew sat around on the benches, laughing and drinking with each other. Antoine had never seen such a variety of different peoples gathered in one place. Immediately recognizable were those of the elven race, their distinctive wings rustling as they moved. There were also men from the eastern continent, the southern continent, and even several gypsies.

In the middle of the gathering stood Rivas and another man Antoine vaguely recognized from the initial attack. The man was tall and lean-looking, with long dark hair held back from his face by a rather flamboyantly colored bandana. Antoine was too far away to make out the details of his face, but there was one thing that stood out clearly: in place of the man's right eye was a mechanical contraption that glowed red in the flickering light of the many lamps, immediately identifying him as a gypsy.

"Quiet down, you damn wretches!" The shout came from the dark-haired man, who kicked an empty wooden box aside. "The loot has been divided. Now it's time to celebrate!" A cheer came up from the entire group, drinking containers raised in salute. There were loud calls for music, and several men began to move around, picking up instruments.

Soon a lively tune with a strong beat from several drums filled the air. A violin picked up a melody and was quickly accompanied by the light, floating sound of a flute. The song was infectious, and soon several people were up and dancing, including the man with the mechanical eye, as the others called encouragement. Watching, Antoine found himself captivated by the man's movements. There were intricate foot and leg movements, some that looked rather impossible, combined with rhythmic slapping motions. More joined in, and Antoine lost track of time as he watched.

It wasn't until the gypsy looked up and smirked that Antoine snapped out of his trance. A startled rustling noise came from nearby, and Antoine saw a flash of gold out of the corner of his eye. Turning, he caught another flash of gold as a figure darted out of a far door. Deciding to follow, Antoine quickly went over to the door. He stepped out to see the figure disappear around a corner. This continued for quite a while, yet Antoine could never seem to catch up to the figure or even get a full image of them, always just a flash of gold to lead him onward.

The longer he followed this person, the louder the sounds of the machinery got. After going down another set of metal stairs, the vibrations from the machinery increased until Antoine could feel them moving up his legs and torso into his very teeth. Rounding a final corner, he saw the now familiar flash of gold vanish behind a slamming door. Hurrying forward, Antoine paused in front of the rounded metal door, trying to find a sign as to what lay behind.

Nothing showed that might indicate what was beyond it, and suddenly Antoine was assailed with nerves. He had no idea who he had been following or what was through the door. It could be the person's private quarters, in which case he couldn't just barge in without announcing himself. He wondered why he had decided to follow this person. Perhaps it was just a desire to have someone to speak with. As far as Antoine could tell, this was possibly the only person on the ship not in the mess hall getting drunk.

Steeling himself, Antoine reached up and hesitantly knocked on the door. The incredibly loud clanking of the machinery made it hard to hear if there was any response. He knocked again, and when there was still no response, Antoine reached up and tried the door. It opened slowly, and Antoine cautiously stuck his head in. The tension in his body eased when he was greeted only by the increased noise of machinery. Not someone's bunkroom, then. Judging by the mind-boggling contraptions, he had stumbled upon the engine room.

CHAPTER FOUR

STEPPING FARTHER inside, Antoine glanced around at the various machines filling the space. The acrid scent of burning coal mixed with oil and heated metal filled his senses as each piece moved through the prescribed circulations. Walking into a maze of moving metal, Antoine followed what looked to be a conveyor carrying coal toward a large furnace throwing off such intense heat it was impossible to get close. Sweat dripped into Antoine's eyes from the heat and he had to back away, which caused him to bump into a metal pipe. The hollow bang the impact created seemed incredibly loud given the amount of ambient noise that was present.

"Who's there?" The voice was strong and sharp, bouncing around the room so that it became hard to pinpoint where it came from. "Is that you, Shandor? I told you to stop bothering me when I'm in here!" The pounding tap of boots moving quickly over metal accompanied the voice, growing louder as both approached. Antoine had never gotten a clear look at who he had followed here, but even having seen the diversity of the crew, he was still taken aback by the person who rounded the corner.

The man appeared to be of medium build, though it was difficult to tell with any certainty since he was shrouded in a baggy workman's coverall. Patches and stains of grease covered both him and the heavy gloves he wore. Messily cut golden hair escaped from under a battered leather cap and goggles, framing a thin face and large eyes the same hue as his hair. He watched Antoine cautiously. The light from the furnace cast fiery highlights over him, causing the numerous piercings on his pointed ears to gleam. But all of these were secondary to the large golden wings arching gracefully from his back. Antoine had seen elves before being brought aboard the *Bloody Aria*, but always at a distance. Those had seemed little more than silent dolls in the company of nobles and wealthy merchants at

11

social gatherings he had attended with his father. The elf in front of him, while stunning in appearance, looked nothing like a doll.

"You... are not Shandor." A scowl crossed the elf's face, and he let out an annoyed huff, crossing his arms. "Are you just going to stand there and gawk? I have better things to do than stand around for your amusement. If you wanted to see an elf, there were plenty on the mess deck. Who are you anyway?" The brash words and voice should have been grating, but Antoine wasn't bothered by the elf's demeanor. He could see the carefully guarded caution in those eyes and the tenseness in the slim body. It was as if the elf was deciding whether to stay or flee.

"My name is Antoine. I'm—"

"He's the captain's *guest*, the big prize from our latest raid. So be polite, Shiv'ren." Antoine stiffened at the sound of the rich voice coming from directly behind him. Turning slowly, he saw that the gypsy that had been dancing in the mess hall was now standing behind him. Up close it was easier to make out the dark olive skin that covered the man's powerful frame. The man could be considered quite handsome with his strong exotic features were it not for the mechanical eye and accompanying white scar that dominated his face.

"Who are you?" Antoine didn't recognize him, but there was a palpable air of authority coming from the pirate leaning against the machinery. It was similar to the feeling he had gotten from Rivas when he had met him.

"I am Shandor, the quartermaster for the *Bloody Aria*. I can see you've already met our cute little engineer, Shiv'ren." Shandor looked over at Shiv'ren, smirking as he raised a dark eyebrow at the scowl that crossed Shiv'ren's face. Shiv'ren turned away, golden eyes glaring sulkily at the ground. Antoine was struck by the strange feeling that there was something more going on between them.

"What are you doing here, Shandor?" Shiv'ren sounded sullen, golden eyes glaring at Shandor. Antoine took a hesitant step back, watching the interplay between the two. There was definitely something between them, and Antoine had no desire to get caught in the middle.

"I came to bring your share, and a gift, of course. Whenever do I come to you without a present?" Shandor grinned, white teeth flashing brightly against his dark skin.

"Whenever you feel like harassing me!" Shiv'ren seemed anything but amused, bringing a gloved hand up and impatiently pushing his hair back from his face.

"I'm wounded, Shiv'ren. I always bring you a present after an attack. Just because I like your company at other times is no reason to get so angry."

"Then give me my share already and be gone. I don't feel like dealing with whatever game you have in mind tonight." Shiv'ren stormed over, wings twitching in agitation or anger, as he grabbed the sack at Shandor's feet.

Shandor let out a sigh, yet Antoine thought he saw something flash in his one flesh eye—something that looked very much like regret. It disappeared too quickly for Antoine to be certain. "There you go, your share of the haul." Shandor stepped back enough to let Shiv'ren pass.

Antoine felt like a voyeur, and he wished desperately that he could leave. There was tension between the two pirates, something unspoken that sat between them. After grabbing his share, Shiv'ren turned away, and stomped back down the hallway. "Thank you for bringing it to me. Now leave." With that Shiv'ren disappeared into the maze of machinery.

"Come along, this isn't really a good place to hang around. Shiv'ren likes his privacy." A somewhat civilly worded command, one Antoine wasn't inclined to argue with. Especially when Shiv'ren had already vanished into his mechanical labyrinth, leaving Antoine alone with Shandor.

Antoine was silent as he followed Shandor through the different corridors of the ship. Slowly the engine noises faded away till it was again just a slight vibration on the plating. When Antoine felt he had finally gathered what wits he had left, they had returned to the captain's quarters. Antoine's gut clenched at the sight of the door, knowing what lay beyond. Antoine hoped Rivas hadn't returned yet. The thought of being alone in such close quarters with him if Rivas had been drinking heavily caused Antoine's stomach to twist.

Shandor glanced over at Antoine as he gave a quick knock on the door. He didn't try to suppress the grin that stretched across his face at the look of pinched worry on Antoine's face. After a muffled response came from behind the door, Shandor reached forward, and pushed it open. Antoine froze in the doorway, unable to make his body enter the room. There was no one visible in the flickering light, but he knew Rivas was in there, waiting for him. Antoine jumped when Shandor placed a hand on his shoulder, the only warning given before Shandor pushed him into the room.

Rivas looked up from where he sat at the desk, green eyes seeming to glow in the flickering illumination of the lamps. Antoine wondered when it had gotten so dark. The sky visible through the portholes was black as pitch, proving hours had passed since he had last looked outside.

"You look exhausted, Antoine." Rivas's words brought Antoine back to himself with a slight start.

His mind felt sluggish, as though he were operating in a thick fog. Given what had happened today, the exhaustion should have been expected, yet Antoine was surprised by how quickly it had come over him. Still, he had no idea where or even when he would be allowed to rest. The idea of sleeping close to someone he was unfamiliar with and could not trust was deeply unsettling. Antoine doubted his host would ask for his feelings on the matter. "Where can I sleep?"

Rivas smirked then, and Antoine shivered as Rivas's eyes purposefully moved over him. Only his exhaustion kept him from reacting more strongly to the scrutiny. "Through that door you'll find my personal quarters." There was a casual wave toward a door in the back of the room. "There's a hammock or my bed if you wish to share it," Rivas said with a leer. Antoine fled through the door to escape the smirk and the bright eyes that caused fluttering in his stomach.

Once in the cabin with the door firmly closed, Antoine closed his eyes, attempting to shake off the strange emotions Rivas conjured inside him. Once he felt more in control, Antoine opened his eyes to take in the room. It was a sparse room all told, hardly what he would have expected from a pirate so successful and infamous. There was a large bed in one corner, covered in a pile of blankets and rugs that trailed off the mattress. Warmth flashed through Antoine as his mind unwillingly conjured images of Rivas in the bed. Shaking them off, he turned resolutely away from the bed. There was a piece of canvas stretched between two beams on the other side of the room, next to a large trunk pushed into a corner.

Antoine spent a minute studying the hammock, trying to figure out how to get in it. It took several attempts before he managed it. Once on it, Antoine barely kept himself from immediately flipping out of it. Gripping the sides tightly, he held still until the swaying stopped. Once it had settled, exhaustion crashed over him like a wave, pulling him into a dreamless sleep.

CHAPTER FIVE

IT FELT like Antoine had just closed his eyes a moment ago, but when he opened them, sunlight was streaming in through the porthole window. Not entirely awake yet, Antoine forgot where he was and tried to roll over. He ended up falling out of the hammock and landing in a heap on the floor with a pained grunt. Carefully Antoine tried to sit up, finding his limbs tangled in a blanket he did not remember having the night before. The fall had shaken the sleep from his mind. After untangling himself from the blanket, Antoine shuffled toward the cabin door. The increased movement reminded him that he should try to locate food before anything else. Absently he pushed his sleep-mussed hair from his face as he stumbled into the other room.

"Good morning, Mr. Suvalese. Nice to see you joining us." Antoine's head jerked up at the smooth and highly amused voice. Rivas sat in a chair at the round table that dominated the center of the room, one booted foot propped up on the edge, a tankard held loosely in his hands. The only change in Rivas's appearance was that he had forgone his coat for a leather vest over a white shirt. Rivas lifted the tankard and took a long pull, the line of his throat as he swallowed catching Antoine's eyes. Antoine quickly looked away when he heard the tankard impact the table, hoping the fall of his unbound hair would hide the flush on his cheeks.

"Good morning." It was a soft mumble, Antoine's throat too dry for more. To add to his embarrassment, his stomach growled again, louder than before. "Sorry…."

Rivas gave a soft laugh, standing up and stretching. "No need to apologize. It's to be expected. Come on, I'll take you to the mess so you can get something to eat." Rivas didn't wait for Antoine to respond, immediately moving toward the door to the cabin. Antoine ran his fingers through his messy hair one final time before he trailed after the pirate captain.

Antoine was more alert as he went through the *Aria*'s passages and stairs, paying attention to each turn. He needed to learn his way around since he would be a prisoner on the ship until his ransom was paid. It wouldn't be a quick process. Antoine would probably be with the pirates for weeks, if not months. He didn't doubt that his father would pay. His father loved him, and Rivas had been correct the night before: Antoine was the favored son even though he was younger. Until the ransom exchange took place, Antoine would need to adjust to his new circumstances.

The route Rivas took to the mess deck was more direct and less winding than the way Antoine had taken last night. He noticed that instead of going in the large doors Rivas went around to a smaller door, which led directly into the kitchen area. Most of the space was taken up by the stove, with cupboards arrayed on the wall above it. A giant man was standing in front of the stove, stirring a pot. A shock of thin blond hair stood up in a greasy halo around his head, and when he swung around to look at them, his belly led the way.

"Well, well, what can I do for ya, Cap'n?"

"Our guest needs something to eat," Rivas stated, staring firmly at the cook as if he expected him to argue.

"Peh." The man looked like he wanted to spit, but held himself back. "Shoulda been here when it was served." He turned away from them, moving from the stove over to one of the cupboards. "Don' have much now, won' have till noon." There was a sound of rummaging and then suddenly hunks of both bread and cheese were being shoved in Antoine's face. He quickly accepted them, giving a slight nod to the cook who had already turned back to the stove and whatever he was cooking. Rivas's hand landed on his shoulder, spreading warmth through his entire body. He led Antoine out of the galley and back into the passageway, moving quite quickly through the corridors. They didn't stop until they were back at Rivas's cabin and the door was firmly shut behind them.

Antoine walked over to the table and set his food down. He quickly began to eat, finding the bread was stale and dry and the cheese much the same. As he ate, Rivas set a tankard by his elbow. Taking a sip, he found it contained water, which he downed greedily. Once he had eaten and drunk his fill, Antoine leaned back with a sigh and looked over at Rivas. The pirate was smirking as he met Antoine's eyes.

Swallowing quickly, Antoine straightened up, unsettled by the look yet not certain what to do about it. He didn't know what Rivas had planned for him while he was a hostage, but so far the crew he had met had either been rude or frightening, which didn't bode well for the coming weeks. So testing Rivas's patience did not seem to be a wise thing. "Thank you, for the food," he said, inclining his head respectfully.

Rivas had a reputation for being completely merciless to the ships he captured. It was rumored he had earned the name Ramshot because he had put spikes on the bow of his ship and used it to ram a naval ship, tearing the hull like paper. Antoine was justifiably terrified of him. Yet the fear kept mixing with another feeling that Antoine refused to identify as attraction. He told himself it was just the shock of his recent events affecting him. His life had just been completely torn apart, and his mind was simply trying to grab hold of anything that seemed stable. The fact that he found Rivas handsome in an unrefined way, that was just physical, nothing more.

"Antoine." The sound of his name made Antoine jump. He looked up to meet green eyes that were much closer than he remembered. Full lips curled into a grin once Rivas knew he had the younger man's attention. "As I was saying, now that you are fed, it's time to let you get used to the *Aria*. Perhaps we'll even find use for you around here."

The words caused a shiver to work its way down Antoine's spine, his entire body going cold. He knew he wouldn't be confined to the captain's quarters, but any freedom would be limited. The thought of the crew finding a use for him brought to mind a variety of disturbing images as to what that use might be.

Rivas must have noticed something amiss with his prisoner, because when he spoke again his voice was much softer. "No need to be going pale like that at the prospect of a little honest work. On a ship like this, everyone has to pull their weight to keep her flying. Even the prisoners. I didn't think you would want to spend your days down here, though if you want to, I suppose we can figure something for you to do below deck."

Antoine took a breath, feeling warmth begin to slowly work its way back through his limbs. "You want me... to do physical labor?" The words came out somewhat stilted, his surprise and disbelief showing through. He glanced up at Rivas, surprised when he saw a dark look cross the scarred face.

"Yes, physical labor. I realize that isn't something the son of a coal magnate would be used to, but here those that don't contribute don't eat. So I suggest you acclimate yourself to the idea of working." Rivas turned on his heel and walked over to the door, flinging it open.

Antoine jumped to his feet, following obediently after Rivas, wondering about the sudden change in his mood. He was acting as if Antoine had insulted him in some way, which was confusing. He had just been overcome with relief that physical work was all that Rivas expected of him, for the present. In truth Antoine didn't mind working as a member of the crew. At home he was treated delicately. His status as his father's favorite meant everything he did was monitored. All of his wishes were met before he had a chance to articulate them lest something displeasing be reported back to Adrian. Antoine disliked being treated as special just because of his father.

CHAPTER SIX

RIVAS TOOK them on an ascending course this time, leading to the top deck of the *Bloody Aria*. Antoine couldn't help the grin that stretched across his face as he stepped onto the deck. A strong wind was blowing, lifting up Antoine's disheveled hair and pushing it back from his face. It carried with it the scent of clouds and burning coal. Antoine had always admired the bustling activity of the aeros. Everyone seemed to have a purpose and a job to do. When he had traveled before, there had never been a chance to take part in it. Instead he was only permitted to watch it from a distance. Antoine was always a guest, the boss's son to be treated with kid gloves and kept away from the rougher elements of any ship he was on.

Rivas strode across the deck with the authority of a king inspecting his kingdom. The crewmen he passed gave respectful nods before returning to their work. Looking around, Antoine was astonished by the truly eclectic nature of the crew. He saw several more elves moving about, their wings rustling in the wind. Occasionally one would lift his face into the wind before turning back to his task. Other pirates he could tell came from the far eastern lands, and a few even had the dark brown skin of the southern continent. Antoine couldn't stop drinking it in, trying to see everything.

Being able to look around now, Antoine remembered that the *Bloody Aria* was a unique aero. She had a strong engine but mainly seemed held aloft by large gas-filled balloons tethered to her main deck and moved by her churning propellers. It seemed most of the activity on the deck was focused on maintenance of the balloon rigging and monitoring of the propellers. While trying to take in everything and attempt to keep up with Rivas's brisk pace, Antoine saw a flash of gold to one side. Antoine saw Shiv'ren standing against the railing, staring out at the clouds sailing by, wings slowly flexing as the wind blew over them.

Antoine didn't get to look for very long before he had to rush to catch up with Rivas, who was approaching what looked to be the wheelhouse. Rivas stepped confidently through the door, expecting him to follow. Inside the wheelhouse was a large bank of windows facing the bow of the ship. A handful of people were there, each focused on a particular task. Innumerable gauges and devices lined the walls, and at the center, on a raised dais, was the helm.

Standing behind the wheel, occasionally making slight adjustments, was a thin, wiry man. He wore a high-collared red shirt with a wide leather sash wrapped several times around his waist and black pants ending in brown boots. Antoine could just make out several items hidden in the sash—one that looked to be the handle of a knife. The clothing, along with his dark hair and almond-shaped eyes, marked him as an easterner. All of the man's focus seemed to be ahead of him as he stared at the bow, at least until he sensed he was being watched. Shrewd dark eyes slid down, taking in both Rivas and Antoine behind him.

"Captain on deck." The voice was accented but clear. Everyone immediately looked up from their assigned tasks.

"Back to work, the lot of you." Rivas's voice boomed through the small space, and everyone quickly turned back to their tasks, except for the man at the wheel. He was watching the two of them carefully, hands remaining steady. The captain gave a slight nod before looking around the wheelhouse. "Can someone tell me where exactly Shandor has gotten to? I need to speak with the bastard."

Chuckling broke out from everyone in the room. Even the man at the wheel gave a brief laugh. Antoine looked around in confusion, only somewhat comforted by the fact that Rivas bore a similar expression. Finally it was the easterner who spoke up. "Shiv'ren's out on deck this morning."

Rivas rolled his eyes then, letting out a long breath. "Oh aye, figures. When attempting to find a dog, look for the person holding the leash." Another round of laughter from the crew. Obviously this was a joke everyone understood, except for Antoine.

"Now if he would only realize he holds the leash, we'd all be better off, I reckon." A different voice this time, but Antoine couldn't figure out who had spoken.

"Oh Christ no, I dread the day that he realizes the real power he has over our quartermaster. I'll be stuck catering to the every whim of my engineer." Rivas sounded incredibly amused by the whole affair. Turning on his heel, he walked back toward the door, opening it and stepping out. "Come on, Antoine, we need to have a discussion with Shandor about where best to put you."

Antoine followed Rivas outside, bringing a hand up to hold back his blowing hair. He idly wondered how Rivas could stand having his hair blowing about like it was. He spotted Shiv'ren still leaning against the railing of the deck, but now, as he looked closer, Antoine saw Shandor leaning against one of the propeller masts several feet behind Shiv'ren. Shandor looked relaxed, arms crossed over his chest, mismatched eyes focused on Shiv'ren.

"Oi, Shandor, stop staring. The subtle approach isn't going to work with him, you know. Try being more direct." Rivas was grinning as he walked up next to Shandor, crossing his own arms. Antoine hung back, not sure what he should be doing but knowing he shouldn't wander too far.

"I tried direct already. He thought I was making fun of him." Shandor tilted his head to the side, several locks of dark hair drifting across his mechanical eye. "So I've gone for subtle and he thinks I'm not serious and still making fun of him. It seems that when it comes to Shiv'ren, I can't win." Shandor straightened up, turning to look at Rivas. "However, you're not here to listen to my troubles. What do you want, Rivas?"

"We need to find something for Antoine to do while we send the message to his father and await the reply," Rivas said, waving a hand vaguely around the deck. The two began an involved discussion that made little sense to Antoine. His input was obviously not needed, so he moved over to the railing, staring out at the rushing sky.

It was different to watch the view from the deck as opposed to a porthole window. The scenery flying by gave a feel of speed and movement that was otherwise lost. Grasslands spread below them, the grass moving like waves on the sea. Far in the distance he could make out mountains and lights against dark rocks. Looking up, Antoine could see an endless stretch of blue with dollops of white clouds. Antoine felt a smile stretch across his face as he turned into the wind and took a deep breath, appreciating the clean, unspoiled air. None of the cloying smoky fumes from massive factories or the stench of open sewage that clogged the air around Laitha.

"Nice, isn't it?" Antoine blinked at the soft voice, turning and meeting Shiv'ren's golden eyes. The elf had moved closer, leaning a hip against the rail now. He seemed less surly this morning than he had the night before.

"Yes, it is. I've never smelt such clean air before." Antoine looked out over the rail again, watching the grassland begin to give way to more rugged terrain.

"It's nothing like you get in Laitha." Shiv'ren turned and leaned far over the railing, his wings arching out behind him. "Almost like flying yourself." It was a quiet murmur—so quiet Antoine almost missed it. Antoine found himself hypnotized by the way that the sunlight created a halo around Shiv'ren. A minute later he pulled back from the railing, his wings folding themselves against his back. "I've got to get back," he said, turning away from Antoine and shoving his hands into the pockets of his smeared coveralls before disappearing below deck.

Antoine watched Shiv'ren go before turning back to watch the scenery. He realized that he didn't actually know where the ship was or where it was headed. When the *Bloody Aria* had attacked, the transport ship had been en route from the Brecker coalmines to Laitha. Antoine wasn't sure if the mountains he saw in the distance were the ones that contained the mines or if they had moved farther west. Of course, knowing where he was wouldn't give him a chance to escape, but it would give him a frame of reference.

Glancing back, Antoine saw that Rivas had finished his conversation and was walking toward him with Shandor a step behind. When they came to a stop in front of him, Antoine was surprised when Shandor was the one who spoke. "Since we don't know enough about your talents to decide what position you might be suited for, we're going to try you out in a couple of positions until you stick somewhere. Of course, some jobs are a little too dangerous for you to be trying." Shandor smiled. "Needless to say, you won't be working with any of the guns."

"I wouldn't want to anyway," Antoine quickly affirmed. Guns were not something Antoine liked, and he never would have expected his captors to give him access to a weapon of any kind. The idea of working other positions, of learning different skills, intrigued Antoine greatly. "When do I start?"

CHAPTER SEVEN

A FERAL grin crossed Shandor's face. He placed a hand on Antoine's shoulder and guided him quickly toward an elf standing on the middle of the deck. A pair of mangled wings rose in twisted ruins from his back, a few limp brown feathers moving weakly in the wind. He was yelling at several of the crew members, bleating at them to work faster. "Lesh'ra! Got someone here for you."

Lesh'ra turned, revealing a grizzled, weathered face with several lines on it and short brown hair matted against his head. Hard brown eyes looked Antoine over, and his wings gave a feeble twitch. "Not very impressive, is he? Don't worry, I'll find out if he's worth anything."

Shandor grinned, clapping Antoine hard enough on the shoulder to knock him forward a few steps. "That's all I wanted. Send him to me if it doesn't work out." With that Shandor turned and left, boots sounding over the metal plating.

"We'll start with the basics, then." Lesh'ra straightened up to his full height, lips twisted in a sneer. "I'm the chief boatswain on this ship, and you'll refer to me as such if you know what's good. You can call me Chief if that's too difficult. Now you're going to learn how to maintain an aero."

Lesh'ra sent him over to one of the other crewmates, ordering Antoine to help check the rigging that tied the balloons down to the deck. There were a lot of complicated explanations about the rigging while dexterous fingers wove the various intricate knots. Antoine tried to follow the explanation, but the words filtered through his brain faster than he could properly process.

"Y'see, in addition to the gas balloons and the engine, we also got a sail. Can't see it really, don't bother trying. Shiv'ren calls it a therma sail. Supposedly the wind most of the time is really good and puts less strain on the engines. Don't really matter how it works, just so long as we keep it working. C'mon, you try the next riggin'."

Antoine stared down at the complicated rope rigging. There was a clamp on the deck connected to a metal pulley that the rope threaded through. He looked from that to the complicated knots on the next one. It seemed to involve tying the rope and then winding it back onto itself to keep it secured. Antoine tried to copy the movements as he remembered the other man doing it.

He'd barely started when the chief made a tutting noise. "No, no, all wrong. No one ever teach you how to tie a proper knot? You trying to kill us or somethin'?" Thus began a long series of similar scenes that took up most of the morning. Antoine would attempt to tie the rigging, only getting partway through before he was told he was doing it completely and utterly wrong. Someone else would take over and do it again properly. After a full half a dozen times of this, Lesh'ra came over and told him to stop trying before he caused one of the balloons to fly away.

Antoine was sent to another worker who pointed him toward a pile of ropes resting in a corner. He told Antoine to check them for damage and rot. It was a tedious job, but Antoine didn't complain. It was better than constantly being told how incompetent he was at tying rope. The new job gave him time to observe the activity on deck. There was constant movement everywhere, which fascinated Antoine, even though hardly any of it was familiar. As he checked ropes, Antoine noticed that one or two crewmates actually climbed over the sides and tops of the gas-filled balloons. It was thrilling to watch, almost like a troop of acrobats performing. When Antoine saw Lesh'ra pass by, he asked what their purpose was.

"Checking the canvassing o'course. If there's a leak we'll lose gas and that could cause a crash. Worse, the leaked gas could cause an explosion if not caught in time. They have to be checked daily for any needed repairs."

Antoine nodded, seeing the sense in that. Any time gas was used on an aero it needed to be monitored. "Why are elves the only ones climbing the balloons?" None of the crew had attempted it even though every other job seemed to be handled by everyone else.

Antoine was taken aback by the snarl that split Lesh'ra's face. "An elf is the only one who wouldn't be afraid of falling if they lost their footing. Now get back to work!" he barked, before stomping off to the other end of the deck.

The words sparked a certain curiosity that made Antoine turn his attention to the elves on deck. There were only four that he could see working on the deck besides Lesh'ra himself. Of those, two were climbing the balloons and one was watching them with a strange look on his face. Antoine had quickly realized the elves were all escaped slaves. There was a defensiveness in how every one of them stood and moved. Even Shiv'ren had shown a similar posture. Now that he was looking closely, Antoine noticed that every elf's wings had been disfigured. Either mangled like Lesh'ra's, missing parts, or on one they had been amputated completely, leaving only small stubs that still twitched slightly.

"Oi you! Get back to work checking those ropes!" Antoine gave a start at the shout, quickly turning back to his work.

CHAPTER EIGHT

ANTOINE WORKED on the ropes through the whole day with a small break here and there. When evening set in, Antoine stood and stretched his back to get the kinks out. He followed the other crew members as they made their way to the mess for the evening meal. It consisted of a thin soup and a slice of very hard bread. Not very filling, but satisfying enough to take the pangs of hunger away.

Now that the meal was done, Antoine was at a loss as to what to do. The air pirates, it seemed, spent the night sitting around and drinking once the meal was over, a pastime Antoine was rather uncomfortable with. A few of the pirates began playing instruments, but none of it was as lively as what had been playing the night before. No one seemed like they would dance tonight either.

Looking around, Antoine realized he hadn't seen Rivas since that morning on the deck. Evidently Rivas trusted his crew to operate without him present at all times. For some reason Antoine missed Rivas. The pirate frightened and confused him, but he was the most familiar thing to Antoine at the present. Like last night, Antoine saw a flash of golden feathers at the side of his vision. He recognized the feathers as belonging to Shiv'ren, and on a whim he decided to follow the winged elf. He headed up to the deck this time instead of the engine room. On deck the wind was blowing as strong as ever, the temperature having dropped considerably, causing Antoine to shiver in his thin shirt. Shiv'ren walked across the deck toward a figure leaning against the railing. Antoine was too far away to make out many details, just the long fur-lined coat and long hair blowing in the wind that made him think it might be a woman.

"You like following me, don't you?" The words were mild, just loud enough to be heard over the wind. There was none of the bite or rudeness that Antoine had started to expect from the golden elf. Shiv'ren was leaning against the railing, his hands shoved in the pockets of his coveralls.

Antoine smiled slightly, giving a faint shrug. "I guess. There isn't anyone else to follow most of the time. You're the only one I ever see wandering around." A small chuckle floated on the wind, causing a small swell of pride inside of him. Antoine had a feeling that Shiv'ren was not someone who laughed easily. "Also I'm not sure I want to be down there with so many drunken sailors. Let alone that many drunken pirates."

"They'll not get that drunk. We've a few more days' flight and no one is willing to face Shandor if they get too drunk and miss their duties," Shiv'ren responded.

"Why would they be frightened of Shandor and not Captain Rivas?" Antoine didn't understand what exactly the balance of power between the two men was. They seemed to be friends and treated each other as equals. It certainly wasn't how he had seen the captain on the transport ship treat his subordinates.

Shiv'ren shrugged a bit, walking toward Antoine. "Rivas might be the captain, but Shandor is the quartermaster." Antoine felt his expression must have been pretty blank because there was a small smile. "The captain has authority in battle and is the head of the ship. Essentially he's a good sailor and soldier who decides on the direction the ship goes. But the quartermaster is the one that delegates work. He handles the distribution of items and spoils amongst the crew. If a crew member is found slacking off, it's the quartermaster they face, not the captain. Any attacks on other ships is decided by the captain and the quartermaster."

Antoine blinked at that, suddenly understanding why Shandor had been the one ordering him around this morning. "So neither of them has complete command over the ship? They have to be in agreement in order to do anything." He shivered against a sharp gust of wind.

"Not just them. If the captain doesn't have the support of the crew, he's not the captain for very long." Shiv'ren gave a smile, feathers fluttering in the wind, a few blowing away.

"Which is why any good captain makes sure he asks what his crew wants before moving forward with a plan." Antoine swallowed when he heard Rivas's voice behind him, the rumbling sound moving through him like a wave. Turning around, he tilted his head back to take in the handsome scarred visage that was currently curled in a sly smile. "A leader should have the best interest of the people around them in mind when deciding something."

"It's a shame more leaders do not follow such a sound philosophy." The voice was lilting, softly accented and female by the pitch of it. Antoine turned toward the voice, watching as she walked up next to Shiv'ren. She had her hands tucked into the wide sleeves of her coat, which besides being fur-lined was quilted in thick brocade material. The moonlight illuminated the soft features of her pale face but did nothing to dampen the sharp intelligence lurking in wide, almond-shaped eyes. The wind stirred her long dark hair, the various ornaments in her tresses chiming musically.

"Your words are too kind for me. I simply have no desire to lose my ship due to the displeasure of my crew." The response was modest in tone, the moonlight turning Rivas's scar into a white slash stretching across his face.

"Not until you've met your goals." She smiled softly, bowing her head slightly before moving past him. "Are you coming, Shiv? You promised me a game this evening, and I look forward to defeating you."

The elf laughed, shaking his head. "Always so confident, Yi. Be careful it doesn't lead to your own defeat." The two of them disappeared below deck, their banter growing fainter.

"I think it's time we retired as well, leave the rest to the night watch. Besides, you're not dressed for the cold of the deck." As if to emphasize Rivas's point, a strong gust of wind came across the deck, causing Antoine to start shivering. He didn't resist when Rivas guided him below deck and back into his quarters. "Sit. Get the blood back in your bones before you shake yourself apart." The words were gruff but not unkind, and Antoine sank gratefully into a chair in front of a grated vent.

Antoine gave a happy sigh when a blanket was draped over his shoulders, enveloping him in additional warmth. As Rivas walked back to his desk, Antoine pulled the blanket tighter around himself. "Where were you all day? I didn't see you after you left me on the deck with Lesh'ra."

"I was making the arrangements for your ransom," Rivas said, settling himself into the desk chair. "After all, your father won't pay if he thinks you're dead. I've arranged to have a message sent informing him of your well-being and what he should pay to keep it that way." With just those words, Rivas reminded Antoine of his true position on the ship. He was a hostage, a way of extorting money from his father.

Antoine slouched over in the chair, wrapping himself more firmly in the blanket. "Until then, you'll use me as just another crew member?" he murmured, carefully lifting his eyes to watch the blond pirate's reaction.

"Until we receive your ransom, you'll be put to work and given an education."

"Education? What are you going to educate me about? The life of a ruffian air pirate?" The words came out more snappish than Antoine had intended.

Fortunately Rivas just laughed, green eyes dancing with mirth. "Life for those outside of Laitha's borders. The life of those who help support that city. The life of a sailor and the workings of a ship, things you might one day find useful when you take over your father's little empire."

Antoine snorted at that, sinking further into the chair. "That's the second time you've stated that I will be taking over my father's company. Nigel is the heir. He's the one that will have the company, not me. Even if you believe that Father prefers me, there is no way that Nigel would just let him name me heir."

Rivas's scrutiny was almost a physical thing, pressing on Antoine's skin. "Nigel Suvalese might be the official heir, but it is a very poorly kept secret that your brother is fond of drink, elf powder, and loose women. It's been whispered he doesn't have a head for making money, only for spending it. He's made no real effort to learn the business, and when he did, he showed no aptitude for it." Rivas clasped his hands together, teeth flashing. "You, however, show an honest desire to learn and a willingness to work hard. You proved that today up on deck. In that alone you have proved yourself better than your elder brother."

Antoine felt himself flushing from the rather blunt assessment of his brother's faults as well as the praise he had just received himself. He wasn't used to hearing things like that spoken so openly, and it flustered him. Antoine pushed the feeling aside, focusing instead on a different facet of the conversation. "How do you know all of this? Nigel's... issues"—because that was what Father called them—"are not something we would reveal to just anyone."

"Information has a way of getting around, especially in a city like Laitha. Aerolines and the wealth of the mountains have made the city important. But it is the trade in secrets that keeps it there." With that, Rivas turned back to his papers, picking one up. "You must be tired. Go and rest. Lesh'ra said he'd not have you on deck again, so we'll be trying you out for some different jobs." The dismissal was quite obvious in the pirate's voice.

Antoine blinked and then sighed softly. "I suppose I wasn't really much use up there? Not like they really needed the ropes checked for rot." Antoine climbed to his feet, wincing when his muscles protested after being still. Walking into the cabin, Antoine stared at the bed for a minute before carefully climbing back into the hammock. Once settled, he wrapped the blanket tightly around himself. It didn't take long for Antoine to drift into an exhausted sleep.

CHAPTER NINE

MORNING CAME far too quickly for Antoine, his only comfort being that this time he didn't fall out of the hammock. His dismount was not necessarily more graceful, but at least he wasn't in a tangled heap on the cold deck. Stretching, Antoine made a face as he looked down at himself. He had never been extremely concerned about his appearance, but the idea of going yet another day in the same clothes was nearly more than he could bear. A quick glance around the room revealed that Rivas was not present, but noises were emerging from the small water closet at the rear of the room.

Running a hand through his tousled hair, Antoine made a face at the greasy feel of it sliding between his fingers. Glancing at the water closet, he shifted on his feet, hoping Rivas wouldn't take much longer. Just when he was certain he wouldn't be able to wait any longer, the door opened and Rivas emerged from it, causing Antoine to almost swallow his own tongue.

Damp blond hair curled over a powerful and equally damp chest. Antoine watched entranced as a water droplet made its way down the tanned neck before disappearing into the thick patch of hair that covered Rivas's chest. Antoine knew he should look away and tried to do so, yet he couldn't drag his focus away. His eye caught a newly revealed scar that went from Rivas's left side, across his abdomen, and stopped above his right hip.

Antoine continued to stare for what felt like a long time, until a stab of pain shot up his stomach, snapping him out of it. He jerked back, looking down and then glancing up to find laughing green eyes watching him in return. Antoine's face heated up, which increased Rivas's amusement. Ducking his head, Antoine darted past him into the water closet, letting the door slam behind him.

Once his morning ablutions were taken care of, Antoine noticed a basin with water sitting off to the side. There was a small sliver of soap and cloth beside it, and upon seeing it Antoine quickly peeled off his shirt to freshen himself up. As he washed, Antoine couldn't help but stare at his own physique, comparing it to Rivas's. He didn't have the older man's muscle mass—not that Antoine was unfit, but his life at home had not required a great amount of physical activity. He wondered if that would change if he was aboard the *Aria* for too long.

Antoine shook off those thoughts, cupping the water in his hands and pouring it over his head to dampen his hair. It wasn't as good as washing it, but it made him feel cleaner. However, the water trickling down his neck and back made him shiver. Quickly Antoine pulled his shirt on, the material clinging to his skin. He would have left the shirt off if he didn't know that Rivas would be outside waiting for him.

Stepping into the cabin, Antoine managed to meet Rivas's gaze for just a moment before looking away, his face heating again. He did his best to move around Rivas in the small space, refusing to make eye contact. Yet as he passed by Rivas, Antoine had to fight not to shiver when he felt the heat radiating from the captain. Once he was in the main room, Antoine felt a little steadier. He made sure to stay several paces behind Rivas as they went to the mess for their morning meal.

After the meal Shandor sauntered over to them, looking as amused as he always did. The mechanical eye focused on them, while his other eye did a quick check of the room. It was unsettling to see his eyes moving independently of each other, and Antoine couldn't contain a shiver at the sight.

"Day two begins, then. Now to see if there is anything good below deck that you might be able to handle." Shandor glanced over his shoulder, where the cook was staring intently at them, his mouth twisted into an unreadable expression. "A job that doesn't involve helping the cook," he said, quickly grabbing Antoine's arm and pushing him out of the mess.

The search for a meaningful job that Antoine could do below deck without damaging the ship started much the same as the day before. The list of jobs below deck contained a greater variety of positions than Antoine had come across above deck. He was given over to someone Shandor referred to as the chief fireman, a gruff man with a full beard and arms the size of cannon barrels. He had promptly taken one look at Antoine and told him to go through the holds and check that the coal piles were level and pushed him toward the front holds. He was also firmly instructed to not try to lift anything.

There were ten holds that contained the *Aria*'s coal supply, each filled practically to the top with coal. Curiously Antoine looked around to try to figure out how the coal was transported to the engine. He found that the *Bloody Aria* had a unique system for transporting the coal that was unlike anything he had seen before in his admittedly limited experience. Instead of a legion of sweaty men shoveling the coal into furnaces, there was an inclined conveyor belt in each room. A wheel of shovels would scoop up coal, dumping it onto the conveyor. The conveyor then carried it higher in a direction Antoine presumed led to the furnaces. He tried to follow the route of the conveyor, but it disappeared quickly into a crawl space between the decks.

Checking the coal and the few other odd jobs that the pirates found for him to do took up the entire morning. When the sound came for the noon meal, Antoine followed the other workers to the mess hall. Upon entering, he quickly separated himself from them, moving to the side. Antoine had gotten the distinct impression that they had given busy work to keep him out of their way. It was frustrating, because it constantly reminded him that not only was he a prisoner, but that they thought him incapable of doing anything more strenuous.

Perhaps they were afraid he would get ideas about escape or attempt suicide, both of which Antoine felt were completely ridiculous ideas. First off, there was no way he could escape, when the aero was hundreds of feet up in the air and he had no idea where they were geographically. He would have no way to get home, and he had seen no smaller aeros that he could use. So unless he suddenly were to seize control of the helm, he wouldn't be able to go anywhere. Since he didn't have the first idea how to pilot the ship, that plan would most likely end with the ship crashing to the ground. Antoine was no hero, nor was he ready to die. His best option was to cooperate with the pirates until the ransom was paid.

Of course there was a possibility that his father wouldn't pay and would alert the Archduke's navy as to what had happened. However, Antoine knew his father, and Adrian Suvalese was the type of man to hedge his bets and probably would go with both options so he would be on the winning end no matter what. Antoine loved his father, admired him greatly for all he'd accomplished in his lifetime, but he was not blind or naïve. He knew that much of his father's success was built on a ruthless drive to win. Antoine had little doubt that his father would do all he could to get him back safely and to not have to pay a single pence of ransom.

Looking around at the air pirates eating and talking in noisy camaraderie, Antoine wondered who would be victorious—though ultimately it would come down to who was more ruthless in attaining their goal. As he watched Shandor step into the hall with Rivas following, Shandor's mismatched eyes sweeping the room, Antoine found himself wondering if this time his father would lose.

Both pirates made their way to the table where Antoine had secluded himself and sat down. Shandor leaned forward, resting his arms on the table. "I suppose you can guess what we're here about."

Antoine pushed the remnants of his meal aside, letting out a heavy sigh. "They don't want me to keep checking coal stockpiles and don't have any other work to give me."

"That's about the tale of it. We can't let you near the gun decks or the powder and not just because you're more useful in one piece. The master gunner doesn't like anyone touching the powder stores, even the two of us." A derisive snort came from Rivas, which he followed by muttering something under his breath that made Shandor snicker. "Don't be sore, Cap'n, doesn't suit you." Shandor turned his attention back to Antoine, a smile stretching his handsome features but somehow managing not to warm his blue eye. "I think I've found the perfect place for you. We just have to convince him to take you on."

CHAPTER TEN

ANTOINE LOOKED between the two of them, his stomach suddenly twisting itself into a hard knot. "Convince who to take me on?"

Rivas flashed a smile, the expression warmer than it had been on Shandor. "Don't fret, it's not that bad. He just gets a little stubborn sometimes. Plus, if it's just Shandor he might disagree to be contrary, so I'm coming along to be sure he behaves." Rivas got up, leaning forward. "Ready to get moving?"

Antoine swallowed, working very hard not to flinch back from Rivas, closing his eyes against the pirate's warmth. "Yes...." He got up and followed after Rivas, distantly aware of Shandor taking up the rear position. As they walked along the corridors, Antoine thought some of the turns looked familiar. A deep thrumming moved up his legs into his chest, and his brain started to work out where exactly they were taking him.

When they came to a stop in front of the door that led to the engine room, Antoine couldn't find it in himself to be surprised. Instead he felt uncertainty rise up inside him. "Are you sure it's going to be all right for me to be here? I thought you were paranoid about keeping me safe?"

Rivas turned to face him, his green eyes shining in the pale light of the hallway. "We are, and believe it or not, this is one of the safest places on the *Aria*. Plus if it's a delicate job, Shiv'ren won't have anyone else handle it but himself."

Antoine let out a small sigh, thinking this would be another afternoon of pointless busy work, only now he'd be in the loud engine room as opposed to on one of the higher decks. Unlike the other jobs he had been given on the ship, he had a feeling he wouldn't really be left on his own here. He would have Shiv'ren nearby, probably snapping at him every time he did something improperly.

There wasn't any time to contemplate it, though, because Shandor was opening the door. Rivas stepped inside, leaving Antoine with no choice but to follow him into the dim, warm cacophony that was the *Bloody Aria*'s engine room.

It was as dark as Antoine remembered from the last time he had been here. Immediately he was blanketed by heat and sweat started to form on his scalp. He walked quietly into the labyrinth, trusting that Rivas at least knew where he was going. Glancing around, Antoine couldn't help but notice how narrow the path they walked was—machinery on all sides. The small space, combined with the heat, made Antoine feel stifled and trapped. The more minutes that passed, the stronger the feeling got.

Just when Antoine thought he wouldn't be able to take any more, they stepped out into an open space. A semicircle of large glass windows stood at the far end of the room, stretching the height of the deck, letting in bright sunlight that contrasted sharply with the previous gloom. There was a table off to one side, covered in what looked to be game pieces. A strange chair was in front of the windows, situated on a raised platform too high to be reached without assistance. In a far corner, a large tarp was draped over something.

Any chance to look around the space more was interrupted by a strong voice from behind them. "What's going on?"

Shiv'ren stood in front of a wall of glass knobs and dials of various sizes, glaring at them. The needles on the dials leapt and fell randomly as if responding to his agitation at seeing them. A clipboard was gripped tightly in his hand. Instinctively Antoine took a step back, wanting to prevent that ire from being directed at him. Rivas seemed completely unruffled, meeting Shiv'ren's gaze with his own challenging look.

"I've brought you some help, Shiv," Rivas said, crossing his arms over his chest and pulling himself to his full height. "You've been complaining about how you can't do everything on your own, so I've finally brought you some help."

There was a dismissive glance in Antoine's direction before Shiv'ren refocused on Rivas. "I'm not that desperate for help,

Captain. What am I supposed to with your little pet anyway? The machines here are sensitive. Do you want me to just let him bang around on them?"

"Nothing of the sort." There was a calm edge to Rivas's voice, the kind Antoine remembered hearing in his father's voice when he was dealing with stubborn investors. Or when Antoine's brother came home belligerently drunk. "I know you have things that he can do down here that don't actually require he take the engine apart. There are any number of small tasks he can take care of, even just checking the readings or greasing the gears if you'd like. All of which you complain you don't have time to take care of on top of everything else."

Shiv'ren scoffed, his face still set in a scowl. "I don't need someone hanging around here with me. I'll be fine. I've done well so far, haven't I? Just because no one else is willing to have your pet hanging around does not mean you get to dump him on me!" Antoine noted that when he was upset, Shiv'ren's wings twitched constantly, a few golden feathers floating to the ground. Mostly, though, Antoine was trying not to let the harsh words upset him or die of embarrassment at having it so blatantly stated that he was only good for busy work on the ship.

"This isn't an offer, Shiv'ren." Rivas's voice was harder, harsher than Antoine had yet heard. It seemed the argument was growing thin. "He is going to be here, and you will find something for him to do during the day, and that is the final word on it." Without waiting for another response, Rivas turned and headed out the way he had come in.

Watching him go, Antoine almost missed the furtive glance Shiv'ren gave Shandor before he resumed glaring at the captain's disappearing back. With an angry huff, Shiv'ren turned his back and strode over to the wall of dials, his wings practically vibrating with tension as he checked his clipboard. Shiv'ren's anger seemed almost alive, engulfing the entire area. He didn't even respond when Shandor walked up behind him. The gypsy leaned over, speaking softly enough that Antoine couldn't hear. The longer Shandor spoke, the more tension drained out of Shiv'ren's wings.

Pulling back, Shandor turned and looked at Antoine, giving him a slight smile as he walked over to him. "Don't be too upset." The words were quiet, gentler than Antoine would have expected from the gypsy. "Shiv's prickly in general, and more than anything he hates being ordered to do something. Give him some time to adjust." Antoine looked over at Shiv'ren, noticing the tension. He briefly rested a hand on Antoine's shoulder, giving it a hard pat before disappearing into the engine's maze.

Antoine watched him go before glancing over at Shiv'ren, who he was now supposed to work under. Shiv'ren wasn't looking at him; he was focused on the place Shandor had disappeared into with a strange look on his face. After a minute he turned away, scowling at one of the dials before setting the clipboard down with a hard thwack. Shiv'ren pulled his cap and goggles off, running a hand through the messy golden curls, leaving a long streak of grease behind. Antoine watched as Shiv'ren paced for a minute or two, seemingly in deep thought, tugging randomly on his loose hair.

Finally Shiv'ren came to a stop, rounding on Antoine, eyes flicking over him quickly. "This won't work at all," he stated flatly, giving Antoine a very intense look. "Not at all. We're going to have to change this."

Anger flared in Antoine's chest at that, hot and sharp. Everyone kept treating him like he was some fragile doll that would break at the slightest hint of rough use. Antoine was a prisoner—he had no say in what was going to happen to him—but they could act like he was a prisoner. If they were going to make him do things around the ship, he should be treated like a normal sailor. It was frustrating to feel as though he was a burden without a chance to prove he could do more. He didn't want to be here, but if he had to be until the damned ransom was paid, he was going to try to make it bearable.

"You haven't even let me try! I'm not going to fall apart if you let me help! I think I can manage not to wreck the entire ship!" he snapped, glaring at Shiv'ren, who looked surprised.

There was a moment of silence when Shiv'ren just blinked at him. "I was talking about your clothes," he said slowly, as though he was afraid admitting this would make Antoine fly off again.

"My clothes?" Antoine looked down at what he had been wearing for the past three days, and then over at Shiv'ren. "What about my clothes?"

"We need to change them." To Shiv'ren it must have seemed obvious, yet Antoine felt only confusion. "They're going to get filthy and covered in grease down here. Come on, I have a set of coveralls you can use." He turned and walked to the other end of the room, entering a narrow corridor that Antoine hadn't noticed before.

It was thankfully only a short walk until they came out into a smaller area without any of the complex turns leading to the main engine space. Shiv'ren immediately went over to a large metal trunk in one corner and began digging through it. Looking around, Antoine noted a pallet covered in blankets and pillows at the back of the room. It was situated in front of a large window that showed the clouds racing toward them. Water beaded on the glass. Antoine saw hand tools and bits of machinery strewn across a long table taking up one whole side of the room. In a far corner, a large piece of flat metal had been set up to create a makeshift barrier. Walking over, Antoine saw that behind it was a small toilet, and directly above was a spout he thought worked as a shower. There was a feeling that this was a personal space, almost like it was a bedroom. Antoine didn't know why Shiv'ren would live in the engine room—he figured Shiv'ren must have his own room somewhere else on the ship.

"Here we are." Shiv'ren straightened, and held out a folded bundle of clothes. "You have boots on, don't you? Because I don't think mine would fit you." Giving a quick nod, Antoine took the clothes. "You can change behind that," he said, waving absently toward the metal divider.

It only took a minute for Antoine to change into what turned out to be a pair of coveralls. While they appeared somewhat baggy on Shiv'ren, on Antoine they were much tighter. Granted, he was several inches taller and longer in limb than the elf. The legs weren't as much a problem because his boots covered that, but the arms were more troublesome. Antoine settled for rolling the sleeves up his forearms before pulling on the heavy gloves that had been included. Once he had changed, Antoine folded his clothes into as neat a pile as he could make.

Shiv'ren was idly twirling a pair of goggles on his finger as he waited. "Set your clothes on the chair." He then tossed Antoine the other pair of goggles. "You'll need those." Antoine took the goggles, slipping them over his head to rest on his chest.

They went back to the main area, and Shiv'ren picked up the clipboard again, tapping it lightly against his thigh. "How familiar are you with engines and machinery?"

Antoine shrugged, putting his hands in his pockets. "Not very familiar. I know some of the parts, but I've never had a chance to work with them. I've been told I'm a quick study."

There was an absent nod. "This is the main hub. These here"— Shiv'ren tapped a finger against one of the jumping meters—"are the main readouts. From here you can check the status of the major parts of the engine. Things like temperature, water level, and the feeding pace of the coal. We can even monitor the level of gas in the balloons if necessary." He moved from the displays and over to a collection of levers and dials. "And here is where adjustments can be made in relation to the engine." Antoine took in the wide array of levers, but he noticed there was a particularly large one set off to the side. He wanted to ask what that one was for, since it didn't seem related to all the others. He didn't have a chance, though, as Shiv'ren continued talking. "Most adjustments are small during the day. It takes a soft touch to handle it, so you won't be doing any of those. Instead you'll give me readings while I make adjustments."

"Is it hard to run the engine on a ship like this?" Antoine had absolutely no idea about the different types of engines on aeros. What he had noticed, though, was that once he started talking, a certain light entered Shiv'ren's face. He definitely seemed much more animated and relaxed.

"On a ship the size of the *Aria* it's not very hard. However, the *Aria*'s engines are special. They've been tweaked and overhauled by myself and the engineer that was on the ship before me. There's no other ship quite like her in the skies." Antoine smiled at the fondness he heard in Shiv'ren's voice.

"What kind of ship is the *Aria*?" Antoine glanced at the wall of dials, trying to figure what function each of the meters correlated to.

"Hmm...." Shiv'ren scratched his head absently. "I believe the ship was originally a dirigible sloop, but that mostly refers to the ship's frame itself, not the engine." He reached out, lightly patting one of the pipes that led out of the engine. "She has a lot of surprises inside her, more than anyone would think." Obviously Shiv'ren enjoyed his work and felt a connection with the ship that might even have surpassed that felt by Rivas or the rest of the crew.

"What should I do for now?" Antoine received a grin at his question, and suddenly he was wondering if maybe he shouldn't have asked. Antoine spent the rest of the day applying grease to various gears and pieces of machinery. It was hard work, and Shiv'ren had been correct—it was incredibly dirty. By the end his coveralls were covered in various spots of grease, and his muscles ached. Antoine hadn't even noticed how late it had gotten until he heard a soft chuckle behind him. He turned to stare at Rivas.

CHAPTER ELEVEN

"YOU SEEM to have settled in well here." Rivas sauntered over. Antoine backed up until his back hit machinery. Rivas leaned in, bringing a hand up to cup Antoine's cheek. The touch was warm and rough, calluses scraping over Antoine's skin as Rivas wiped a smudge of grease from his cheekbone. Antoine wasn't able to suppress a shiver and swallowed thickly when Rivas didn't move away.

"It's… it's interesting…." Antoine wanted to wince at his stuttering words and breathless tone. He looked up, meeting those intense bottle green eyes watching him. Rivas hadn't moved away, his thumb still stroking over Antoine's cheekbone, even though Antoine knew the smudge of grease had to be gone by now. Antoine swallowed again. "I… I seem to be p-passable at it." He managed to get the words out, barely aware of what he said. He just knew he needed to say something to break the thick tension.

"I'm sure it's more than passable." Rivas leaned even closer, full lips stretching in a slow, seductive smile. That smile sent an unexpected spark of heat shooting through Antoine's body. "I would have heard if you weren't." His low, silky voice was like a caress, and Antoine fought against the desire to close his eyes and relax into it.

Antoine's eyes had fallen halfway closed when there came a sudden, extremely loud banging noise. He jumped, heart skipping a beat and his adrenaline spiking as the noise came again. He turned in the direction it came from to see Shiv'ren standing behind him. Shiv'ren held a length of metal pipe against one of the large pipes that carried steam from the engine to the rest of the ship. He had an annoyed scowl on his face, golden eyes flashing as he looked at Rivas.

"Captain! If you're going to seduce the hostage, you will *not* do it in my engine room! You have a goddamn bedroom for doing that shit. Plus you're blocking the way, and I want to get to the mess

hall before that greasy bastard decides he's not feeding latecomers."
Antoine realized he hadn't heard Shiv'ren sound this brisk or angry
since he'd first been brought here.

Rivas seemed supremely unaffected, even letting out a small
chuckle. "My apologies, Shiv, I'll be more careful next time." He
gave a slight bow that Antoine was certain was somewhat mocking.
"I suppose we'll be going now and letting you get to your meal. I
know how much you enjoy the cook's creations." Rivas stepped
back and wrapped a strong hand around Antoine's arm, pulling him
along. Antoine was too stunned to fight against the hold, not that he
would have been able to. Instead he focused on getting his still
racing heart to calm down. It wasn't until they were back in Rivas's
quarters and he was released that Antoine was able to feel his pulse
return to normal.

Absently he rubbed at the spot where he'd been grabbed,
trying to erase the feel of Rivas's hand. The heat from it was still
there, imprinted on his flesh like an invisible brand. In fact, his
entire body had felt flushed and overly warm since running into
Rivas in the engine room. Antoine quickly scrubbed his face, the
rough gloves giving him a different sensation to focus on.

This was crazy. He should not be feeling like this. It had to be
some kind of madness brought on by the whole ordeal. Antoine
glanced over at Rivas, and stared at Rivas's broad back before
turning away again. He pulled off his gloves, jamming them in a
pocket before running a hand through his limp brown hair. Antoine
paced over to the window. The sun was setting, lighting the clouds
on fire as they streamed by the ship. It was beautiful, yet also
frightening. Antoine thought there must be something primal in
humans that reacted to the appearance of the clouds being on fire.
Hadn't there been an old saying about red skies and sailors? Or
perhaps it was a nursery rhyme? At least his heart and body felt
calmer now that the unnatural warmth Rivas gave off had finally
faded.

"It's beautiful, isn't it? The sunset from inside the clouds."
Rivas's voice came from behind him, causing Antoine's eyes to shift
and focus on his reflection. Rivas was staring out the window as

well, taking in the movement of the clouds and the color. "If there was no other reason, this alone would keep me in the sky. The sunset from the ground is too tame in comparison." Rivas moved closer, and now Antoine could feel the heat radiating off him.

"I never noticed the sunsets before, seemed such a small thing to take notice of in the city. But you're right, this is so much larger than what I ever saw in Laitha." In Laitha, the clouds of black smoke from the factories and workshops often obscured the sky on the lower terraces. Even on the upper terraces by the Spire, the hazy clouds would often drift up to discolor the sky. The colors were never bright, the aesthetics of nature dwarfed by the advances of man.

"I'm not sure there is a sunset in that city anymore. Even when it is night, parts of it seem to be lit up as though the sun were still overhead."

"You're not fond of Laitha? Have you been to the city?" The view of the clouds slowly faded, and Antoine was left with just the reflection of Rivas standing behind him. He saw the full lips curling in a faint sneer.

"Often enough. Mostly in the lower terraces, where a man's face and name are less important than the coin he carries. I've not ventured to many of the upper terraces, barely up to the market terrace." Rivas's sneer transformed into a smirk. "Not reputable enough to venture out where proper society would see me."

That startled a laugh out of Antoine, seeing the scene clearly in his mind. Rivas would no doubt horrify the gentle ladies of Laitha who frequented the shops of the market terraces. Especially if he went dressed in the tight breeches and white linen shirt he wore now. Antoine tried to imagine Rivas dressed in more formal attire and found he could envision it, but somehow Rivas still looked disreputable.

"Could a pirate ever be considered reputable? I thought your stock and trade was being thieves and scoundrels."

"You would be surprised. There is at least one pirate here that, if he wished to, could blend into the highest society gatherings. However, he doesn't care to do so. I believe he described it as being boring."

That drew another laugh out of Antoine. "I would have to agree with him on that. More than that, it can be exhausting. Everyone has an agenda, trying to find something they can use against you. Some make me think of snakes just the way that they look at you." Antoine shivered, remembering the cold, reptilian looks in the eyes of the nobles at different parties his father would take him to.

It was most disturbing to see women looking as if they wanted to devour him alive, combined with their thinly veiled offers to help him become a man. Antoine often felt slightly dirty after speaking to them. The very idea of doing anything with them made him feel ill. Especially since he knew it was nothing more than an attempt to gain influence with his father through him. While Antoine might have been rather sheltered, he wasn't naïve. He only wished Nigel would be more careful about his own dalliances.

"That's the problem with Laitha. The entire city is dishonest, everyone with secrets of their own or the secrets of others they want to sell." Rivas leaned against the bulkhead, arms crossed loosely across his chest. "Everyone attempting to get ahead at the expense of another."

Antoine shrugged, turning away from the darkened window. "Where do you hail from, then, if not the city?" He noticed food had been laid out on the table. He picked up an apple, glancing over at Rivas questioningly. After getting a nod, Antoine took a bite. The work earlier had left him starving, and he quickly devoured the apple in a few bites before grabbing another. Besides the fruit, there was also some bread and hard cheese, nothing fancy but still infinitely better than the bland gruel he'd had previously.

"We'll be making a stop soon, to resupply." Antoine glanced up, surprised by Rivas's words. Any aero would need to resupply at some point, but he'd never thought about where exactly a pirate ship would do so. It wasn't as if it could just pull up to any aerodock it came across.

"Where?" Maybe he could figure out exactly where they were now. Then he could finally figure out how far from Laitha he was.

There were several towns that had aerodocks, but none were as big as Laitha's.

"Tyrnium," Rivas said, reaching over, snatching up a handful of figs, and then popping one in his mouth. "We'll dock and resupply, give the men a chance to relax away from the *Aria*. A chance to spend their shares on what they wish."

Antoine was surprised. The name of the town was familiar, but it took a couple of moments to think of where exactly it was located. "I thought Tyrnium was in ruins?" It was supposedly an ancient outpost on the northern ridge of mountains on the plateau. It had been a bustling city long ago when a trade route had run between the Archduchy of Laitha and the eastern kingdoms. A landslide had destroyed the best mountain path centuries ago, causing the city to eventually be abandoned, or so he believed.

"Tyrnium is abandoned to normal society, but its location is perfect for docking aeros. The belief that it's a pile of ruins is a boon for those who wish to stay unnoticed of the Archduke's navy." Rivas smirked a bit, popping another fig in his mouth and chewing slowly. "You'll find that a lot of things aren't quite how they seem."

Antoine sighed, stretching his sore muscles slowly. Twinges of pain flashed through his back and shoulders. "When we arrive, am I to stay on the ship?"

Rivas didn't respond right away, thinking it over. "We'll have to see. It will take another day to get there. If I allow you to leave, it would be under supervision. There are many dangerous characters in Tyrnium." With that, Rivas stood and walked out, leaving Antoine alone in the cabin.

CHAPTER TWELVE

THOUGH HE was tired and sore, Antoine wasn't ready to sleep yet. Instead he prowled around the cabin for several minutes, searching for something to occupy his attention, but there was little to be found in the way of amusement. There were a few books scattered about the cabin, mostly on geology, of all things. It seemed unusual for the captain of an aero and completely unrelated to the activities Rivas engaged in.

A few titles were familiar from his father's library, and eventually Antoine settled on a book entitled *The Mountains and Minerals of the Laithu Mountain Range*. If Antoine remembered correctly, it was a rather dull tome with little interesting about it. His memory proved correct, and after nearly an hour of reading, Antoine could no longer keep himself awake.

When he woke several hours later, the cabin was dim and the only light came from a gas lamp on a nearby table that had been turned down. Antoine rubbed his eyes, which felt gritty from sleep, and a heavy blanket slid off him. A glance at the porthole showed the sky to be completely black. Yawning, Antoine stood, wrapping the blanket around his shoulders to keep warm. He shuffled across the room and picked up the lamp, using its faint light to navigate toward the bedroom. It was a slow pace, Antoine having to keep blinking in order to make his eyes focus.

Upon stumbling in, Antoine reflexively glanced toward the bed. What he saw made his breath hitch, temporarily chasing the sleepiness from his mind. In the flickering light, he could make out the massive shape of the pirate captain. Moving closer, he could see that Rivas was naked from the waist up, his lower half hidden by the blanket. The light glinted off the thick golden hair that covered his muscled chest and abdomen. Rivas's skin was tan, lines of scars crisscrossing his skin like lines on a map. Some were pink and new-looking, others white and faded from age. Antoine swallowed, his mouth suddenly dry.

Antoine was riveted by the muscles that rippled as Rivas breathed. It wasn't until the lamp began to sputter that he realized how much time had passed. Turning away, he quickly went over to the hammock, hanging the lamp on a nearby nail. Once safely in the hammock and wrapped in the blanket, Antoine extinguished the lamp, allowing the darkness to hide him.

IT WAS morning when he next woke, and Rivas was not anywhere to be found. Antoine dressed quickly, grabbing some bread that had been left out. Since he hadn't seen Shandor yesterday, Antoine could only assume he was to return to the engine room. Finishing the hurried breakfast, he descended the decks, wondering what exactly Shiv'ren would have him do today.

Antoine checked that his goggles were secured around his neck. He pulled on his gloves before making his way into the catacomb of tunnels that made up the engine room to reach the rear. Walking in, he immediately saw Shiv'ren at a table in the corner that was covered with game pieces. Shiv'ren had a look of deep concentration on his face, the golden wings rustling softly. Sitting opposite him was the woman Antoine had seen on the deck his second night aboard the *Aria*. Without her coat, he could see she was wearing a long dress of blue brocade covered in embroidery with a high collar and slits up the sides. Her stocking-clad legs were crossed neatly as she watched her opponent study the board.

"You should decide your move quickly, Shiv'ren. You have company."

Shiv'ren glanced up, and blinked as he focused on Antoine. "You're here sooner than I thought you would be." Turning back to the game, he picked up a piece and swiftly moved it to a new position. Then he stood and flashed Antoine a quick smile. "She's going to defeat me in four moves."

"Three moves actually." The voice was light and confident, the click of the piece being set on the board only just audible over the ambient noise of the engine.

"No need to be quite that blatant about it, Yi."

"There is no reason to be untruthful about your chances either." She glided over to stand in front of Antoine, the decorations in her hair swaying gently. "It is a pleasure to see you again, Antoine Suvalese."

A lifetime of manners instilled by his mother took over. "It is my pleasure, madam," he said, bowing politely like he would to one of the ladies he had met at his father's functions. The fact that they were in an engine room and she was a pirate and not a noble lady was hardly important.

"Lovely manners, something that has been missing from here." There was a faint snort from Shiv'ren, causing her delicate eyebrow to arch. She held out a slim hand clad in a black glove. "I do apologize, I have not properly introduced myself as yet. I am Yi, the Gunnery Master of the *Bloody Aria*."

Reflexively Antoine took the hand, bowing over it, as her words began to penetrate his mind. "The Gunnery Master? I thought that was a man's position." Antoine was completely surprised that the pirates would allow a woman to hold such an important position. He would have thought air piracy was a male-dominated society. Certainly Yi was the only female pirate Antoine had ever heard of. Besides being a woman, she was also from the far eastern kingdoms, a land not known for encouraging independent women.

She laughed, and Antoine felt his face heating at the slightly mocking tone. "It never fails. Once someone knows my gender, they immediately believe it is impossible for me to do anything except look pretty." Yi smiled as she spoke, her head tilting slightly to the side.

The words only increased Antoine's embarrassment. "I apologize, I didn't mean to be disrespectful of your position, I just... I wasn't expecting...."

"Expecting to hear that a woman was in charge of guns. The explosions would no doubt frighten us too much. Not to mention the dirt and soot." Yi made a face, waving a hand dismissively.

A wave of panic broke over Antoine, eyes widening as he shook his head. He had never handled women very well, especially strong-willed women. In both good and bad ways, Yi reminded him of his mother. Both were strong-willed, strong-minded women with no problem going after exactly what they wanted. No man would get in their way, and no man could intimidate them.

"Stop teasing him so much, Yi. It's not nice, and I don't need him so flustered he can't work." Shiv'ren didn't even look over, seemingly preoccupied by what the different readings were telling him.

"Very well, Shiv." Yi gave a light pat to Antoine's shoulder as she walked by him. "You handled it better than most do, which says something about your character. Let me know when you've decided your next move, Shiv'ren."

"Good-bye, Yi." Shiv'ren's response was distracted, his attention absorbed by the various dials and gauges. "Antoine, come over here. I need you to check some of these measurements for accuracy." He marked something on the clipboard before running a hand absently through his hair, leaving a long smudge of ink high on his cheekbone.

"Which ones am I checking?"

"You're going to be checking the readings on these gauges." Shiv'ren pointed to five different dials clustered together.

Antoine looked at the dials but had no idea what exactly he was seeing. "What am I supposed to be checking?"

"These give the pressure and temperature for the main furnace." There was an absent gesture toward the large furnace. "You need to monitor and be sure that none of them go into the red area."

The monotony of the task helped calm and steady Antoine's nerves. He found his mind drifting from one subject to another as he worked. He wondered if his father had received the ransom demand yet, and if so how he had reacted. From there his thoughts drifted to his mother and brother, wondering how they would react when they found out. No doubt this would create quite a scandal. The papers would no doubt be covered in bold headlines about the kidnapped son of an influential man at the hands of dastardly air pirates. The thought of air pirates brought his thoughts back to the subject of the infamous pirate captain, Rivas the Ramshot, and they stayed there for longer than he wanted to acknowledge.

CHAPTER THIRTEEN

RIVAS BENT over the map in front of him, doing his best to ignore the smirking of his quartermaster and friend. He knew that growling or otherwise making his displeasure known would just encourage the gypsy. "If you smirk any louder, Shan, the whole of the ship will know."

That brought a rich chuckle, the sound soothing in its own way. "I apologize, I've simply never seen you so besotted before. You can't blame me for finding it amusing, Rivas. Especially since you've been calculating our trajectory for the past thirty minutes without a single change. It hasn't taken you this long to do it since you started growing fur on your body."

Rivas snorted, straightening up and glaring at his longtime friend. "Need I remind you, I'm hardly the only one besotted on this ship?"

"Oh aye, but it's never interfered with my work either. Also, I've never been hankering after a hostage before." Shandor picked up the calipers, carefully measuring the distance between the two points that Rivas had marked. "So tell me, did we choose young Mr. Suvalese because of his family connections, or because his pretty brown eyes caught your attention?"

Rivas's first instinct was to tell Shandor to shut his damned mouth. Except that wouldn't work with someone as familiar with him as the gypsy. "I saw him once before, when we were last in Laitha proper. I was scouting out the Suvalese family, trying to figure out which one would be the easiest to kidnap."

"Then you saw the pretty brown eyes and your choice was set," Shandor teased before frowning at the map.

Rivas felt his face twist into a scowl, the old scar on his cheek pulling with the motion. He knew Shandor was teasing him, a bit of petty revenge for all the times Rivas had mocked him about his dogged pursuit of Shiv'ren. Yet the words hit closer than he would

53

like, so he altered the course of the conversation. "The way you keep going on, perhaps you're the one who's become entranced by Mr. Suvalese," Rivas said, crossing his arms over his chest.

"I don't go for the naïve innocent type. You know that." There was the familiar whirring sound of Shandor's mechanical eye adjusting itself. No matter how many times over the years Rivas had heard the sound, it was still disconcerting. Watching the eye adjust and telescope was equally as strange, even though he had seen that quite often too. "So, you're planning on stopping in Tyrnium and then continuing onward to Black Rocks."

Rivas nodded, straightening up and turning back to the map. "We've taken several ships. The men need time to unwind and debauch themselves. Lighten their purses and give us time to receive a response to our demands." Shandor turned his head to the side, and Rivas felt the weight of those strange eyes resting on him. "How long did you give them to respond?"

"I gave them five days to respond with a time frame of how long it would take to get the money together. Given how close Tyrnium is to Laitha, it shouldn't take that long for the messenger to return with a response." Rivas traced his finger from Laitha up the mountain pass to the small dot that marked their destination. "So you figure two days at Tyrnium while we wait for a response?"

"Two days there, then upon receipt of our response we head to Black Rocks and stay there until the time for the exchange. Hopefully he won't make us wait too long, or we'll have to go out to keep the crew from becoming difficult."

"Considering by that point we're likely to have a large part of the Archduke's navy hunting for us." Shandor's lips twitched, but the expression didn't reach his flesh eye. "More than they have tried to do so far. Who did you send to deliver the demand?"

"I sent Ciel in the small aeropod." Rivas tapped the table lightly before glancing over at the voice tube that ran from the rear of the bridge to the various parts of the ship. Including the engine room, where he could hear Shiv'ren's garbled voice in the middle of some type of explanation.

"Ciel?" Shandor's voice was sharp, pulling Rivas's attention back to him. The gypsy's dark eye flashed in the light, wariness flitting briefly across his face. "Are you sure that's a wise decision, Rivas?" Rivas paused, turning to look at his friend. Shandor in general was content to leave the decision making in these situations to Rivas. If he had concerns or didn't agree, he would wait until they were in private before bringing it up. Shandor understood that they had to keep a united front to the crew to maintain order. So whenever he saw fit to test his judgment where others could hear, it made Rivas pause and reevaluate.

Ciel had been on the *Bloody Aria* for just over a year, which made him a veteran as far as crewmen went. He was an adequate sailor, good at his job and a crack shot when battle came. Off duty, Ciel tended to be quiet, even reclusive, but there was no reason not to trust him. On any kind of aero, trust was the most important thing to have amongst a crew.

Rivas trusted Ciel, not on a deeply personal level, but enough to follow the orders he was given. The main reason he had sent Ciel was his ability to easily blend in. He was to deliver the ransom notice, receive Mr. Suvalese's response, and then slip away without being followed. Unlike many pirates, Ciel was rather unremarkable in appearance, and that meant he could blend with the crowds of the city.

Shandor was staring intently at him, his very stillness giving tell to how important Rivas's response would be. "Ciel was the best choice I had, Shandor. I needed someone what would be able to move through the city without drawing undue attention. We don't have many crew that can do that."

Rivas watched as Shandor scowled, turning his head away. "I don't trust him, Rivas. There's something off about him. There always has been." His voice was gruff, hands moving restlessly over the table.

"Nothing to be done about it at this point. Ciel should have reached the city already and be preparing to deliver the ransom note," Rivas said with a sigh. "So you'll have to trust him now."

"Or make contingency plans."

"That's what I've always enjoyed about you, Shandor, the optimistic outlook you have upon life." Rivas walked toward the platform that held the wheel. "Li, continue on course for Tyrnium. I want to reach it by tomorrow."

"Aye, aye, Captain." Rivas left the wheelhouse and stepped out into the sun, the wind blowing his blond hair back from his face. His crew was working steadily at their various jobs, not even glancing up when he passed them. It was strange at times, to think he was in charge when he could still clearly remember being a lowly sailor himself.

It was said once a person got a taste of the freedom given by the wide blue sky and the ships that sailed her, the sky became their home. Rivas believed it, because he had been in these skies since his eleventh year and still had no desire to return to a life on land. For as long as he had been sailing the skies, he had been on board the *Bloody Aria*. He knew for many of his crew it was exactly the same. Even the very enigmatic Shandor. Rivas had known the gypsy for ten years and had already been a seasoned crewmate when the younger man had come aboard.

Rivas had served under six different captains before being voted into the position himself. Under his command, the *Bloody Aria* had become more infamous than ever before. The main source of their notoriety was that they were unafraid to take on larger ships. Especially those belonging to the Suva Coal Company, which wielded power second only to that of the Archduke of Laitha. Rivas knew that with his latest move, his name was certain to be cemented as a legend amongst air pirates. Though, to be truthful, creating a legend for himself was not his motivation when he planned this particular scheme. His reason was much more personal.

Rivas paced the deck, making sure everything was in position and taken care of. The crew was glad to hear that they would be pulling into port soon. Their loot was burning holes in their pockets, and boredom was beginning to peak, which was never a good thing. Everyone might have a designated job onboard an aero. However, none of the jobs were so involved that it took the entire day to complete. Boredom was a captain's worst enemy. Bored crew had time to talk to each other. Talk led to complaints, and then to dissatisfaction, and ultimately a call to install a new captain on the ship. Good pirate captains made sure the crew had few chances to grow bored.

Rivas joked with his men about what he would do when they reached Tyrnium. He made it sound like he'd be right there with them in the pubs and the whorehouses, sharing the drink and merriment. He never did, though, at least not to the extent that the others would when the *Aria* pulled into any of the safe ports. Rivas would go to the pubs and drink heartily, but he never went to the whorehouses. A decision to which he attributed his continuing good health. It was tempting to spend all day on the deck and leave the others to the work of preparing for entering the port. There were many tasks to be completed before reaching port and still more once they reached it, besides giving the men a chance to unwind. After returning to his quarters, Rivas strode over to his desk, and pulled out a small inkwell and pen before sitting down. The ship needed supplies, which meant he needed to put together a supply list. The list distracted him for several hours. After that, there were other tasks to occupy his time. Before Rivas even realized it, the daylight had begun to fade, washing the cabin in spots of color. Rivas stood and stretched, his back giving a creak and pop, a reminder he wasn't so young anymore. At twenty-seven most would not consider him old, but amongst air pirates, he was very old indeed. That Rivas had lived so many years doing it was a testament to both his toughness and his luck.

Looking around, Rivas realized Antoine hadn't returned yet. Moving to the door, he yanked it open and looked out into the corridor to determine if Antoine was nearby. When he couldn't find the younger man, Rivas decided to find out where he had gotten to. Rivas went to the mess hall, figuring Antoine had followed Shiv'ren there for the evening meal. The mess was as chaotic as ever, so instead of looking for Antoine, he scanned for the distinctive golden color of Shiv'ren's wings. It took only a moment to spot the elf off in a far corner, and next to him sat Antoine, picking at whatever gruel the cook had created that night.

Rivas made his way over to the corner, dropping down heavily onto the bench next to Antoine. He watched those large, fathomless brown eyes fix on his face for a moment before quickly looking away. Antoine's face was smudged in various places with grease from the engine. The recently acquired goggles were pushed up on his forehead, keeping strands of sweaty brown hair back from his narrow face. It gave Antoine a certain ruggedness that Rivas felt suited him better.

"Here is something unexpected, the captain joining us in the mess. Normally you eat in your cabin and refuse to touch this stuff." Shiv'ren's voice was mocking, golden eyes focused on Rivas.

"One of the benefits of being the captain is not having to eat the swill the cook calls food," Rivas replied, looking down at the unappetizing plate.

"The captain is too good to eat normal food like the rest of his crew," Shiv'ren said, leaning over the table and rolling his eyes for Antoine's benefit. The words from anyone else would have been scathing, but there was a glint of amusement in Shiv'ren's eyes. This was a conversation they'd had before.

"I'm not the only one who objects to calling that food. Li and Yi don't eat here either if they can avoid it."

"No, they eat in a cabin because they have strange food traditions. I tried it once, too much boiling and excessive spices." Shiv'ren made a face, shaking his head.

"To each their own. The fact still remains, if the men want to bring their own rations onboard, they're welcome to. I would welcome it if they chose to spend their shares on fine food rather than whores and drink," Rivas replied, glancing at Antoine out of the corner of his eye. He was growing quite fond of the delicate blush that colored Antoine's cheeks at the crude conversation.

"As if they would partake in something like that. A few coppers for a warm meal, strong ale, and a few more to buy some willing company for their bed. That's all they care about." Shiv'ren waved a hand vaguely at the rest of the people in the mess, most of who were done with their meals now. Tables were moved aside to allow for the playing of music as the sailors drank and danced the night away.

"Then it is their loss and they've no need to complain about me not dining here all the time," Rivas said, standing up. "We dock tomorrow. We'll be there for at least two days. If there is anything you need that you haven't already mentioned, you'll be responsible for purchasing it." When Shiv'ren nodded in acknowledgment, Rivas smiled, turning to look at Antoine.

Antoine looked excited at the prospect of the ship arriving in Tyrnium. It was obvious he had lived a sheltered and secluded life before becoming Rivas's guest aboard the *Aria*. Yet Rivas sensed a desire for adventure deep within Antoine, a potential for great passion that had never been tapped. The idea of bringing that passion out of Antoine, in any number of ways, was enough to cause Rivas's blood to quicken.

CHAPTER FOURTEEN

THE NEXT morning Antoine woke without any prompting. Honestly his body had been thrumming with energy since Rivas had told him they would be docking today. He had no idea what to expect when they arrived, which only enhanced the excitement twisting his gut. Rivas hadn't been in the cabin when Antoine woke, but there was food laid out. Antoine ate quickly then headed to the engine room.

When he made it to Shiv'ren's little control center, the winged elf was already a flurry of activity. Levers were pulled, adjustments made, and sweat had already dampened his golden hair. "Good, you're finally here. We're going to begin the descent and docking soon. I need you to go and watch those gauges over there." He gave an absent wave to a set of gauges connected to the furnace. "Make sure they don't drop below the second black mark."

Antoine watched the gauges for an hour, calling out the readings when requested. Messages reverberated down the speaking tube, which Shiv'ren responded to. Eventually a shudder ran through the entire ship, followed by a jerking stop that almost knocked Antoine off his feet. A hand came to rest on his shoulder, giving him some support until he managed to gain his balance again. "Come on, we're docked now." Shiv'ren patted him lightly on the shoulder before pulling away. "Time to get off and go into the town." Shiv'ren went behind the metal sheet, emerging a few minutes later. He had two belts slung low on his hips, each holding a pistol and a large wrench that he put through the belt loop of his coveralls. Antoine was curious about the sudden addition of weapons to Shiv'ren's attire, but when he stopped to think about where they were going, he decided it made sense. Shiv'ren gestured for Antoine to follow him out of the engine room.

Soon they were out on deck, and Antoine was getting his first look at the pirate port of Tyrnium. The *Aria* was tethered to a makeshift dock constructed on a plateau. A gangplank led to the ground and sailors were disembarking, talking boisterously about what they were going to do first. A quick glance around showed that the only people Antoine recognized were Shiv'ren and Yi, who was waiting by the gangplank.

Yi smiled, the expression beautiful and slightly cold because it did nothing to warm her eyes. She was dressed in the same coat as before, looking as regal as any noble Antoine had ever met. Antoine wasn't able to actually see the town until they were on a steep set of stairs that led down the mountainside. The ruins of older buildings spread out, showing the history of the town from when it had been a stopping point for trade through the mountain passes. Throughout the town were signs of continued occupation in the remaining buildings. The places that didn't have usable walls but solid foundations had newer buildings erected over them, though they didn't seem exceptionally sturdy. The closer they got, the more noise that began to crescendo around them. Drunken laughter, thin music, and, most unexpectedly, the calls of merchants lining the streets.

"How do the navy patrols miss this place?" Antoine wondered out loud, only to give a slight hiss when a hand grabbed his arm, his eyes locking on Yi's black ones.

"Keep your voice down, and do not mention such things. You do not want your life ended prematurely, do you?" When he nodded, she released him, turning forward again. "The reason they do not notice this place is because they do not patrol this area. It has no value to Laitha anymore. Why waste resources patrolling empty space?"

"The few ships that do come through, well, watchmen are easily bribed. So instead of a bustling town, they report just a small village sparsely inhabited." Shiv'ren smirked, stretching his arms and wings with a sigh. "Always something different about the air on the land than on the sea."

Antoine stayed close to the two air pirates as they moved through the town. He thought perhaps his eyes would fall out of his head as he tried to take in all of the different sights. It wasn't the wide variety of items available for purchase that surprised him—the markets in Laitha had more. Instead it was the acts taking place all around him. There was fighting, cursing, and he passed more than a few spaces where he swore he saw people having sex against the sides of different buildings, and once he thought he saw them lying in a dirty alley.

"Don't gawk so much, Antoine," Yi said with amusement, placing a hand gently on his arm this time and pulling him along the road.

They turned off the main thoroughfare and stepped into a twisting set of alleys that Antoine was unable to keep track of. Eventually they stopped in front of a door with no sign. This was the parting of ways, it seemed, because Yi went inside and Shiv'ren went onward, leaving Antoine to follow after him.

They moved through the town most of the day, Antoine trailing after Shiv'ren as he went to various places. Shiv'ren would buy random items, some of which Antoine heard him arrange to have delivered to the *Aria*. Eventually they ended up in a pub off the main road, sharing a hard wooden bench with two tankards of some type of alcohol in front of them. Shiv'ren had said it was rum, but all Antoine really knew was one sip of it had him coughing and sputtering for several minutes. It caused a few of the patrons to laugh, which in turn caused Antoine to turn red with embarrassment. He hadn't tried to drink any more of it.

Food was placed in front of them, a meager fare of bread and some roasted meat whose age could not quite be hidden by the amount of spices the cook had put in it. Still it was better than what he had gotten on the ship, and he ate it with gusto. Antoine had worked his way up to taking another, more cautious sip of his drink. This one he handled better than the first. Shiv'ren had already gone through two tankards, but didn't seem at all affected.

"How do you drink this... swill?" Antoine asked, looking over at the winged elf he had started to consider a friend. Or at least as close to one as he could get given the circumstance of his capture.

"It's more of an acquired taste, one you learn after drinking it a long time," Shiv'ren said, grinning slightly. "Still, in places like this you don't want to drink what passes for water." He took another drink, grimacing a bit and then shaking his head. "Also, the more alcohol you drink, the longer it takes to affect you."

"At least that's what the old timers say." The sound of Rivas's voice gave Antoine a start. Rivas stood beside their table, his familiar smirk making Antoine's stomach turn over in a not unpleasant way.

"I'm not sure I'll ever have the stomach to build up that kind of tolerance," Antoine replied, taking another sip of the caustic drink.

"You're doing it wrong, Antoine. You don't sip something like this! That gives you a chance to taste it. You need to just swallow in one pull, so you don't have to actually deal with the taste." To demonstrate, Rivas picked up his own tankard and took a long pull before setting it down with a strong thump. A cheer went up from several of the nearby pirates, followed by calls for more drink to be brought out as Rivas dropped onto the bench next to Antoine.

Three on the bench made it a rather close fit, and Antoine became keenly aware of the heat from Rivas's thigh pressing against his. In an effort to distract himself, Antoine grabbed his tankard and took a large swallow, letting out a gasp as the alcohol burned down the back of his throat. Rivas was correct—downing it quickly kept you from really tasting it as much. Antoine thought that was mostly because your throat was on fire more than anything else. He was still working on getting his breath back when a hand clapped him roughly on his shoulder. The hand didn't withdraw. Rivas left it there, leaning forward on the table and grabbing a remnant from their meal.

Antoine tried to distract himself from the feeling of that strong hand on his shoulder. He gripped his tankard harder, his whole body warm now. Why hadn't he felt how warm the pub was before now? Words were being said, but none of them really penetrated Antoine's suddenly fuzzy mind. Since the conversation didn't seem to involve him or require his attention, Antoine focused instead on his drink. He took a few more gulps, finding that the more he drank the less it burned. The overall heat seemed to increase, and his thoughts stopped making sense entirely. Also Antoine thought at one point some inconsiderate person had tilted the entire pub on him, so now everything was at an angle. At least he had found a comfortable place to rest his head.

"I think he's a bit drunk, Captain." The voice floated through the white noise that made up Antoine's thoughts. He frowned a bit, opening his mouth to tell Shiv'ren that he was not drunk at all. What ended up coming out was a rather undignified belch. He brought his hand up to hide his mouth, scowling at the laughter he heard.

"'M not drunk...." Antoine scowled harder when the words slurred as they passed his lips. He was not drunk! His body just didn't want to cooperate with him.

"It seems our guest can't handle his liquor very well." Rivas's voice seemed much closer than it had been before. A calloused hand came up and gently brushed Antoine's hair back from his flushed cheek. Antoine realized his comfortable pillow was rhythmically moving up and down. Was he leaning on Rivas? Antoine turned his head a bit, spying Shiv'ren leaning back against the wall, wings slightly spread. That meant he was definitely leaning on Rivas, which for some reason his mind was telling him was not a good thing. However, Antoine couldn't think of precisely why it wasn't good.

"Ish... not good." Antoine waved his hand a bit, though it ended up being more of a flail than anything else.

"What's not good?" More amusement, which was just annoying.

"Feeling good... like...." Antoine gestured again, the precise words escaping him. "This!" There was more laughter, softer this time.

"You're thinking too much. Just relax." A calloused hand brushed his cheek, stroking the hair from his face. A shiver moved down Antoine's spine, and he let out a small sigh as the caressing continued. All the strength seemed to leave his bones, and Antoine decided not to let the wrongness bother him. Time lost meaning again, though he was aware of another glass being pressed into his hand at one point. When he drank it, it didn't burn as badly as the previous drinks. Instead it actually cooled his throat, and for that Antoine was grateful.

"I think it's time that we got you home, Antoine."

Rivas's voice caused Antoine to peel his eyes open, unaware that they had even closed. He blinked slowly, the room swimming into focus. Antoine tried to straighten his body, but the room slid sideways in a rather dizzying fashion. His stomach churned a bit, and he closed his eyes again until the nausea passed. As the churning died down, he again felt Rivas steadying him. Even in such a short period of time, the touch had become both familiar and comforting.

Antoine moved to stand up, and Rivas's arm slipped around his shoulders, bracing him as the room started to whirl like he was riding a carousel. This time he had to bring a hand up in an effort to keep the contents of his stomach from coming up. It most likely wouldn't have been noticed or even considered unusual for someone to be sick in this type of bar. Antoine just wasn't sure his pride would be able to stand the embarrassment of it. Walking proved no easier than standing had been. It felt like his legs had been replaced with springs, and he was certain it was mostly Rivas that kept him upright and mobile as they left the pub.

The cool mountain air helped to remove some of the alcohol-laden fuzziness from Antoine's mind. As he became more aware of the world around him, he realized they were walking down the main boulevard in the direction of the *Bloody Aria*. There were a few sputtering gas lamps giving off faint, greasy light, but most of the light came from the nearly full moon hanging over the town.

As they slowly headed back toward the ship, Antoine's attention was caught by a brightly colored bandana at the edge of one of the lamps. Blinking, he forced his eyes to focus on the figures, and quickly found that it was actually two men standing together. His sluggish mind told him one was Shandor, but the other was a man he didn't recognize. He wore a long, rather flamboyantly colored frock coat, and a long queue of curling black hair fell over his shoulder. The alley was too dim to make out anything of his face other than the vague impression of strong features and a bearded jaw.

"Who'sh that?" The words were a slur, and Antoine stumbled as he tried to keep looking even though they were past the alley now. "That man talking with Sh-Sh-Shandor...." He was really starting to hate how his tongue felt too big for his mouth.

There was a pause, and Antoine felt Rivas pull away slightly and crane his neck around to see. After a minute of watching, Rivas returned his gaze forward, renewing their march. "That's Beznik."

"Beshnik...." Vaguely Antoine was aware he had horribly maimed the pronunciation, but again his tongue felt too large for his mouth, lips too clumsy to form proper words.

"Yes, Beznik. Shandor meets with him every time we come here. He's some kind of information dealer. I've heard he mostly operates in Laitha, but it seems the gypsy can get anywhere he likes."

"Why would Sh-Sh-shandoor need to shpeak with him?"

"Not sure. I've known Shandor for ten years or more, yet sometimes I'm still not sure how much I actually know about him. He keeps things very close to his chest, which makes him hard to read. It also makes him a great pirate."

Antoine made a soft noise of agreement, his eyes getting heavy again. As they came to the stairs, his neck was suddenly unable to support the weight of his head. Words were being said, but his mind wasn't deciphering their actual meaning. He could feel the change under his feet from the solid ground to the ship's deck. It was a change in how their footsteps echoed, and the way things seemed to sway in a manner that had nothing to do with his poor balance.

The trip from the deck to the cabin was a blur that he wouldn't remember later. All he really was aware of was a change from outside to inside, and then being laid on something soft, and warm being draped over him. Then he wasn't aware of anything else for a long time.

THE SEEDIEST bars of Laitha were located on the lowest of the terraces, close to the ground but kept away from the still functional seaport. It was the location of the city's underbelly, where getting an answer to a question depended on how much coin the person asking was holding. It was a place to be seen and also a place to disappear.

Which was why Ciel had informed Suvalese to have his messenger come here to deliver his response to the ransom demand.

Nursing a tankard of the thin ale they served, Ciel scanned the people in the room. The agreed-upon time was approaching, and he had to admit to a certain anxiousness about who would be sent to deal with him. He hid his nervousness, though, years of practice making it easy. He gestured to the serving girl for a refill to his drink, idly drumming his fingers on the table.

Fortunately he wasn't forced to wait long before a new figure walked in. There had been an effort made to blend in with the other patrons, but it was still obvious that this person was not a regular. The clothing, while not of a great quality, had obviously been recently purchased. Still, it was enough to not stand out blatantly. No doubt some would think it was some merchant's son come to slum in the lower terraces. As he came closer, Ciel saw that it was Rupert, Nigel Suvalese's valet. This development was not unexpected, and Ciel hid a grin behind his mug.

Rupert dropped down onto the opposite chair, signaling for the serving girl to bring him an ale. Nothing was said until Rupert had his own drink, which he carefully pushed aside after taking an initial sip. It was becoming obvious that Ciel would have to be the one to begin.

"What is Mr. Suvalese's response to our demands?"

Rupert's face briefly twisted into a sneer before smoothing out. "Mr. Suvalese will meet your demands regarding his son. However, he asks that he be given time to gather the money."

Ciel nodded slowly. "Captain Rivas anticipated that you would require time. He is willing to give you up to a month to gather the ransom and bring it to the rendezvous point."

"Very well, I will pass this along to Mr. Suvalese." Rupert cast a quick glance around before leaning forward. "There is another matter I have to discuss with you, on behalf of the younger Mr. Suvalese."

This time Ciel didn't bother to hide his smirk. From the moment he had stepped into the Suvalese manor and presented the neatly written ransom note to Adrian Suvalese, he had sensed there was something else going on. When Adrian had read the letter aloud to his firstborn, Ciel had caught the look of surprised glee on Nigel's face before it was quickly masked. Right then, he had known Nigel would be sending a special request to Ciel.

"The younger Mr. Suvalese would be quite pleased if it could be arranged for his brother to have an unfortunate… accident, before the exchange was finished."

Ciel chuckled a bit, playing with his tankard. "I might be able to arrange something. However, if he wants it to be convincing, I'll need his assistance." With luck he would not only be able to give the spoiled Suvalese son what he desired, but line his own pocket and advance his ambitions all at the same time.

CHAPTER FIFTEEN

THE NEXT morning, the sunlight slanting through the portholes felt like hot knives being stabbed into Antoine's skull through his eye sockets. A whimper worked itself out of his throat, the soft sound causing needles of pain to pierce his skull through his ears. Antoine carefully moved further under the blankets, trying to escape the painful brightness.

It worked briefly, but soon the uncomfortable pressure in his bladder forced him to move again. Very carefully Antoine sat up, quickly overbalanced, and fell out of the hammock with a pained grunt. Lifting the covers away, he kept his eyes firmly shut against the pain and brightness, even though it did little to help. Slowly Antoine climbed blindly to his feet and bumped into various items as he shuffled to the water closet. After bumping into the washstand hard enough to nearly knock the basin off, Antoine finally slitted his eyes open enough to navigate to the water closet.

After relieving his bladder, Antoine felt slightly more awake and able to face the day. It did little to lessen the pain vibrating through his head, though. Returning to the washstand, he found a pitcher of water along with a heavy mug waiting for him. He drank several glasses and poured the rest into the basin. The cool water splashing over his face helped to clear more of the cobwebs from his mind and dulled the pain somewhat so it was easier to think. Shuffling back to the bed, Antoine ran his hand through his tangled brown hair, trying to recall what had happened.

Vague memories from last night began to return, causing Antoine to groan slightly. He couldn't remember drinking that much, but he had quite obviously been completely drunk. After the first large drink of alcohol, Antoine could only remember pieces of the previous night. It might be for the best that he couldn't draw up more details as to what had happened, because Antoine had a feeling it was embarrassing. At least he had woken up completely clothed, so he was certain nothing indecent had happened.

The gurgling of his stomach drew Antoine out of his musings and into the main part of the cabin in search of food. There was some bread laid out on the table, along with another pitcher and some cheese. The first few bites were careful, in case his stomach rejected them. Once Antoine was certain his stomach wouldn't rebel against the food, he began to tuck in. The pitcher ended up containing milk, no doubt a rare treat on a ship. Antoine wondered how exactly Rivas had obtained it. He felt better after eating, his headache lessening to where he felt able to leave the room.

Upon stepping out of the cabin, he found the *Bloody Aria* deserted. As Antoine walked around, he briefly considered trying to escape while the pirates were preoccupied with their debauchery. The thought lasted just long enough for Antoine to realize that even if he were to escape, there was little hope of actually getting anywhere. Tyrnium citizens would offer no help, and Antoine didn't have the slightest idea how far away the next town was. Antoine also realized that he had no clue how to survive the trek to a different town. So far Rivas and his crew had been decent to him, and the pragmatic part of Antoine's mind knew that attempting to escape was a good way to lose that goodwill. Antoine climbed the stairs to the top deck, hoping that fresh air would help clear the cobwebs from his mind. Cool mountain air ruffled his hair and clothes, soothing his headache even further. He took a deep breath, walking over to the railing as his chest expanded with the clean air. Even though he was still sore, there was a strange sense of peace to be found—something he had never felt before. Antoine refused to think about why he felt at peace when he was a prisoner and just decided to enjoy it.

The sound of approaching boots broke Antoine's sense of peace. Antoine thought he would see Rivas, or perhaps Shiv'ren, when he turned around. Instead he was greeted with the dark-haired figure of Shandor sauntering toward him. He seemed different today, and it took Antoine's still slightly befuddled mind to realize what was different. The black curls weren't bound by their normal bandana but twisted freely around his shoulders. There was a pensive look on his face as he leaned against the rail next to Antoine.

They stood there in silence for several minutes, the only sounds coming from the town below and the birds. When Shandor finally spoke, Antoine gave a startled jump. "You often attend society functions in Laitha, don't you? As the son of the great coal tycoon, yes?"

It was such a strange question, Antoine answered without thinking. "Somewhat often. They are not something I enjoy, but Father and Mother insist I attend."

"When was the last time you saw the Archduke at one of those functions?" Shandor never looked at Antoine as he spoke, just stared into the horizon.

"I can't recall. I know the Archduchess was at a ball I attended last month."

"Was the Archduke by her side? Or did she attend alone?"

The question gave Antoine pause and made him think about when he had last seen the Archduke of Laitha out in society. "She was alone at that ball." He frowned as he continued to think back. "I can't remember the last time I saw him out in society... I remember hearing a rumor that he's been in ill health for several years. I suppose stepping out would be hard on him."

Shandor snorted, looking away from the mountain. "I'm certain it is," Shandor muttered, more to himself than to Antoine.

Something in Shandor's voice made Antoine turn to look at him. The comment wasn't strange exactly, yet he could tell there was a lot more to it than Shandor was revealing. Antoine wondered why Shandor was so interested in the comings and goings of the ruling noble family.

"When you are in Laitha and walking its streets, how does the city feel to you?" This time Shandor turned to look at him, the full force of his mismatched eyes making Antoine squirm under the scrutiny. He looked away, trying to focus on the question without facing that unnerving gaze.

"It feels...." Antoine fumbled with his sluggish brain to give him the proper words. "Quiet in a way. There's activity and people move about, but it always feel a little... furtive?" Antoine sighed, shaking his head. "It just feels like the people are on edge all the time." He shivered a bit, running a hand through his hair then pausing to rub his temples. "Every time I see the Archduchess, I get a strange chill. Her eyes are so cold...."

Shandor gave a brief nod before turning away, arms crossing over his broad chest. He seemed to lose himself in thought, staring off toward the east. Shandor's expression was hard and closed, giving away nothing of his thoughts. Antoine felt there was some greater meaning to all these questions that he was missing—something he was getting just a small glimpse of. All of this thinking was making his headache return, pain building behind his eyes.

"How are you doing there, Antoine?" Shiv'ren's voice broke through the increasing pain, making Antoine open his eyes in surprise. "Did the captain get you back to your bunk safely?" He was coming up from the lower decks, adjusting the aviator cap on his head, looking bright and alert. Perhaps alcohol affected elves differently? Honestly Antoine had never really thought about it before.

"My head hurts," he muttered darkly, glaring when Shiv'ren started to laugh. "Why did you let me drink so much?" There was more laughter, which made Antoine scowl more. "It's not funny! I thought I was going to die when I woke up this morning!" This time even Shandor couldn't hold back a laugh. With that much laughter, Antoine felt himself beginning to smile as well.

"You're hardly the first person to wake up in such a state. In fact, I don't think you were the only person on the ship to wake up in such a state today," Shandor said, the previous seriousness seeming to have left him. He walked over, reaching out as if he was going to ruffle Shiv'ren's hair, which the elf quickly avoided, glaring at Shandor. "Besides, V'ren has always handled alcohol differently than other people. Never seems to affect him at all, so we don't get to see him be a fool."

The glare intensified, gold eyes focused solely on Shandor. Now that he was a little more familiar with Shiv'ren, Antoine realized there was no real heat behind the glare. He thought maybe there was something different in the elf's eyes when he looked over at Shandor, but Antoine couldn't determine what it was.

"There's no reason for me to lose my head to drink when there are so many others willing to do so." Shiv'ren scowled, turning away from Shandor. "I came to get Antoine. I'm heading into town and I didn't think he would want to be stuck on the ship all day." A quick glance was cast at Antoine. "Feel like going through the town, or do you want to nurse your sickness some more?"

"I've nursed my sickness enough. I think some new air would probably help me," Antoine said quickly, running a hand through his greasy-feeling hair. Maybe there would be a place in Tyrnium where he could get a bath for himself.

IN THE end, there wasn't a place for bathing, at least not one that Shiv'ren was willing to go to. Instead they wandered through a different market, with Shiv'ren digging through piles of manuscripts at various stalls. Evidently they were part of the loot taken by different air pirates that they would exchange for hard coin. It seemed the less scrupulous traders knew this was where the pirates came to debauch and spend their treasure, so they would come and offer hard coin for things the pirates viewed as less valuable.

Of course, they weren't above selling those manuscripts to other sailors that might know their worth. Antoine really thought it was a waste of time since none of the merchants seemed to have what Shiv'ren was looking for. At least until he heard a triumphant shout and turned to see Shiv'ren holding up a book.

"What did you find?" Antoine asked as they walked away, Shiv'ren eagerly flipping through pages.

"It's an engineering book from the eastern country of Xu. I've been wanting to look at one for ages."

"Xu?" He looked over Shiv'ren's shoulder, noting the strange characters that covered the pages he was examining with such rapt attention. "You can read it?"

"Somewhat. Li and Yi are both from Xu, and they've taught me a little bit. Their engineering ideas are unique, different from what comes from the western cities. It's fascinating to study. Some of it is really elegant in comparison to the larger, more clunky machines that we have."

"You really enjoy this, don't you?"

"Hmm? Enjoy what?" Gold eyes finally looked up from the page they'd been studying.

"Engines, mechanical contraptions, machines and the like. I don't think I've met anyone who's so excited about these things before."

There was a pause before the book shut with a snap. "Maybe. I've always been interested in machines, but there's always more to learn." Shiv'ren shoved the book into a pocket of his coveralls. "Tell me, Antoine, do you have anything you like to study?"

Antoine shrugged, shoving his hands in the pockets of his own coveralls. "I like to read about history, but it's not something I have time to indulge in. Father says I have to keep my eye on the future, not keep looking back at the past."

A large hand fell on his shoulder, making Antoine jump in surprise. "Yet those that don't understand the past tend to repeat the same mistakes." Rivas's voice rolled over him like a velvet wave, caressing his ears and even his skin. Antoine flushed as he remembered what it had felt like to have that rough hand running through his hair in the pub last night. The flush grew worse when Rivas walked into Antoine's line of sight.

"Good day, Captain." Antoine hated how his voice wavered. "Thank you for taking care of me last night."

Rivas's tanned face split into a smile, green eyes glinting in the sunlight. "Of course. I couldn't leave you where someone could take advantage of you in such a state." He leaned down so their faces were closer, warm breath washing over Antoine's face "You're far too cute for others to resist."

"So, then, I should be lucky you have such admirable self-control?" Antoine was amazed his voice didn't shake. Having Rivas so close caused his stomach to churn in a not entirely unpleasant way. Heat was slowly spreading through his body before pooling in his groin. The low chuckle he received did nothing to dispel the feeling.

Before Rivas could respond, there came a shout from down the street, followed by one of the *Aria*'s pirates running toward them. "Captain! Captain, Shandor told me to inform you that Ciel has just returned in the aeropod with a response to the ransom demand."

CHAPTER SIXTEEN

THE WORDS forced all of the air out of Antoine's chest. For a while he had forgotten he was just a prisoner, a hostage to be exploited for the money his father had. The people around him had felt like friends, and the journey had felt like an adventure. But they weren't friends and it wasn't an adventure. They were watching him, making sure he didn't get into trouble, that the precious hostage wasn't hurt before they collected their money. A slow flush of embarrassed anger crawled up Antoine's neck. He turned away in disgust, feeling like an utter fool.

This time, when Rivas's hand fell on his shoulder, Antoine shrugged it off, and then walked away without another look. They might have gotten him to forget for a while, but that didn't mean Antoine would let it continue. A small part of him said he was being irrational, letting his embarrassment color his view. That knowledge did nothing to quiet the anger now churning in his gut. Antoine also didn't want to think about why exactly he felt so betrayed by it all.

RIVAS WAS annoyed as he stormed back to the ship. He knew his dark expression was a warning to those that crossed his path to get out of his way. As soon as he was back at the ship, the few pirates still around quickly found other places to be. All of them except Shandor.

Shandor was leaning casually against a wall, arms crossed as he watched Rivas with a smug look. Rivas clenched his hands to prevent himself from giving in to the urge to punch his longtime friend. Instead he strode past him, throwing open the door leading below deck. The sound of a second set of boots falling into step behind let him know Shandor was following him. Rivas had to grit his teeth to keep from snapping. It wasn't Shandor's fault, and he couldn't go into this meeting at odds with his fellow leader. Shandor must have sensed the fraying thread of Rivas's patience because he wisely kept his comments to himself, but the bastard didn't stop looking smug.

It didn't take long to reach their destination. Rivas had ordered that Ciel be taken to the mess deck until he returned to the ship. A quick glance showed Ciel sitting at one of the tables, a tankard of drink in front of him. He stood when he saw Rivas, shaggy dark hair falling into shrewd brown eyes.

"Captain. I've returned as ordered. I've got a response from the Suvalese household to your demands."

Rivas nodded, letting a smile stretch his mouth. It wasn't welcoming or nice, but it fit his current mood perfectly. "Excellent, Ciel. What was their response?"

Ciel bowed slightly, pulling out an envelope and presenting it with a small flourish. After opening the envelope, Rivas quickly scanned the letter to get the main points. Antoine's father had agreed to the ransom, but requested a month to gather the hard coin. It was what Rivas had expected. He had never doubted that Adrian Suvalese would comply with the demands if it meant the return of his favorite son.

"Did there seem to be anything unusual with the house when you were there? Anything that might cause a hindrance with our plan?"

Ciel shook his head. "Nothing unusual. The eldest son did not seem pleased with how quickly his father agreed to pay for the return of Antoine. However, I doubt that it will come to much." Ciel looked through his bangs at the blond captain, and Rivas felt those dark eyes measuring his reaction.

Rivas nodded, folding up the letter. "Very good. Your efforts shall be remembered and rewarded. You're dismissed. Go, enjoy yourself in the town tonight. We leave tomorrow."

Ciel bowed respectfully before quickly leaving the mess, passing Shandor without even a glance. He missed the suspicious gaze that followed him as he disappeared. It didn't go unnoticed by Rivas.

"I wish I could understand why exactly you distrust him so much," Rivas remarked as he held out the folded letter. He felt calmer now that he had the letter and the report from Ciel.

"I can't explain it. Just something in my gut tells me there's something not quite right about him." Shandor took the letter, scanning it quickly before going back and reading in more depth. "It all seems to be in order. He even agreed to the meeting point you gave. He says he will send the money with a designated representative that shall be escorted by the Archduke's navy. To ensure we keep our word. Certainly doesn't seem to believe that we won't harm the little lord."

"Well, we are a group of infamous air pirates, well known throughout the continent for our ruthless ways." Rivas's voice was dry as he sat on one of the tables, one booted foot coming to rest on the bench. "Of course, most of that is the creation of newspapers, but that isn't really important."

"Of course it isn't. It's not about truth, just the perception of truth." Shandor handed the letter back then crossed his arms over his chest. "Of course, a fearsome reputation has yet to be a hindrance." There was a pause before the gypsy spoke again. "You don't really believe that it will be that simple, do you?"

"Of course not. Suvalese will try and double-cross us. He'll probably send orders through the navy. It will be cautious, though. A full-on fight might lead to someone being injured in the cross fire."

"Too bad he doesn't know that you'd never let anything happen to Antoine." Shandor's smirk was back, and with it returned some of Rivas's earlier annoyance.

"Smugness is unattractive, Shandor." He folded the letter up, and slid it into a pocket of his pants. "Besides, how are you so certain that it's not just a passing entertainment?"

"Because if it was you would have had him in bed by now, and you wouldn't be quite so angry about a few thoughtless words uttered in his presence." The words were confidently spoken.

Rivas sighed, shaking his head ruefully before resting his chin on his palm. "That obvious, is it?"

"Only to me, but then I know you better than almost anyone." Shandor laughed a bit, blue eye twinkling. "It's nice to not be alone in endlessly pining over someone."

"Except I'm not as patient as you are. I'm not going to sit there and wait for him to get over his scared rabbit tendencies. Don't have the time for it," Rivas shot back.

Shandor scoffed. "Just because you set a time limit for yourself doesn't mean the rest of us are so unromantic."

"Oh aye, and look where romance has been getting you there, Shan. The elf will only look at you to glare half the time. How he hasn't realized you'd do anything he asks is beyond me."

"At least he'll be convinced I'm serious once he stops fighting me." Shandor put a hand on his hip, head tilting to the side. "How exactly are you going to convince Antoine that he's less than just a passing fancy while being held here? That this is about more than just profit?"

"How do you know it's about more than profit? Do please explain my motivations to me, then, Shandor. Sometimes I can't keep track of all my different machinations." The sarcasm was thick. Of the two of them, Rivas wasn't the one who wove complicated plans.

"If you insist, my captain," he said, walking over and sitting down next to Rivas. "This was never just about the profit you could get from the ransom. This is political, always has been. Why else would you make our next destination Black Rocks, a former coalmine and mining town that you are very familiar with? Run by the Suva Coal Company no less, until the mine was no longer prosperous. You want to show the heir apparent what his father's company is like, what Adrian Suvalese's practice of profit at any cost is truly about. If the more tenderhearted son sees what the situation is like, he'll be more apt to change things once he assumes control of his father's dominion."

Rivas had to give a soft laugh at that, shaking his head. "Indeed, you know me far too well, Shandor. That is part of my motivation, I won't deny it. It's not the entire reason I decided to do this, though." He closed his eyes, smiling a bit. "Maybe I'm just a fool." A friendly hand came to rest on his shoulder, squeezing gently. "I guess then we're both fools."

"Aye."

CHAPTER SEVENTEEN

HOURS LATER, when Antoine was sitting in the pub with Shiv'ren again, the anger was still moving through him. It had died down a little as time passed, but it sat in his gut like acid, eating at him. Antoine could only pick at the food Shiv'ren had purchased and take halfhearted sips of his drink. He didn't taste any of it, and the more he ate the more his stomach churned, making him feel sick.

The worst part was, by this point Antoine wasn't sure who he was angry at. He felt like a fool for forgetting he was ultimately a hostage. Worse than that, he was furious that they had treated him like an equal, as if they enjoyed having him around. Shiv'ren, Shandor, even Rivas had all treated Antoine like he was another crewmate. Like he was a friend. Every time Antoine thought about it, a new surge of anger came forward. With the anger came something else, something dark he didn't want to put a name to.

"Stop sulking already." Shiv'ren's voice cut through the haze of Antoine's thoughts. When he glanced up, Antoine was pierced by gold eyes staring intently at him. "What are you so angry for anyway?"

Antoine scowled, looking back down at his glass. "It's none of your business." He grabbed the tankard, gulping half of it so he wouldn't have to respond.

"Actually, it is my business when I have to put up with your damned mood all day." Shiv'ren grabbed the tankard, pulling it away with a firm yank. "Especially since it obviously has something to do with what happened with the captain."

"Give that back." Antoine made a grab for the tankard, scowling when it was calmly taken. "Very well, then, it is your business. You, all of you going around and acting like I'm something I'm not. I'm your profit, that's all, something you can exploit for money. You didn't... you shouldn't have treated me any different!" Antoine was surprised by how much his chest was heaving when he finished. And damned if he didn't want to try to punch that inscrutable look off the elf's face.

"You're angry that we didn't treat you like a prisoner and keep you chained up? You're worried that it was all just some kind of act, a lark we were all having at your expense." Antoine stiffened at the biting words, the action followed by a heavy sigh from Shiv'ren. "It wasn't, you know. It was never an act or a lark. Rivas isn't that crude." There was a rustling sound that Antoine recognized as Shiv'ren's wings. "If you truly want to know, you're the first hostage Rivas has ever taken."

"So? That supposed to make me special?" Antoine was getting the familiar fuzzy feeling from the drink he'd taken before. He wanted more of it so it could blot out this whole day from his memory and leave him with only the happy but painful fogginess he'd had upon waking.

"Yes, it makes you special." Shiv'ren was still holding his drink out of reach. "Rivas doesn't do things without a reason."

Deciding that scowling wasn't enough, Antoine stood, grabbing his drink back. That some of it sloshed over the sides and onto his hand didn't bother him in the slightest. After gulping down the remainder, Antoine smiled as the fire burned away all his feelings, leaving only pleasant numbness behind. It prevented him having to think about Shiv'ren's words. Antoine barely reacted when the empty cup was wrenched out of his hand, the sound of it slamming down on the wooden table hollow and far away.

"It's not going to go away with drink, Antoine."

Instead of calming him, Shiv'ren's words angered him further. Antoine glared at the scarred table, focusing on a long, unidentifiable stain on the wood. He hoped it would give him a reprieve from the swirling mix of emotions he couldn't properly understand. Antoine didn't want to be a plan or a reason. He didn't *want* Rivas to see him as just a business transaction, a spoiled rich brat that had to be babysat until his father paid for his release. Antoine wanted Rivas to look at him and just see Antoine. For a while he had thought that perhaps Rivas did see him. Now, though, he wasn't certain, and it only fueled his anger. Since Shiv'ren had stolen his previous cup, Antoine waved a hand for another. Right as it was set in front of him, the door opened, and the object of all of Antoine's grief and consternation came waltzing in. Green eyes swept the pub before landing on Antoine. The intensity in that gaze made Antoine shiver and look down, biting his lip. To distract himself, Antoine took a long pull, barely noticing the burn of the alcohol searing his throat. He refused to look up when he felt Rivas sit down next to him, the warmth from the large body next to him causing more heat to rise in Antoine's cheeks.

Conversations went on around Antoine, but he refused to focus on them. Instead he wrapped himself in the warm haze seeping into him from the alcohol. He found a new appreciation for the strong drink. It took away the tangle of emotions that twisted him up. Closing his eyes, Antoine let himself drift as he listened to people shouting and in a few cases even singing, though quite badly. Oddly it was this chaos that helped to ground him.

It lasted until a large, rough hand came to rest on his shoulder. He turned at the touch, and looked up into Rivas's scarred face, brilliant eyes watching him with something that resembled concern. That look blew away the peaceful numbness. Reflexively pulling away from the touch, Antoine almost fell off the bench. Hard, calloused hands caught him, though, pulling him back onto the bench.

With his emotions running high thanks to the alcohol, Antoine was robbed of his normal good sense. Shaking off the hands, Antoine managed to get his legs working enough to reach his feet and stumble toward the door. He didn't want to be there with Rivas around. In fact, currently, he didn't want to be anywhere the pirate captain was. Though if he had been thinking clearly, Antoine would have known better than to try to leave the bar on his own.

Stumbling out into the night, Antoine tried to get his bearings so he could get back to the ship. There he could at least pass out and not have to face Rivas until the morning. This was easier thought than executed, because Antoine could not properly remember which direction the *Aria* was, except that it was up. With that in mind,

Antoine began to walk with a purpose. It didn't take him very long, though, to get utterly lost. It took only slightly longer to realize it, which he blamed on the fact that the town was listing alarmingly to one side.

Right when he thought he was going to fall over, or just fall off the world and float away, a pair of arms wrapped around him, anchoring Antoine to the ground. He didn't need to look up to see who it was. There was only one person that would have come after him. "Go away. Just leave me alone."

"I can't do that, Antoine. You're too cute to be left to wander around in your current state." Antoine hated that soft, almost teasing tone that Rivas always used when speaking to him. It felt like the older man was mocking him.

"Don't! All I am is a way for you to extort money from my father! So stop acting like it's something else!" Antoine snarled the words, struggling futilely against the arms holding him.

Rivas didn't let him go. Instead he tightened the hold, pulling Antoine flush against him. Antoine shivered, Rivas's body heat burning away the chill that had begun to settle over him. "That's not all of it." The rough voice caused more shivering and a new warmth to spread through his body. "There is so much more to it than just that."

"Like what?" Antoine's voice was harsh and raspy, his throat closing up on him so that it was hard to speak. His gut churned constantly from both the anxiety and the drink, leaving him uneasy. "What could possibly be more important to a pirate than money? That's all you pirates care about, money and treasure."

"Not every pirate, Antoine." Again Rivas's voice flowed over him, bringing warmth at the same time that it caused goose bumps to rise up on his skin. "There is so much more than just money that was involved with my capture of you." Antoine felt Rivas's lips and nose brushing against his hair as he spoke, reminding Antoine of how close they actually were. "The first time I had ever laid eyes on you, it wasn't on that transport aero. I had seen you long before, and I knew then that I had to see you again."

It was important, what Rivas was saying, Antoine knew that. However, the churning in his stomach had gotten worse, and he started to struggle with renewed vigor. It surprised Rivas enough that he relaxed his hold, allowing Antoine to break away. He stumbled forward before bending over, his throat tightening again before he proceeded to lose everything that had been in his stomach. Antoine remained bent over, retching at intervals as his body continued to heave. A soothing hand ran over his back, offering comfort. Antoine wanted to say something, at least a few words of thanks, yet he feared opening his mouth.

Many interminable minutes later, Antoine felt secure enough to stand up again. He still felt green, his stomach continuing to churn but not bad enough to cause further illness. Rivas's arm slipped easily around his waist, helping to keep Antoine upright. He was grateful for the support, since he now felt like he might pass out. It only took a few stumbling steps before Rivas let out a small sigh that sounded almost like a laugh. Antoine felt Rivas shift his hold, looping Antoine's arm over his shoulder to better take more of his weight. Antoine surrendered it gladly, eyes drooping as he tried to stay awake. Ultimately it was a futile gesture, his consciousness fluttering away on the cool breeze.

CHAPTER EIGHTEEN

RIVAS WAS glad when Antoine finally passed out. He carefully gathered the younger man into his arms, lifting him off the ground. Rivas had certainly not expected Antoine to consume that much alcohol and remain upright. That he had endured this long was quite a feat, especially given how much of a lightweight Antoine had been yesterday. Now if only Rivas could find out what exactly had set him off on this little binge.

Making his way back to the ship, Rivas grinned when he saw the sailors on watch give him a speculative look. He ignored them for the most part, just carted his human cargo down to his cabin. Once inside, Rivas thought of trying to pour Antoine into the hammock, except a look at his still slightly green face deterred him. Rivas doubted the rocking movements of the hammock would help settle Antoine's stomach. Instead he laid him down on the bed, ignoring the small whimper the drunken man gave.

Once that was done, Rivas straightened, pushing his hair back from his face. He paused to watch Antoine sleep, absently running a finger over the scar on his cheek. Even asleep, Antoine was beautiful, with lightly flushed skin and his coveralls slightly unbuttoned. It was tempting to unbutton it further to reveal the hint of smooth, pale skin beneath the coarse material. It took great effort to keep his hands by his sides, clenching his fists to keep from reaching out. Antoine was too tempting for his own good, especially since he had no idea of his own appeal.

With a sigh Rivas sat on the edge of the bed, reaching down to pull off Antoine's boots. It would be easy to think that his father's status was the only reason Antoine was taken. Even Rivas's attraction to him could simply be seen as a nice benefit of taking a prisoner. Sometimes he wished it was that simple, because if it was he would have long since gone ahead and seduced Antoine into his bed for the duration of his time with them.

It wasn't that simple, though. Nothing ever was. The complexities of the situation meant Rivas didn't get to just seduce the rather attractive Antoine Suvalese. Rivas had known the plan to take Antoine hostage would be dangerous, but he hadn't anticipated how hard it would be to stay in control of his own emotions and libido. Even now, having removed Antoine's boots, Rivas still cradled his foot, a hand slowly working its way under the leg of Antoine's coverall, exploring the texture between soft skin and crisp hair. There was a fine layer of light muscle under the skin, not incredibly developed but not something to be found on a completely idle man of means.

"You have no idea what this whole thing is about." Rivas kept his voice quiet, not wanting to disturb his guest. "Perhaps you won't even remember this night when you wake up, given the amount of alcohol you downed tonight." Antoine shifted, head turning to the side, causing locks of brown hair to fall across his forehead and cheeks. Leaning forward, Rivas pushed them back from his face, letting a calloused finger trace the slope of a cheekbone. "I can't decide if I want you to forget or to remember. We leave this place tomorrow, moving on towards the next destination."

Rivas allowed himself one last touch before he pulled back and stood with a sigh. He wasn't tired enough yet to try to sleep. He also didn't trust himself to be in the same bed with Antoine and keep his hands to himself.

Leaving the cabin, Rivas made his way up to the top deck, taking a bracing breath of the cool air. The town was still bustling. Even this late at night the various rogues and outcasts that made up Tyrnium were still carousing. It would continue all night, only slowing when the sun began to rise over the mountains. However, the *Aria* would not be around to see much of the town's recovery from another night of carousing. He had given orders for the aero to depart early in the morning so the sunrise would hide their departure from passing patrols.

From Tyrnium he planned to continue on to the settlement of Black Rocks and wait until the appointed time of the exchange. In a few more weeks all would be taken care of. Antoine would be delivered back to his family, hopefully a little wiser about the true workings of his family's business. Meanwhile, Rivas would continue on with the *Bloody Aria* to a life of plunder and notoriety. Strangely the idea did not fill him with the sense of freedom it had previously.

"You think too hard, Rivas." Shandor came up behind him, slinging an arm over Rivas's shoulder, waving a bottle in front of his face. "Have a drink before your brain burns out." Rivas gave him a glare before taking the bottle and gulping some of the liquor down. Seemingly satisfied, Shandor pulled back to lean against the railing.

"I'm not the only one who has a habit of thinking too hard." Rivas took another drink from the bottle he had been given. "Sometimes I think you are a dyed in the wool schemer, Shan."

"A schemer? Nonsense! Schemers have agendas and plans for power. Those are called politicians."

"Oh? I know for a fact you have plans and some kind of agenda that you won't let people know about."

"But I have no plans for power. If I wanted power, I would have taken control of the ship already." Shandor brought his own bottle up to his lips and took a drink.

"I'm not certain you don't want to have control of the ship sometimes. One of these days, you will have to let someone in on your plan." Rivas cast a sideways glance at his old friend.

"One of these days," Shandor said, inclining his head. "But not this day. After all, this is your show, Rivas. Maybe you should stop hiding up here and go back down there." There was a wry smile on the gypsy's face as he spoke.

Rivas looked away from his friend, taking a long drink to brace himself. "He's passed out drunk, passed out in my bed no less. I'm not so hard up that I'm going to just take advantage of someone too drunk to remember the event. I'm not sure my ego could take that."

Shandor gave a rather crude snort, tilting his bottle a little. "Your ego is not that fragile, Rivas. You just don't want to consider that he might not remember." He swirled the amber-colored alcohol around before taking a drink. "We're not so different in that respect."

"No, we're not." Except that Shandor's situation was simpler than his own at the moment. Shandor kept trying and getting shot down, and then trying again. Rivas was not sure he would be able to take rejection so easily. "However, I am better-looking."

"Only in your daydreams. Exotic charms beat rakish good looks."

"If you're blind perhaps," Rivas said, relaxing into the teasing that the two of them shared. It let him focus on something else for the rest of the night.

CHAPTER NINETEEN

ONCE AGAIN Antoine woke up feeling like he was being stabbed by the sunlight. He tried to roll over, pulling the blanket over his head to block the light. His sluggish mind tried to point out something about the current situation. Thinking was painful, though, so Antoine was not going to do so until absolutely necessary. He burrowed even further under the blanket, trying to will oblivion to take him again. The next time Antoine was conscious, the light was no longer hitting directly in his eyes, making it less intense and therefore less painful. Carefully emerging from his cocoon, Antoine finally registered the lack of a rocking motion. His place of sleep was not swaying in the now familiar motion of the hammock. A quick look revealed that he was in Rivas's bed.

A quick pat down showed he was still fully clothed, only his boots having been removed. Antoine let out a long breath, trying to remember how exactly he had come to be in Rivas's bed. The last thing he could accurately remember was going into the tavern upset and ordering a drink. After the first drink, the rest began to blur together with no distinct memories standing out. He remembered feeling incredibly angry at everyone in a way he was not used to. He also had a vague feeling of being wrapped in strong arms, followed by a feeling of safety. It was all rather confusing, and thinking of it just made his headache worse.

After climbing off the bed, Antoine shuffled around the room to get ready for what was left of the day. After washing himself, he drank some water and managed to eat some bread that was left on the table. Antoine decided to head down to the engine room. He was certain he owed Shiv'ren an apology for his previous behavior.

By this point Antoine was familiar enough with the layout of the Aria to navigate without too much thought. Finding the engine room was especially easy. He simply followed the increasing vibrations moving up his legs until he came to the familiar metal door. Stepping inside, Antoine maneuvered through the maze of machinery until he came to the main area of the engine room. Looking around, Antoine realized Shiv'ren wasn't there. Normally the elf was moving around, going over his various dials and readings that seemed to be everywhere.

Rubbing his tired eyes, Antoine considered that maybe Shiv'ren had gone to another part of the ship. Before leaving, though, he decided to thoroughly check the area, in case Shiv'ren was somewhere. Swallowing a yawn, he walked over to the metal sheeting that served to separate the space. The sight that greeted him behind the sheet made him stop in surprise. Shiv'ren was sitting there, though really it seemed more like he was perching on the ground. His knees were drawn up to his chin, wings wrapped around himself with a blanket draped over his shoulders.

Moving carefully, Antoine worked his way closer. He was curious about what he was seeing, but he didn't wish to disturb Shiv'ren either. The position reminded him of a bird perched on a branch, not something he would have thought was comfortable. Watching Shiv'ren, Antoine realized he'd never considered the mechanics of what it would be like to try to sleep with large wings coming out of his back. Maybe it worked well for elves to sleep like that, or maybe it was just Shiv'ren? He had to admit the elf was definitely unique.

As the thoughts chased themselves in his head, Antoine realized he was babbling in his own mind. Rubbing his face vigorously, Antoine hoped the motion would help to clear up his head. It didn't really, so he headed back to the main area and made his way to the windows. The sight of the clouds and land rushing by underneath the aero finally calmed Antoine's racing thoughts. The lower perspective gave the ship a feeling of speed as it moved that couldn't really be felt when above deck.

"Are you going to stare out the window all day?" The words were meant to be sharp, but the voice was fuzzy with the last dregs of sleep.

"Well you weren't awake. I'm not foolish enough to touch anything here without you."

"Good, I've no desire to end my life in a fiery crash in the middle of the mountains." Shiv'ren ran his fingers through his hair to straighten it before tugging on his goggles.

Antoine continued to look out the window, spotting something in the distance. He squinted, leaning forward to try to get a better look. It was something in the sky, possibly another aero moving along the shipping routes. He was about to mention it to Shiv'ren when a sudden banging sound came from the speaking tubes.

"Shiv'ren." The accented voice echoed out of the tube. "There's a merchant transport ship on the port side. It's flying the flag of the Amelito Federation."

Shiv'ren moved quickly over to the window, a pair of binoculars in his hand. There was about a minute where he peered through them, tracking the ship. When he finished, Shiv'ren shoved them into Antoine's chest as he walked back to the speaking tubes.

"It's about seven miles away, not moving very quickly. Are we going to hit it?" Antoine lifted the binoculars to his face, focusing them and scanning until he found the ship. The aero was definitely flying the tricolored flag of the Amelito Federation, a small but rich federation of islands and cities located to the south.

"We will be hitting it, given the distance we need to increase our speed to catch it." Li's voice echoed hollowly down the tube.

"Ramming or flanking?" Shiv'ren asked.

"Flanking. Captain wants it in one piece and to stay in one piece."

"Roger that." Antoine noticed Shiv'ren was grinning with a lot of teeth as he pulled his goggles over his eyes. "Get over here, Antoine! We got to get to work!" He started pulling several levers, gesturing over to his right side. "See the large dial over there? Watch the marker, tell me when it hits that point." He tapped the dial in a certain spot.

"All right." Antoine was quiet for a minute before he spoke up. "What are you going to do to that ship?"

"Attack it of course." Shiv'ren said it like it was to be expected. "That's what we do. I don't think they had planned to

91

actually hit another ship on the route to our destination, but if it's there… no reason not to take advantage of it."

"Is that how you find most of the targets of your raids? You just find them as you're flying around?"

"Sometimes. Shipping lanes are pretty set between the major ports in the different countries. All you have to do is watch those to find any number of merchant vessels. If you want ships from a certain place, the best way to do it is to stake out the ports they tend to trade with," Shiv'ren explained easily, moving the entire time.

Antoine blinked, keeping his focus on the dial in front of him. "That's very… sensible." It was incredibly sensible, in fact, which took away a lot of the romance and the mystery of an air pirate raid. It also took away some of the blinding terror of an attack. It was hard to be frightened when you realized the tough, cutthroat pirates that terrorized the merchant class of Laitha were a bunch of men who flew around, got drunk, and really just took whatever ships they stumbled across.

"Seems a little strange, doesn't it?" Shiv'ren said, continuing to make adjustments. The sounds from the engine picked up noticeably, the ship shuddering under their feet. "Pirates are opportunists. Another raid will help keep the crew content."

Antoine fell silent after that, focusing on the task he'd been given. The practices of his captors were not something he really needed to know about it, plus his head was still hurting quite a bit from his overindulgence. When the dial finally reached the requested mark, he notified Shiv'ren, who flashed him a quick grin before turning from what he had been watching. He grabbed a wrench, went over to the speaking tube, and banged on it twice before turning back to the engine's readouts.

"Get ready, we're about to catch up to them." There was banked excitement in the elf's voice. It peaked Antoine's interest, causing him to turn toward the large windows to see what was going to happen. The other aero was much closer now. The *Aria* approached from behind in an effort to achieve greater surprise for their attack.

Antoine had a moment where he marveled at how quickly they had bridged the gap. He remembered Shiv'ren saying the *Aria* was one of the fastest aeros in the sky. As they got closer, the *Aria* started to swing to its side, lining up to run parallel. The reason for this quickly became clear when the ship shuddered under Antoine's feet, knocking him backward onto his ass. Several cannonballs hurtled toward the other ship, impacting it without doing a great deal of damage.

"Sorry about that." A hand was thrust in Antoine's face, helping him regain his feet. Of course as soon as he was back on his feet the ship gave another shudder. Antoine held tightly to Shiv'ren's hand as he struggled to maintain his balance. "Sorry, I forgot to warn you that when we fire a broadside you need to brace yourself on something. We're right below the main gun decks, so it can get a little rough."

Antoine was feeling a little tossed around, quickly placing a hand on the window to brace himself. Just in time, as the ship shook as the cannons went off yet again. "Does it always happen like that?"

"Usually it only takes a couple of volleys as we pull up next to the ship. It's not like we're really trying to sink them. A lot of it is intimidation in the end—make them afraid before we even board."

Another shudder wracked the ship, slightly different because they were pulled up right next to the other aero. They were so close Antoine thought he could reach out and touch the other aero. There was one last shudder before it stopped, leaving only the familiar engine vibrations. Antoine leaned forward, trying to peer up through the gap between the two ships. He remembered that when they had raided his transport, there had been grappling hooks used to connect the two ships. He assumed that had been the last shudder he had felt.

CHAPTER TWENTY

"SO, DO you want to go up and take a look?" Shiv'ren's voice sounded both amused and excited. When Antoine turned around, the elf was putting a large wrench through a loop in his coveralls, a belt with two pistols already slung around his hips. "We can't go all the way up on deck, but if we're careful, we can go and take a peek. You have to stay behind me, though."

Antoine nodded quickly, straightening up from the windows. His heart thudded heavily, excitement flooding his system until he thought he might start shaking. The trip was quick and quiet, the sounds of the engine fading to be replaced with the sounds of battle. As they came up to the deck, Shiv'ren stopped at the door, peering out. Antoine carefully peered around him, trying to get a view of what was going on.

Even though they were up on deck, they were still a fair distance from the actual fighting. A majority of the pirates were on the other ship, all of them blending together to make one mass melee. It was pure chaos with the smell of gunpowder and the shouts of the men creating a disorienting cacophony.

Antoine squinted, trying to make out the individual figures in the melee; though with his untrained eyes it was nearly impossible to follow. Eventually he was able to locate Rivas at the edge of the deck. The captain was standing by the railing of the ship, shouting orders over the rest of the noise. He wore a red coat with a pistol in each hand, occasionally taking aim at someone and firing. Looking at him in the heat of battle, Antoine understood how Rivas had received such a terrifying reputation.

Antoine continued to watch Rivas, entranced by this different side of him. Rivas was lethal, with coiled strength that moved with an uncanny grace. After a few shots, he exchanged one of the pistols for a cutlass, cutting through the few sailors still attempting to fight him. Soon enough, the merchant aero's captain dropped his sword, surrendering.

"Antoine.... Antoine!" A strong hand gripped his shoulder, shaking him firmly. It was enough to snap Antoine out of his daze. "Are you well? You're flushed. We should head back inside." Antoine realized then that his face, in fact, his whole body, felt warm, and most of it was centered on his cock. Shiv'ren was giving him concerned looks as he pulled him off the deck. Once back below, Antoine tried to shake Shiv'ren's surprisingly strong grip. He felt unsteady, his body vibrating with unused energy that he was desperately trying to understand. Antoine followed Shiv'ren without thinking, shoving his hands into the pockets of his coveralls. His erection was pressing against the front of his coveralls, and he tried to subtly ease the cloth away from it.

After the chaos up top, the inner decks seemed almost too quiet, their boots echoing on the metal plates. Instead of being soothed by the quiet, Antoine grew more uneasy. The silence offered no distraction from the feelings running through his body or the thoughts chasing themselves in his head. And Antoine desperately wanted a distraction from his current condition.

"Are all raids like this?" Antoine tried not to be embarrassed when Shiv'ren turned to look at him, gold eyes staring right through him. He wasn't sure what exactly the elf saw in his face before he turned away and started walking again.

"The amount of fighting changes. A lot of ships surrender after a few broadsides. Some continue to fight until we board them. Most are clever enough to realize that their cargo is not worth their lives."

"Will you sink their ship once you've taken everything?" Antoine remembered seeing his own transport aero burning as it sank toward the ground.

"No. Destroying ships is wasteful and rarely done. Ships and crews are hard to replace. We want trade to continue, not stop." There was a pause as Shiv'ren looked over his shoulder. "Only in certain situations would a ship actually be sunk and everyone killed."

"Certain situations, eh?" Antoine tightened his fists in his pockets, taking in a deep breath through his nose. His mind supplied ideas as to what those situations might be. Like when they didn't need witnesses who would report the kidnapping before a ransom demand could be made.

"It varies" was the response he received. "Everyone on the *Aria* has an agenda they're working toward. Even Captain Rivas, though he won't admit it openly. Shandor is more blatant about it. He has some kind of connection with Laitha, which he never really explains. He just seems to collect information from anyone he can find." Frustration laced the words, the rustling of Shiv'ren's wings another hint to his agitation.

"Different layers to everything, huh?" Antoine followed Shiv'ren into the engine room, feeling more relaxed in the cramped space. He took a deep breath, taking in the scents of warm metal and burning coal, already feeling less jittery and more in control of his body. His erection, thankfully, had subsided enough that he could pull his hands out of his pockets. "Seems like there is more to air pirates than one would at first think."

Shiv'ren leaned against one of the large pipes running through the engine room, wings shifting and spreading to each side. "I think there's more to a lot of people than would first be apparent, whether they are pirates or the sons of rich mine owners." The grin was sharp and immediate, something Antoine found himself returning. "It might not seem like it, but the *Aria* is a place of vendettas and revenge. Nearly everyone has one here."

Antoine blinked, a little surprised by that. "Revenge? Vendettas?" He thought back to the crew he had met. None of them had seemed particularly angry or vengeful. Though Antoine had to admit his contact with most of the crew had been rather limited after his first few days aboard. He remembered working with Lesh'ra on the rigging and the few sad brown feathers hanging onto the mangled remains of his wings. "Revenge against whom?" Antoine asked tentatively, a little frightened of the answer.

"Depends on the person really." Shiv'ren straightened, walking over to the windows, staring out at the aero they were moored to.

"Everyone's reason is different. Li and Yi came aboard from an orient merchant aero. They were being sent somewhere when the ship was attacked. Yi immediately volunteered to come aboard and Li followed her. I think it was something their family was forcing them to do."

"Are you out for revenge?" Antoine asked. Honestly he was conflicted about how exactly his friend would answer and whether he wanted to know the answer. He liked Shiv'ren, but he could also sense that there was a story to the surliness the elf often exhibited. That it was rooted in events from the past that Antoine didn't know about and perhaps might not truly understand. He wanted to try to understand, even if it was a small part of the whole. Antoine sensed that trying to understand was important, that it would help him to better understand everything about Rivas. Including the reason he had kidnapped Antoine.

There was a long pause, so long that Antoine began to think that Shiv'ren wasn't going to answer him. "Did you know that none of the winged elves on the *Aria* can fly any longer? That's why there are so many here. It's the closest to flying, to touching the sky that we can get. Especially since we can't return home."

Antoine's stomach gave a harsh twist at the words, his mind flashing the images of the elves he had seen on the deck. He remembered how Lesh'ra had said that only elves were able to climb the balloons to check them for leaks. Now he was forced to look at the situation in a new light, wondering if Lesh'ra only allowed the winged elves to do the climbing because it allowed them to have the illusion of flight.

The rustling sound of wings moving drew Antoine from his contemplation. Shiv'ren had shifted away from the window, his wings flexing as he walked by. It brought to mind what he had said, about none of the winged elves being able to fly. The other elves on the crew Antoine had met were all obviously injured in some way. But Shiv'ren's wings looked perfectly fine. In fact, they were the only wings he had seen that looked relatively normal. "You said all of the winged elves... does that include you?" he asked timidly.

"Of course it does!" There was anger and resigned bitterness in Shiv'ren's response. Suddenly, without warning, his golden wings flared out to their full span, stretching as wide as Shiv'ren was tall. It was a magnificent sight, one that took Antoine's breath away as he watched the light catch and glitter off the feathers.

"They look good, don't they? No sign at all that they're completely useless now, clipped forever." The wings snapped closed in an angry movement. "My former owner had me pinioned, took away my ability to fly without actually destroying my wings. I was too unique and beautiful to permanently maim, unlike others. Most owners find some way to limit the ability of the flight of their winged slaves, so that they can't escape." Shiv'ren paced away from the window. "It's more than that, though. It's done to break our spirits, destroy the very thing that makes us what we are. I've even heard of cruel masters completely removing their slaves' wings. Not enough that you come to our land and take us away at a whim, they have to make sure we can never go back or risk our kin meeting a similar fate."

Antoine recoiled from the angry bitterness that radiated from Shiv'ren. He swallowed. His mind felt like a top that was spinning out of control. New ideas were running through his head, each of them greater and greater in ugliness. The ugliest part of it was the truth Antoine had to face about himself. He had never really thought about the plight of the winged elves he had seen in Laitha. They had often seemed more like strange living dolls, exotic pets that some of the people he saw at high society functions liked to parade around. That they came from the western continent and that they were slaves with no freedom of their own had been something he'd only been aware of in an academic sense.

It was entirely different to have evidence of it thrust into his face. No longer an academic situation kept at a safe distance, but something very real that had happened to people he knew, people he liked. Antoine would always wonder now how they suffered.

"I'm sorry...." The words felt pathetically small and inadequate for what had happened.

Yet they, or perhaps the sheer miserableness behind them, seemed to reach Shiv'ren. He turned, and quickly Antoine began to intently study his boots.

"It's… it's not your fault, Antoine." There came a loud sigh, followed by a familiar rustling noise. "You're not like those that did this. You could never be like them." Shiv'ren's smile was tinged with sheepishness. "I tend to get caught up in things and let them affect me too much."

Before Antoine could respond, a shudder went through the ship, and two loud bangs rumbled down the speaking tube. The sound caused Shiv'ren to let out a relieved breath, rushing over to the engine controls. "C'mon! They've uncoupled from the other ship. We need to get the engines back up to steam! Pull those two levers over there!"

The process of bringing the engines back up to full power so the *Aria* could make a quick escape provided a suitable distraction from what they had been discussing. Yet even as he focused on the instructions Shiv'ren yelled at him, their conversation lingered in the back of his mind the rest of the day.

CHAPTER TWENTY-ONE

ANTOINE WAS still thinking it over later when he went up with Shiv'ren to the mess deck. Even before entering the room, the sound of the crew celebrating and carousing could already be heard. Still lost in his thoughts, Antoine didn't immediately notice that Shiv'ren had not followed him. Looking around, he couldn't find any sign of his friend in the corridor. Before he could search further, he was pulled bodily into the mess hall. The change from the bright hallway to the dimness left him blinking rapidly to adjust himself.

"Just in time, I was about to go and get you." Rivas's warm breath washed over his ear, causing shivers to wrack his entire body. A large calloused hand settled on his shoulder, the warmth spreading through his body as he was steered through the gathered pirates. Antoine's mind flashed back to the scene he'd witnessed on deck, the raw strength Rivas had shown earlier. "We wouldn't want you to miss the festivities. It's the best part of a successful raid," Rivas said, guiding him onto a bench on an area of deck that had been cleared of all else.

It was similar to his first night on the ship, only instead of watching from up on a balcony, he was now in the thick of it. Evidently the loot had already been divided up, because everyone seemed in good spirits. Instruments were brought out, and the music when it began, was slow and then built to something faster. Rhythmic clapping joined, which seemed to be the sign, for those who wanted to, to begin dancing. The entire mood was infectious, and Antoine joined the clapping without even realizing it. When Shandor stood up and started dancing, a shout came from the whole group. Watching him move about in such a graceful, energetic manner, Antoine felt his breath catch.

"Amazing, isn't it?" Rivas whispered the words in Antoine's ear, hot breath tickling it. "Few things are as entrancing as watching a gypsy dance. Everyone is transfixed when Shandor dances. No exceptions…." Antoine blinked, his mind flashing back again to that first night when he'd watched Shandor dance… from the balcony.

Quickly he turned and looked up, catching the familiar golden flash of Shiv'ren's wings. He was leaning over the railing, golden eyes following every movement. It made Antoine want to start laughing. Especially when he remembered how smitten Shandor was with the engineer and how Shiv'ren rebuffed him at every turn. It seemed, even though he would not admit it, the attraction was mutual.

"Are they always like this?" Antoine leaned back to ask the question over the noise, his back pressing against Rivas's side.

"Pretty much. Shiv'ren is the only one in denial about it. I suppose he has his own reasons for it. In the meantime, the rest of us get something amusing to watch. I have to admire my friend's patience, though. When there is something I desire, I find it exceedingly difficult to hold myself back." The words caused a shiver to go through the whole of Antoine's body. Reflexively he shifted away, trying hard not to think about the implications behind those words.

When a tankard was pressed into his hand, Antoine took it gratefully. As he took a healthy drink, it occurred to him that he had drunk more in the past few days than he had in the preceding months in Laitha. He felt he should worry about developing an addiction to strong drink, yet he realized such a concern was foolish. He was being held hostage by pirates. Antoine felt he might as well live the pirate life while he was here. Also it had the wonderful ability to keep him from thinking too hard about things, something he was coming to truly appreciate.

After a few songs, Shandor stopped dancing, laughing as he came over and accepted a tankard of his own. There was a lot of excited talk before another got up and started dancing. He was a tall man with dark skin and long hair held back from his face. His dance was completely different than Shandor's. It was more staccato, lots of stomping but entrancing in its own way.

The celebrating and drinking went on for hours, alcohol flowing like water. Depending on the perspective, it was either a good thing or a bad thing that Antoine was prevented from getting drunk. Once his words began to slur and his calls became more raucous, Rivas refused to give him any more. With no more alcohol to be had, Antoine tried to get up to do his own dance. He was less than successful at it, requiring Rivas to catch him before he went ass over teakettle.

"I think it's time that you were put to bed." Rivas gave a laugh as he wrapped his arms around Antoine's waist. "The third time in as many days, it seems to have become a bit of a habit." He brushed some of Antoine's tangled hair back from his face. The hand was cool, a nice contrast to the flushed heat Antoine felt on his face. Unconsciously Antoine gave a small whimper, moving his head to keep the contact when Rivas pulled back.

There was the rumble of words, but most of their meaning escaped Antoine's jumbled brain. Instead of focusing on it, Antoine allowed his mind to drift on a cloud of contented warmth—a stark contrast from how he had been the night before. He was aware he was being led through the ship by a strong guiding hand wrapped around his bicep. He allowed his mind to drift happily, until the warmth of Rivas's hand left him.

Looking around the room, he saw again the books that lined the shelves, the map that covered the main table, and yet there was a lack of personal touches in the cabin. A glance toward the bedroom showed a similar lack of personal touches. Shiv'ren's earlier words floated back to him. *It might not seem like it, but the Aria is a place of vendettas and revenge.* He wondered what vendetta Rivas had. A question his mouth decided to ask before his mind could stop.

"How did you become an air pirate, Rivas?" The words came out slightly slurred, but they were still enough to stop the larger man in his tracks.

Slowly Rivas turned to look at Antoine, green eyes seeming to glow from his tanned face. A smirk crept across his face, the scar on his face pulling into a white slash in the faint light. "Well, there is an interesting story behind that. However, I don't feel like telling it just yet, especially when one party is drunk."

"Will you tell me eventually? There are so many secrets on this ship. It seems like everyone has one. I want to understand what you're hiding." Antoine met Rivas's eyes intently, trying to transmit his earnestness to the older pirate in a look.

Something must have come through because Rivas's expression changed, the look becoming slightly darker, heat entering those green eyes. "Damn, you have no idea what you're asking for, or what you're making me want to do to you." Rivas stalked forward, making Antoine aware that he was now the sole focus of Rivas's attention. "You are sorely tempting the control of my better nature, Antoine." He stopped in front of Antoine, placing a rough hand on his chin, tilting it up so that Antoine had no choice but to stare directly into that heated gaze. "I don't think you are quite ready to face the consequences of that."

Antoine swallowed, reflexively licking his lips in an effort to moisten his suddenly dry mouth. However, when he saw Rivas's attention zero in on his lips, he suddenly realized it might not have been the smartest thing he had ever done. Swallowing again, Antoine backed up a couple of steps in an effort to get some space between them. He felt that he was quickly approaching a precipice from which there would be no turning back. Even in his inebriated state, Antoine wasn't sure he was ready to jump.

Rivas seemed to realize as well because he stopped just before he would have completely boxed Antoine in. His green eyes still seemed to glow with latent heat, but he made no further move toward Antoine. "Sorely tempting...." The tone was rough, rubbing over Antoine's skin before Rivas turned and marched out of the room.

Once he left, the strength left Antoine's legs, and he slowly slid down the wall until he was sitting on the floor. He ran a shaky hand through his hair, wondering if the flush of heat in his body was from the alcohol or something else. Taking a deep breath, Antoine tried in vain to cool his body down enough to be able to think clearly. Unfortunately, no matter how long he sat there, no clarity was forthcoming. At least the shaking in his legs had stopped, which he took as a sign to get up from the rather uncomfortable floor.

Since Rivas did not seem likely to return for some time, Antoine decided to go to bed. He had heard some of the pirates mentioning that they should be reaching their destination tomorrow, some place called Black Rocks. It took several attempts to climb into the hammock, and once he was settled Antoine decided he definitely was going to cut back on the amount he drank.

UP ON the top deck of the *Bloody Aria*, Rivas was working very hard to get his emotions and libido firmly under control. Something that was much easier thought than done. Especially when it felt like he had already used up most of his control to keep himself from acting on the impulses Antoine unknowingly stirred in him. Rivas felt his control when it came to Antoine had been herculean in its proportions thus far, yet there seemed no end in sight. Frankly Rivas wasn't sure how much longer he would be able to maintain his control. If Antoine continued to look at him with those endearingly sincere brown eyes, Rivas knew he wouldn't be able to hold himself back.

The air cleared his head and helped cool his wayward body. Rivas tilted his head back, staring up at the clouds as they streamed across the stars. The sky always brought a sense of calm to him, giving clarity to his thoughts—something he seemed to be lacking of late. Especially in regards to his prisoner, who was so much more than just a prisoner, even if he didn't know it yet.

Rivas's mind turned to Antoine's earlier questions about secrets on the *Aria*. Something had obviously happened earlier to cause Antoine's sudden curiosity. To Rivas the questions were a good thing, and he hoped that Antoine's newly awoken curiosity would lead to more questions. Perhaps he would even start to question the things around him that he had not considered before.

The arrival at Black Rocks would come sometime tomorrow. They would hide there until the time came for the ransom to be picked up. The ransom money was the reason he had given the crew for the kidnapping. Of course, there were a couple of crewmembers that thought their captain might have ulterior motives; however, those motives did not matter as long as they got their share. Shandor knew the most about Rivas's plans, but not even the gypsy knew everything. Rivas trusted that Shandor would keep any knowledge to himself. Beyond having his own agendas, Shandor was a friend, one of the few on the *Bloody Aria* that Rivas knew he could trust without question.

As Rivas considered all of his plans, a cloud blotted out the moon, casting darkness over the entire deck. A chill passed over Rivas as he stood there. He wondered if this could be considered an omen of some sort. He hoped not, because if it was then it was not a good omen for him and his crew. After a minute the moon reemerged, and Rivas reminded himself that thoughts of omens were foolish talk for mystics. His fate was his own to make, not to be decided by clouds and whimsy. Nodding vigorously, Rivas turned and headed back below deck.

CHAPTER TWENTY-TWO

"WHAT KIND of place is this Black Rocks that we're going to?" Antoine's head was not hurting as badly as it had the other days he had drunk, something for which he was profoundly grateful. He stared out the view port in the engine room, watching as the high plains gave way to rocky foothills that led up to more impressive mountains.

"It's a place we go to hide out between flights. It gives us a chance to rest and perform any repairs or maintenance that is needed." Shiv'ren's response was vague and distracted. He was tinkering with the large contraption he kept covered in a tarp.

"So, it's like your base?"

"Sort of, but not exactly. The *Bloody Aria* is our base, but there are ports where we go to hide and rest in between expeditions." A hollow clunk echoed in the space as Shiv'ren set down one tool for another.

"This isn't like Tyrnium, is it?" Antoine wasn't sure his mind, or his liver, could take another visit to a den of depravity so soon after the first.

There came a laugh that echoed metallic as Shiv'ren's head had disappeared into the internals of whatever he was working on. "Not at all. You'll see, it's very, very different."

Antoine watched Shiv'ren tinker, gold wings twitching every so often before he faced the windows again. The mountains were much closer now, the sharp peaks and crags clearly defined. In a couple of places he could see signs of mining activity on the mountains they passed above. It raised questions in his mind about just what kind of place it was they were going to.

Mentally he added it to his list of things to try to get Rivas to answer when he saw him again. Thoughts of Rivas caused Antoine to let out a heavy sigh, leaning forward and pressing his head against

106

the glass. He hadn't seen Rivas at all today. The captain had already left when he woke up this morning, or maybe he had never come back at all. Antoine had felt at a loss when he realized that Rivas wasn't there. In such a short amount of time, Antoine had gotten used to seeing Rivas when he woke up, his solid presence in the room.

The comfort of Rivas's presence, the fact that he missed it when it wasn't there, filled Antoine with confusion. At least that's what he was calling it. Confusion was a lot easier to deal with than some of the alternatives. However, nothing competed with just not thinking about it, which was what Antoine was attempting to do. What he needed was a nice distraction so he could focus on something else entirely.

As if in answer to his silent prayer, there came an echoing voice down the speaking tube. "Ascension degree is 6.5. Destination height, 10,000 feet."

Shiv'ren emerged from what he had been tinkering with, scratching his head and smearing grease over his cheek and ear. "Antoine, go over and tell me what the current speed is. Need to figure out the speed needed for the ascent."

Seizing the distraction, Antoine immediately ran over to the wall of gauges and dials. It took a few seconds to locate the one that indicated speed, plus a few more to figure out what exactly it was saying. "Speed is thirty aeroknots."

Shiv'ren walked over to stand next to him, wiping his hands on a rag. Antoine felt him lean over his shoulder, squinting heavily at the dial for a minute, making a tsking noise before straightening up again. "Very well, given the ascension degree and our target height, we need to increase our speed by about five knots. Climbs like this take more power from the engines, so we need to increase the coal feed accordingly."

Antoine blinked a bit, filing the information away. That was something he'd found he enjoyed about being down here with Shiv'ren. He explained things, and he showed what exactly he was doing as he did so. It was certainly interesting while also letting Antoine feel he was being genuinely useful.

The time passed rather quickly after that, the rate of ascension increasing steadily as did the angle. Antoine shifted his feet farther apart to keep the proper footing. Right when he had found his balance, the aero suddenly leveled off. It knocked Antoine back a couple of steps, flailing to grab one of the pipes to correct his balance.

The sound of Shiv'ren's laughter made him turn once he was certain his feet were under him. Antoine was confronted by laughing gold eyes, a gloved hand clasped useless over Shiv'ren's mouth to try stifling the sound. Antoine scowled, not enjoying being the source of Shiv'ren's amusement, even if it was the first time he'd seen him laugh.

"It's not that funny to see me get knocked around, is it?" Antoine knew he was grumbling, which he shouldn't be doing. It was just that he felt like he had been adapting pretty well all considered, and now the elf was laughing at him.

"A little bit. It's been a while since I've seen someone knocked around by an ascent like that. I tend to forget how rough it is." Shiv'ren was still snickering as he pulled one of the main levers up to almost vertical. "Anyway, we've reached our destination."

"Really?" Antoine briefly wondered if it was supposed to distract him from the fact that he'd just been the subject of his friend's mirth. Even if it was, Antoine's curiosity was too great to resist. He walked quickly over to the windows, only to be confronted with a view of rocks and clouds that revealed nothing. "I'm going to go up on deck to take a look. Are you going to come?"

"No, I've already seen it before. I don't really want to see it again. I'm just going to get some other work done, but go look to your heart's content. Shouldn't take that long."

It struck Antoine as an odd thing to say. Still, the engineer was kind of strange, so he shrugged it off. Turning from the windows, he made his way through the maze of machines to the main door of the engine room. Once he was in the corridor, Antoine gave in to the excitement, racing up to the main deck. Stepping out, Antoine was greeted by bright sunlight along with a cold breeze. While his eyes adjusted, he made his way to the railing, eager for his first sight of their new destination.

When his eyes finally adjusted, he was met with an unexpected sight. Antoine thought he'd see something similar to Tyrnium, even though Shiv'ren had warned him that it was different. What he saw instead was a town that looked like the mining towns he'd seen when on trips for his father.

There was one difference though—Black Rocks seemed entirely deserted. It was perched on a flat outcropping that had been blasted out of the side of the mountain. The few buildings he could see were ramshackle, some in such obvious disrepair that they were barely standing. There was a feeling of despair and desolation hanging over everything like a miasma. Suddenly Antoine wasn't so enthusiastic. The lifeless town spread in front of him, causing a chill to settle in his bones. Antoine knew it wasn't from the wind, and he wasn't sure he would ever get warm again. Even feeling Rivas's hand settle on his shoulder barely had any effect.

"Not very impressive, is it?" Even the sound of Rivas's familiar voice was not enough to soothe him.

Antoine didn't object when he was pulled away and guided back below deck. In fact, he was grateful they were leaving it behind, before the numbness completely engulfed his soul. Antoine didn't come out of his daze until a hot mug was pressed into his hand. The feel of steam and the scent of something bitter drifted up to wreathe his face, and reflexively Antoine took a large sip. The coffee burned his tongue but brought a searing warmth to his body, from the top of his head all the way to his fingertips. He kept drinking until it was all gone, his body and mind slowly returning to normal.

"Feeling better?" The words and the concern behind them made Antoine jump a bit.

"Somewhat…. What is this place?" It felt like a dangerous question, because while Antoine wanted to know the answer, he was also afraid of it.

"It used to be a mining town. They mined coal and iron out of the mountain for years on end. It was never a large mine, but it had a steady output."

"What happened to it?"

"Several things, the iron veins began to run dry. The coal veins were deeper and more difficult to reach. Which meant it was harder to extract and required more dangerous methods in order to reach it. Not exactly profitable, especially if you could get it easier from a different mine. But the miners had pride in their work, and the fact was that their entire livelihood was dependent on the mine." Antoine could hear Rivas pacing slowly through the room, even though he didn't look up. "One day, they misjudged the amount of explosives used and there was a cave-in and the coal caught fire. They say it's still burning, even all these years later. After that, the company that owned the mine shut it down and abandoned the miners. Those that could leave went to other towns; those that couldn't were just left here, stuck in a dying town."

Rivas's voice trailed off after that, leaving Antoine with silence and his own swirling thoughts. Eventually one thought rose above the others. "Were you one of those who managed to leave? Or did you end up stuck here?"

Silence greeted the question, stretching uncomfortably between them for many minutes. When he couldn't bear it anymore, Antoine looked up, meeting the green eyes that were studying him so intently. Being the focus of such scrutiny made Antoine want to shrink back into himself, while at the same time it sent a flush of heat through him that was becoming very familiar. Even that did not distract from his desire to know the answer. So Antoine forced himself to continue meeting Rivas's gaze, refusing to look away until Rivas answered.

"Do I look like someone who was stuck?" It was a response, but not a response as well.

"You shouldn't answer a question with a question. And no, I don't think you were stuck here, not physically at least."

Rivas let out a hoarse chuckle, walking over to the port windows. "I wonder if your family realizes how smart and perceptive you really are. If they do, they probably don't appreciate it like they should." He let out a controlled breath. "I grew up here. My father was a miner. I worked there too, as a child, hauled the

110

carts of slag rocks from the shafts and shoveled the coal and ore into the transport containers. It was hard work, didn't pay very much either. It was all we had, me and Pa. The mine and each other, until...."

Antoine swallowed, his mouth feeling like it had been filled with sand. He knew, or thought he knew, what was going to come next. Even then, he couldn't stop himself. It felt like there was something else that was driving him, pushing him to ask even as a large part of him didn't want to hear the answer. "Until what?"

"There was a cave-in while Pa was working. The shafts weren't supported properly. It was considered secondary to getting to the coal. Eleven miners were trapped with no way out. It took days to clear the tunnel enough to reach them. By the time they were reached, there were only four just barely alive. Pa was one of the first to die. He was crushed under the falling rocks."

Rivas paused there, lost in his memories.

"I think that was the beginning of the end for Black Rocks. After that the attempts to reach useable ore became more dangerous until the whole mine caught fire. I didn't hear about it until months after it had happened. I'd stowed away on one of the transport aeros a few months after Pa died. There was nothing for me here. I had no way to support myself. Eventually I got picked up by a crew of pirates, and it's been all I've done since. The infamous Rivas the Ramshot, who could never forget one insignificant mining town."

"You wanted me to see this, didn't you?" Antoine's voice was quiet, yet it seemed to resonate through the entire room. "To see what my father... my family's business has done to people." He wrapped his arms around his stomach, seeking some kind of comfort.

When his father talked of the various mines that they owned, they were just marks on a map. Numbers on a ledger to show which ones were improving, which were not performing up to the required level. Changes to them were brought up in terms of money saved, increased earnings, better productions. Rarely, if ever, was it spoken of in terms of how it affected the workers. Concerns of what might happen to the towns that lived off the mine were never brought up, at least not in Antoine's presence.

Now that he began to think about it more carefully, Antoine realized that he wasn't surprised his father had never brought it up. Looking back, there was a host of other incidents he had witnessed that he had never questioned. The casual way his father would dismiss people they passed in the street with a sneer or harsh word. How his father never acknowledged the servants that crept around their home. Antoine felt a flush of shame when he realized how dismissive his father was of anyone he didn't consider an equal. The shame only deepened as he realized that until right then, he had never questioned those actions. The behavior of his father and others had never struck him as unusual.

Pieces began to fall into place for Antoine, things that Rivas, Shandor, and others had hinted at since he had been taken prisoner. "This is it, isn't it? The real reason that you attacked the aero and kidnapped me. It wasn't just the ransom you think my father will pay, you wanted to make me see just what it is my family has done."

Emotions battled inside of him, leaving Antoine's stomach churning.

"You thought you would teach me some kind of lesson, didn't you?" The words came out bitter and angry, taking even Antoine by surprise with their vehemence. He waited for a response, a confirmation or a rebuttal from Rivas, though Antoine wasn't sure which he wanted to hear. The silence that stretched out between them was its own answer. "Poor little rich boy who needs to be educated in the real world. Make him see what a monster his family and their business is." Antoine couldn't explain where the anger was coming from, but he was powerless to stop it from pouring out.

Antoine forced his mouth closed, locking more ugly words behind his teeth before they spilled out. The cabin felt too close. Everything feeling like it was pressing against him. He looked up at Rivas, taking in the grieved look on his face. Rivas looked as though he were trying desperately to come up with something to say, something to contradict what Antoine had just accused him of. All of the air seemed to leave Antoine's lungs, and there was no air to replace it.

He bolted from the room, running down the corridor and up onto deck. The ship was docked now, a gangplank having been placed between the dock and the ground. Antoine ran down it, ignoring the shouts from the pirates. It wasn't like there was anywhere he could really go. The town was abandoned, and if he tried to hide they would find him quick enough. Antoine wasn't trying to hide. He just needed to get away until he could draw a deep breath. Until the rage of emotions in his chest finally calmed.

What ultimately stopped Antoine's flight was the stray stone he tripped over that brought him crashing to his knees. The pain made Antoine suck in a deep breath, and then another as he realized he could breathe again. His knees and palms burned, giving him something to focus on beyond the churning of his gut. He whimpered, and then a choked scream came up followed by another. Once he started, Antoine couldn't stop himself, the screams continuing until they caught in his throat and turned into strangled sobs. He didn't know where it was all coming from, but as the sobs slowly eased up, it felt like a storm had settled inside him.

CHAPTER TWENTY-THREE

EVENTUALLY THE pain of his injuries overrode everything else. Carefully Antoine shifted so that he was not kneeling then moving slowly until he was sitting up. His gloves were still intact, but his palms burned. His knees were worse—the coveralls were torn and blood had seeped out around the edges. There was a fair amount of gravel that clung to the scrapes, making it difficult to see how bad they were. Antoine tried to brush the worst of it off, but all it did was change the pain from dull to sharp.

Antoine let out a sigh, finally starting to take in his surroundings. Evidently in his blind running he had worked his way through the abandoned town all the way to the mouth of the mine. There was debris from the mountain scattered around him, not just rocks but carts and tools. An acrid stench drifted up from the mine, the familiar smell of burning coal almost comforting if not for the reminder that he was next to a burning coal mine. Carefully Antoine scooted backward until he could lean against one of the boulders, letting out a slow breath to combat the pain.

Once he was standing again, Antoine was left wondering what he would do now. He knew that someone, most likely Rivas, would come looking for him. Even if there was nowhere for him to go, there were enough ways for him to get injured without proper supervision. Which Antoine sheepishly realized he had just proven. So the question became should he leave now, or stay and wait for Rivas to find him? Eventually it was the ache in his knees that decided it. Antoine was going to stay put for the moment.

Mercifully he didn't have to wait very long before he heard the sound of boots crunching over the ground in his direction. Antoine refused to look up, though, even when he saw the boots walk in front of him, stopping short of him. It was petty, but Antoine decided he wouldn't be the first to break the silence. Also given the amount of ugliness he had spewed out earlier, Antoine really thought it would be better if he stayed quiet this time.

"You do not make things easy, do you, Antoine?" Rivas's voice was a mixture of fond and frustrated.

Antoine didn't feel like a reply was really needed, so he didn't offer one. Instead he tilted his head back to take in more of the looming figure. When Rivas shifted and crouched in front of him, it made them eye level with each other.

"Well, since it seems like you're not going to say anything for once, I guess it's my turn to speak." Rivas pulled a canteen off his belt. He set it aside, reaching out and grasping Antoine's knee in a warm grip. "You're right, I did plan ultimately to show you this place. I wanted to show you what it is like for those that work to make the Suva Coal Company successful. But honestly, I didn't do it out of cruelty, not intentionally."

There was a pause as he carefully brushed the gravel out of one of the scrapes.

"I wanted you to see it, so that when you take over you'll keep it in mind, perhaps even change it." Rivas unscrewed the canteen and used the water to clean the wound. "Things won't change if you're not aware of the problem." Rivas released the leg he'd already treated, moving on to the next one. "I will admit, though, I didn't handle it that well."

Antoine winced, both at the words and the sting from his scrapes. "I'm sorry, I don't know what got into me. I'm not even sure where it all came from really. It just seemed... once I started I couldn't stop it."

"You wouldn't be the first. Sometimes you just need to let it out." Rivas frowned, pulling back. "However, I could have done without the theatrics of you running away from me through the entire town."

"Ah, I think I could have done without that too." He stared down at his stinging knees. "Certainly wasn't the best idea, I'll admit."

Rivas let out a startled laugh, which made Antoine laugh in return. It was a strange, small bubble of happiness that just seemed to burst inside of him. The laughter was as overwhelming as the anger had been before, yet this time instead of weighing him down, it seemed to lighten him.

When it finally subsided, Rivas straightened, holding out his hand. "Well, since we're already here, would you like the tour of the town? There isn't much to see, but I doubt you saw it when you were tearing through here before."

Antoine took the hand, getting to his feet with a small whimper. "If my legs will let me."

"If they won't then you can lean on me." Rivas's smile was warm and made Antoine's stomach flip pleasantly.

Ultimately it seemed that Rivas was right: there wasn't a lot to the town itself. The buildings were abandoned, covered in dust with several seemingly barely held together. The best maintained buildings were the few that were close to the aerodock itself.

Rivas led him to a house on the western side of the town. It looked like all of the other buildings, yet Rivas said it was the house he had shared with his father when he was a child. The idea of seeing the feared pirate captain's childhood home was simply too tempting a location to not visit.

There was little evidence remaining of the occupants of the house. Some beaten-up and broken furniture, a small coal stove tucked in a corner, and moldering bedding. It was anticlimactic in a way that Antoine didn't really understand. There were no grand revelations about Rivas waiting to reveal themselves. Rivas did get a nostalgic look on his face as he stood in the center of the house, green eyes slightly unfocused, as if he was seeing something from his past.

There were stairs leading to a second story, but most of the middle steps were missing, and those that remained did not look very sturdy. Antoine decided that his curiosity was not worth the probability of further injury. All told it was a quick exploration of the house for Antoine, though Rivas was obviously taking a bit longer.

Antoine settled onto the lone chair in the room to wait for Rivas to finish his reminiscing. He had just gotten comfortable when there came a rumbling sound from the ground. Antoine tensed and glanced around nervously as he tried to find the source of the sound. Rivas had just stepped outside, and when he didn't return Antoine figured he must have imagined the sound. Until it came back, louder than before, accompanied by the ground shaking dangerously.

"Rivas!" Antoine leapt to his feet, trying to maintain his footing as the world seemed to shake apart. Panic was clawing at his throat, especially when he heard the building creaking around him. He had a brief glimpse of Rivas rushing in as the creaking got louder, now followed by a far more ominous sound akin to dry twigs breaking.

What followed after, Antoine would only ever remember in broken images. A glimpse of Rivas's face, for once raw with panic and concern. Looking up to see the ceiling approaching his head. The impact of another body knocking him hard to the ground. The crushing feel of an entire house falling on them. After that, there was only the blackness.

CHAPTER TWENTY-FOUR

SHANDOR SAT on a rock by the *Aria*, enjoying the silence that the abandoned town gave. Most of the crew was below deck drinking heavily, leaving only Shandor and a few others relatively sober. With Rivas having run off after Antoine, Shandor was in charge of the ship. Hence why he had basically given everyone leave to drink until drunk. Not that he particularly minded being one of the few sober people aboard the *Aria*. It gave him privacy—time to think away from everyone else. No need to keep the façade up like he normally did.

He had just started to settle in and relax, perhaps even catch a quick nap, when the earthquake came. The ground shaking knocked him off his perch, taking the breath from his lungs. When it finally stopped, Shandor scrambled to his feet, taking in the damage to the town. Several of the buildings had collapsed, and a small fissure had opened in the middle of the street, spewing noxious-smelling gas.

Shandor quickly scanned the area, searching frantically for any sign of Rivas or Antoine. He knew they had been wandering through the town earlier. He'd seen them briefly before losing track of them through the buildings. Now he was scared his friend had gotten trapped under the debris.

"Shandor? What's going on? What happened to the town?" Shiv'ren's voice came from the deck of the ship, his tone filled with shock at what had happened.

"Shiv'ren, come with me. The rest of you, stay on the ship until it's safe. Was anyone else in the village besides Captain Rivas?"

He waited for the negative response before he started to move through the buildings, trying to figure out where Rivas would have taken Antoine. The sound of boots following him was reassuring. It meant that V'ren had followed after like he had ordered. It would take more than just himself to search the town, and if either Rivas or

Antoine were injured, Shandor would need another set of hands. More important than all that, he needed someone he could absolutely trust.

"What happened, Shan? What's going on?" The worry in Shiv'ren's voice had increased greatly, making Shandor wish he had something positive to tell him.

"There was an earthquake. Rivas and Antoine were in the village when it happened."

"Where are they, then? You don't think they were caught in one of the buildings, do you? Do you?" Shandor didn't respond. There wasn't any response he could give, positive or negative. Of course, he knew not responding would do nothing to ease the worry. "Say something dammit! Don't just stay silent like this!"

"I don't know." Shandor forced the words out slowly, doing his best not to let his own frustration turn to meaningless anger. "I don't know where they went or if they were in any of the buildings. I wasn't watching them." Shandor paused at a side street, looking around, trying to think clearly.

If he were Rivas, where would he take someone in this dump? He took a minute, tried to think like his friend. If he was trying to calm down and get back on the good side of a person he was enamored with who was upset with him, where would he go? Well, the situation wasn't that hard to imagine, given the way his overtures to the winged elf beside him were received. Except he had to think about how Rivas would handle it….

Shandor turned on his heel, running down the cross street. He hoped he remembered the location correctly. He had only seen the place a few times, Rivas pointing it out in an offhanded manner. He skidded to a stop in front of the house that he remembered Rivas mentioning as the one he had grown up in.

"Oh god…." There wasn't a house there any longer, at least nothing that looked remotely like a house. Shandor approached the rubble cautiously, trying to figure out the best way to search without dislodging more rubble onto anyone who might be inside.

"Rivas! Antoine!" He knew it was probably futile to call for them, but Shandor couldn't help the small kernel of hope that prayed one of them would answer.

ANTOINE'S MIND felt sluggish as he woke up. There was a heavy pressure on his chest and torso, making it difficult to get enough air in. Briefly he wondered why that was, but then something else drew his attention—the feeling of something wet dripping onto his face. It was irritating, and he tried to bring his hand up to wipe it away, but his arm wouldn't move. Whatever was weighing down his chest had also pinned his arm.

Forcing his eyes open, Antoine tried to make out his surroundings. It took a few moments for his eyes to fully adjust to the uneven lighting, but once they did he looked up. His heart stuttered when he saw just what was pinning him down. Rivas was sprawled on top of him, his larger body shielding Antoine. The wet feeling was blood dripping off Rivas's head and onto his cheek. Memory returned in a rush, of the house shaking around them, Rivas throwing himself on top of him as the walls began to collapse.

"Rivas?" Antoine tried to move, wriggling a bit in the hope of getting one of his arms free. "Rivas, come on, wake up. We need to get out of here...." He hated how his voice was wavering as he spoke, catching slightly as he said the name.

The lack of response made him start to panic. Antoine tried to reassure himself that Rivas was just unconscious, knocked out from the collapse of the house. There was no way the strong air pirate could be dead. Not like this, not protecting someone like Antoine. If he was going to die, it should be in a blaze of glory, some great battle, any other way but like this.

His breath hitched, coming harder and shorter the more Antoine tried to draw in a full lung of air. Just as it felt like the panic was going to drown him, a sound cut through it. Faint at first, but it grew stronger, followed by the rather worrisome sound of shifting rubble. "Rivas! Antoine! Where are you?"

"Here...." The words were weak, barely audible. Antoine swallowed, giving another try. "Here! We're here."

The sound of shifting rubble grew louder, footsteps carefully picking their way toward him. "Antoine? Antoine, can you hear me?" Shandor sounded worried, something Antoine didn't let his mind focus on.

"Here…. You've got to hurry. Rivas is… I think he's hurt. He's not waking up."

"Stay still. Antoine, you've got to stay calm, we're going to get you both out as quickly as we can."

"Hurry, please. I can't tell if…." Antoine cut himself off, couldn't bring himself to say the words out loud. A small, childish part of him was afraid that if he gave voice to his fear, that would make it real. His chest felt like it would cave in on itself even thinking it. To say the words would rip it completely apart.

"Shiv'ren, go back to the ship, get Li and tell Sawbones to be ready. Try not to let on to anyone else what has happened, all right? I'm going to work on clearing the rubble." Shandor's voice was tight with control.

Clearing the debris was a hard, slow process. Even more worrisome: as pieces were moved, other pieces became dislodged and moved on their own. Each time it happened, Antoine winced and held his breath, afraid there would be further instability. Soon more sunlight began to filter in, giving Antoine a better view of his situation. A cut ran along Rivas's hairline, ending at his temple. It had been the source of the blood that had continued to drip onto him, but now it had stopped. The fact that it had stopped dripping onto him was not as comforting to Antoine as it should have been.

"Antoine, can you hear me?" Shandor's voice was back, closer this time.

"Yes. We're still here."

"Good, just stay awake. I've gotten a lot of the debris removed. I'll have you both out soon."

"Please, hurry."

It was getting harder to breathe, to pull in a good breath. Even though he could see the rubble being removed, his lungs felt like they were on fire. He must be getting weaker from trying to breathe through the weight that had settled on him.

Soon, though, he could see Shandor's face peering down at him, sweaty and coated with dust. "We're here. Just hold still, we're going to try and move Rivas." The scrambling of booted feet was followed by a grunt. It seemed to take agonizing minutes before he felt Rivas's weight being shifted off him.

Antoine started to move, to sit up on his own when a soft voice spoke. "Don't move, Antoine. It's very unstable beneath you, so if we're not careful it will collapse even further. Wait until we have the captain moved." Looking up, Antoine saw that Li was staring down at him, perched on the edge of some boards. He gave a slight smile, which surprisingly did a lot to reassure Antoine.

"We're clear, Li! Get Antoine now." At the sound of Shandor's voice, Li moved quickly, reaching down and grasping Antoine's arms and pulling up. His legs felt shaky as he stood up, leaning heavily on Li. The other man moved quickly over the rubble with surer feet than Antoine possessed.

As soon as they reached firm ground, Antoine collapsed to his knees, not even feeling the sting of previous injuries as he dragged in lungfuls of air. He saw Shandor leaning over Rivas, a hand resting on his chest. Carefully Antoine crawled over to Rivas, placing a shaking hand on the captain's shoulder. He looked beseechingly at Shandor, hoping for some kind of reassurance.

"He's breathing, but his heart rate is slow," Shandor said, when he saw that Antoine was staring at him. "We need to get him back to the ship." Shandor shifted, placing one of Rivas's arms around his shoulders, and then he wrapped his own arm around Rivas's waist.

"Can you walk on your own, Antoine?" Li crouched down next to him, black hair shadowing his eyes as he held out a hand. Antoine swallowed, taking the offered hand to pull himself upright. His legs were shaky, but they held, and once he was sure that they would continue to do so, he gently shook off Li's hold on him.

"I'll be fine. Help Shandor," Antoine implored, wanting more than anything else for Rivas to be safe. He watched as Li went over, moving to support Rivas's other side. The two men were able to move quickly with their burden, leaving Antoine to limp after them. Despite the aching in various parts of his body, he refused to be left behind.

By the time they reached the *Aria*, Antoine could barely keep up with the two other men. Thankfully having to navigate through the ship corridors made the going a bit slower, allowing Antoine to catch up. When he realized they were heading for Rivas's stateroom, Antoine let himself go at a more moderate pace, knowing their ultimate destination.

Upon reaching the cabin, Antoine was greeted by a rather motley group of people in the main room. Li and Yi were there, as well as Shiv'ren. The winged elf was over by one of the round view ports, staring pensively out of it, the constant twitching of his wings the only sign of his great agitation. The two easterners were much more reserved, better at concealing whatever emotions they felt.

Distressingly there was no sign of either Shandor or Rivas in the main room. Without pausing, Antoine began to limp over to the sleeping cabin. It was only when he reached the entrance that he paused, leaning heavily on the doorway as his eyes swept across the room. Rivas was laid out on the bed, Shandor standing off to the side with another man who was examining the captain. He was tall and broad with darkened skin and long dreadlocks falling over his shoulders. Antoine vaguely recognized him as one of the men who had been dancing the other night in the mess hall.

Shandor glanced over at Antoine, his mechanical eye making a soft whirring noise before he refocused on the other man. "How is he, Sawbones?"

The man, Sawbones, let out a snort, rubbing his face. "You know it not that easy to tell, Shandor. You got enough knowledge of healing for that. Cap'n asleep for now, several of his ribs be broke, makes his breath short. Leg be broke as well, and the wound on his side is not so good. Cap'n won't be up and about for a good while."

Shandor let out a heavy breath, head falling forward as he cursed softly under his breath. "Can you treat him?"

"I can make him comfortable, keep the pain back. I bandage his wound and splint his leg. The only real cure gonna be time. Someone got to keep watch over him, though. He ain't gonna be able to move." Sawbones had propped his chin on his hand, his long wooly locks of hair almost brushing the floor.

"Do what you can, Sawbones." Shandor straightened, hands falling to his sides. He glanced over at Antoine again. "When you're done taking care of the captain, take a look at Antoine. I want to be sure that he isn't more injured than he appears."

"Aye, aye. You go do what you got to." Sawbones stood, stretching his back before he picked up a satchel that had been resting by his feet. He began to sort through it, pulling out various items and setting them to the side. Shandor brushed by them both, making his way back out to the main room.

"You should sit down before you fall down." The words made Antoine jump, gripping the edge of the doorway to keep himself from falling over. He carefully limped his way over to a chair, and then sat down heavily.

There wasn't any more speaking for a long time. The murmur of voices from the main chamber drifted by, but the words were too muffled for Antoine to make out. Sawbones didn't seem concerned, though. Instead he continued putting different dried plants into a shallow bowl.

The purpose of the plants wasn't readily apparent until Li walked in, carrying a small kettle. He poured steaming water into the bowl, smiling slightly at the darker-skinned man before slipping out of the room again. Antoine noticed the smile, but his mind was too preoccupied with the bowl Sawbones was holding to think more on it.

"What is that?" The question slipped out as Antoine watched the contents of the bowl being stirred. A fragrant bitterness began to fill the cabin.

"Medicine" was the terse reply. "Strong medicine to help block the pain. Best to give that first before setting the bones. It better for everyone this way." With that they lapsed back into silence until the medicine was done steeping. Then Sawbones pulled out a bottle that was half full of a familiar amber liquid, filling the rest of it with the liquid from the bowl, before swirling it all together. "Rum helps hide the taste, 'cause the medicine, it taste horrible." There was a smile that flashed bright teeth before Sawbones turned and set the bottle aside.

Antoine swallowed a bit, his stomach twisting as he looked over at Rivas. "Why hasn't he woken yet?" The question was quiet, and Antoine despised how his voice quavered.

"Any number of reasons really. Judging by the wound on his head, he took a nasty blow. No way to work around that until his body decides to wake. Which may be soon once I get to work." There was a shifting, Sawbones moving to sit on the edge of the bed. "Prop him up for me. We gonna give him medicine."

Antoine stood up, shakily walking over to collapse on the bed by Rivas's head. Carefully he lifted the pirate's head up high enough that he wouldn't choke, bracing it against his chest. Sawbones leaned forward, pressing the bottle to Rivas's lips, forcing the concoction down his throat.

After a few sips were forced down his throat, Rivas finally stirred, letting out a haggard cough. He turned his head to the side, coughing some more.

"Cap'n, good you awake now."

"That shit… tastes horrid." Rivas's voice was hoarse and weak, but his green eyes appeared sharp and bright.

"A common complaint, tough pirates always bellyaching. You be grateful for it soon," Sawbones said, leaning over his leg. "Now I need you to stay still. Antoine, you got to hold him back, so he don't move on me."

Antoine swallowed, bringing his arms up around Rivas. It would have been tender, if not for the guilt twisting his stomach. He had a horrible sense that the feeling would only get worse when he saw Sawbones leaning over Rivas's right leg. Sawbones placed strong hands on the leg before pushing down. Rivas let out a pained scream that had Antoine closing his eyes and turning his head away.

When it was finally over, Rivas was sweaty, pale, and panting in obvious pain. Antoine turned, fumbling for the bottle and holding it up to Rivas's lips. This time there was no complaint about the taste, only quick sips between pants for air. While this was going on, Antoine was aware of Sawbones fastening a splint to Rivas's leg.

"Part done, more to come, Cap'n." There was regret in Sawbones' voice when he spoke. He reached down and pulled out several additional rolls of bandages, setting them on the bed as he scooted forward.

"In that case… I want some more medicine," Rivas panted out. Antoine immediately lifted the bottle, watching as Rivas took several grateful gulps before closing his eyes. "Do it."

Before the broken ribs could be wrapped, Rivas's shirt had to be removed, a process that was slow and awkward. The sight of Rivas's bared chest would normally have flustered Antoine, but that response was stifled by the slowly blooming bruises on Rivas's sternum and abdomen. Fresh guilt flooded Antoine's system, forcing him to look away.

Mercifully bandaging the ribs took much less time than the leg had. It was hard to tell if it was more or less painful since Rivas was stubbornly gritting his teeth to keep any possible sound from escaping. When it was finished, he collapsed backward onto the bed, covered in a sheen of sweat. He managed to take a few more sips of the medicine before he closed his eyes tiredly. Antoine gently wiped away the sweat with his sleeve, trying to make Rivas more comfortable. Antoine was so focused, he barely noticed when Sawbones left.

"I'm sorry. This is my fault… I shouldn't have run away like I did. I always seem to be causing trouble for you, Rivas." Antoine swallowed, blinking back wetness from his eyes. His mind told him feeling guilty was foolish. He'd had no control over what happened. Even knowing that, it did nothing to stifle the guilt.

"If you feel it's your fault then perhaps you'd like to do something to make it better?" Shandor's voice startled Antoine enough to make him jump. He turned quickly to look at the gypsy standing in the cabin's doorway. There was a tenseness to Shandor's stance that Antoine hadn't seen before. It was matched by a new weariness shown around his mouth and his one flesh eye.

Antoine swallowed, his response automatic. "What can I do?"

"Come out here when you're ready, and I shall explain." With that, Shandor turned on his heel, leaving Antoine alone again.

CHAPTER TWENTY-FIVE

ANTOINE STAYED for a minute, staring down at Rivas, who was sleeping uneasily. He made sure the captain was completely covered, so he could rest as comfortably as possible. Then Antoine stood and made his way into the main part of the cabin. He had expected to see the other crewmembers that had been present earlier, but they were all gone. Only Shandor remained, sitting behind the desk with his fingers steepled together in front of him.

"Sit down, Antoine." The gypsy's voice was heavy and tired.

Antoine followed the order, sitting stiffly in the chair, curling his fingers into the material of his coveralls. Shandor didn't speak again for a long, painful moment.

"I'm going to be blunt, Antoine, because you need to know all the facts and there isn't time to soften it. We're in a precarious situation. The captain's injuries mean he'll be incapacitated for a while, unable to move or do his duties. The crew's faith in the captain is going to be stretched thin. What we need to do, what I need your help with, is to make sure that it does not snap entirely. If the crew votes to remove Rivas from his position as captain and replace him, well, it won't be good for you. Most likely the ransom deal will fall through entirely, which means either death or worse for you."

Antoine swallowed thickly, his voice a bit hoarse when it came out. "What could be worse than death?"

Shandor's mismatched eyes flashed briefly "A lot of things, none of which you want to experience. That's not the point, though. The point is that we're going to have to play at a bit of mummery for the next few weeks. I'm going to downplay Rivas's wounds, in an effort to keep the crew from getting restless. Unfortunately news travels fast on a ship, so the crew already knows that he's injured. Which makes your position even more tenuous than before."

"Tenuous?" Antoine felt like the world was slipping around him, all of the new information making his head spin.

"The crew will blame you for what happened to the captain, so in order to keep them from doing anything, I'm going to have to take certain measures. The first of which is this: you will be the captain's caretaker." Shandor let out a breath, leaning back in the chair. "To the crew it will be a form of punishment, and for us it will be a safeguard against word getting out about how serious the damage to Rivas really is. You won't be leaving the captain's quarters for a while, probably not until we do the ransom switch." Shandor leaned forward, resting his hands on the desk.

Antoine swallowed, a fierce ache moving right across the front of his head as he thought of it all. "So I'll be taking care of Rivas until he gets better, or my father sends the money to free me?"

Shandor let out a long breath, rubbing his forehead. "Yes, for now. It's the best way to both keep you safe and the *Aria* functioning."

Antoine leaned forward, meeting the gypsy's gaze. "I know I don't really have a choice, but I'll do it." It would ease his guilt greatly to know he was doing something for Rivas. That he was protecting him, even if it was by being a nursemaid.

Shandor sighed, deflating a bit. Antoine thought he could almost see the weight dropping off his shoulders. "Thank you, Antoine." The sincerity was palpable. Antoine knew then that whatever else was going on, whatever hidden agendas Shandor might have, he did truly care about Rivas as a friend.

"I hope you understand that this means you won't be leaving this room for any reason. Food will be brought for you and Rivas each day. Sawbones will also be visiting to check up on both the captain and you. You took quite a nasty tumble yourself. Sawbones said he'd be back soon to check on you."

Antoine blinked, raising a hand to his head. "My head has been aching quite a bit." He took a deep breath, wincing when pain lanced through his sternum. "Also it hurts to breathe too deeply."

"I would imagine so, given what happened." Shandor stood up, stretching slowly. "I'll send Sawbones up to take a look at you." He smiled slightly, walking over to Antoine and patting him on the shoulder. "Would hate to have all of Rivas's work be for naught. Rest for now, alright?"

Antoine nodded, getting to his feet with some difficulty. It wasn't helped by the room spinning as he stood up. He was grateful when Shandor's hands came to rest on his shoulders, providing a steady point. Antoine let himself be guided until he was able to collapse onto his chair. Once seated, Antoine closed his eyes and leaned forward to rest his head on the mattress.

Time moved strangely for Antoine as he drifted between awake and asleep. He didn't try to think because it caused the ache to increase a great deal. Instead he just listened to the murmur of the *Aria*'s engines and the faint echo of Rivas's breath.

It seemed he'd just closed his eyes when he felt a hand on his shoulder, gently shaking him. Yet when Antoine opened his eyes, the color of the light coming through the porthole had changed. There was a reddish cast to it now, the shadows having lengthened considerably. His gaze settled on the still sleeping form taking up the bed. Rivas's brow was creased in apparent pain. However, he seemed to be breathing well, which loosened some of the knots in Antoine's chest.

"C'mon, get up. I needs t'look at you." Sawbones was standing behind him, his long dreadlocks bound back from his face. A small smile creased his face, his white teeth flashing in the dim light. He reached down and helped Antoine to his feet and out into the main part of the cabin.

Antoine didn't argue when he was again guided to a chair and forced to sit. Hands ran lightly over him, poking gently at various spots. When Sawbones got to Antoine's ribs, Antoine couldn't resist letting out a small gasp of pain.

"Like I thought, bruised in the fall, probably from the cap'n falling on you and staying for so long. Shirt off."

Antoine blinked, sluggishly obeying the instruction and stripping off the top portion of his coveralls, leaving himself bare from the waist up. Warm hands were pressing firmly against his bruises. Antoine could only gasp and grit his teeth against the pain. When Sawbones finally moved away, Antoine sucked in a deep breath and let out a muffled curse at the pain that raced through him. He steadfastly ignored the amused laughter coming from Sawbones.

"Nothin' broke, only some bruises. Will fade quick enough if y'don't strain yourself too greatly. Which accordin' to Shandor y'shouldn't have a chance to." Sawbones turned away, walking over to the desk where there was a surprisingly wide assortment of containers lined up. "I make you some more medicine for the cap'n when he wakes. You tell him it's Sawbones' special medicine. He won't object to taking it then."

"Why do they call you Sawbones? That's not your actual name, is it?" Antoine asked, stepping forward to stand near the table, watching as the different items were mixed together.

There was a rich laugh as something green and strong-smelling was added. "No, Sawbones not my name, it my title. They call me Sawbones, because I can saw the bones when needed. On ships like this, it's the closest to a doctor you'll find."

"A doctor... who saws bones?" Antoine was trying to follow the logic, but the images that came to mind were not encouraging.

"Yes, sometimes when the hurt is bad, only thing to be done is take it off. Saw the bone off if needed." He didn't look up as he continued to work, mixing different things. "We be lucky here. I's know more than how to just saw bones."

Before Antoine could even begin to think of a response to that, there was a soft knock on the door. The person on the other side didn't wait for a response, pushing the door open gently. Li stepped in, nodding to Antoine as he walked over to the desk, sliding a package over to Sawbones.

"Here, this will help with the pain. It is a special plant that grows in the east." Antoine had to strain to hear the softly spoken words. What he did notice, though, was the way that Li and Sawbones locked eyes for a minute. Their fingers seemed to linger slightly before pulling away. The moment felt intimate.

Antoine turned away, walking back into the cabin to check on Rivas. He felt he couldn't draw a full breath until he saw the blond air pirate. Antoine thought he would never get used to seeing Rivas so still and vulnerable. Even in such a small time, Rivas had taken on a near invincible status in Antoine's mind.

Antoine sat down, taking a little bit of extra care when his chest gave a twinge of pain. He watched the slow rise and fall of Rivas's bare chest, the white bandages contrasting with the tan of his skin. A maelstrom of emotions swirled through Antoine, guilt and worry the strongest. Yet in a far corner of his mind, there was a strange warmth when he contemplated Rivas and what he had done for him. Rivas had sacrificed himself to make sure Antoine was safe. Antoine couldn't think of anyone else he knew that would do the same. It gave him a small burr of pleasure that only increased his guilt. He shouldn't feel happy that Rivas was willing to do so much to save him. Logically he should have been upset that Rivas hadn't died when the building had collapsed. The man was his captor after all. Only he wasn't, and he wasn't happy Rivas had been injured either. It was why he hadn't complained about being forced to take up the role of nursemaid. Antoine leaned forward, burrowing his fingers into his hair in frustration. The more he thought about it, the more tangled up it all became inside of him.

The feel of a calloused hand wrapping around his arm brought Antoine back to awareness of his surroundings. Antoine slowly looked up to meet tired, concerned emerald eyes.

"Rivas…." Antoine swallowed quickly, forcing his brain to start working properly. "How are you feeling? Do you need anything?"

Rivas shook his head slightly, even though his eyes were lined with pain. "What… is wrong, Antoine?" His voice was hoarse, cracking partway through.

"Stay put, let me get some water." Antoine stood up, gently working his wrist free of Rivas's hold. It seemed a sign of how weak he was that Antoine was even able to force his arm free.

Antoine swiftly moved into the main room, grateful to find that a tray laden with both a pitcher of water and some food had been left on the desk. A folded piece of paper was propped up against the lamp. The handwriting was a clear, ornate scrawl listing precisely what medicines had been left for them and how they were to be administered. Next to the note sat several small earthen containers, unevenly made but brightly colored, each bowl representing a different tincture.

Antoine decided to forgo the mixtures until Rivas requested them. He had already taken a great deal of medicine previously, and Antoine didn't want to cause more harm by giving Rivas too much. Instead he poured the water into a cup and carried it back into the bedroom.

After setting it down on the table by the bed, he moved to help Rivas sit up. It was easy to tell that he hated having to accept help with such a simple task, but it was also obvious that he wouldn't be able to support himself for a while. Once Antoine had him positioned, he held the cup up so Rivas could drink. After a few sips of water, though, Rivas pushed Antoine away.

"Are you hungry? Are you in pain? Sawbones left some medicine for when the pain gets too great." Antoine forced himself to stop talking before he began to ramble.

"No, I'm all right. Still feeling the effects of the last round." Rivas's voice was steadier now, his eyes moving over Antoine. "Were you hurt, when the building came down?"

Antoine felt himself flush a little at the concern. "I'm fine. Sawbones said I just have some bruises and scrapes. You, you protected me. Thank you for that."

A calloused hand came up, wrapping around Antoine's wrist, squeezing gently. "What happened out there?"

"Evidently there was an earthquake. Several buildings collapsed and part of the ground split open as well."

Rivas winced, shifting a bit as if he were trying to get more comfortable. "I suppose it was inevitable. The entire mountain range is unstable. The mining doesn't help with that—this is hardly the first earthquake."

Antoine leaned forward, moving to prop Rivas up against the wall. "You're very educated for a pirate," Antoine commented distractedly, moving to arrange the blankets around Rivas.

"When I was first taken onto a ship, I couldn't read or anything. I didn't think I needed it, but the captain at that time wouldn't stand for ignorance simply for ignorance's sake. He insisted I learn." Rivas winced, taking a slow breath. "The engineer we had before Shiv'ren, he was a man of learning. He taught many of the crew their letters and numbers."

That brought a smile to Antoine's face as he tried to imagine a younger Rivas bent over books, working studiously. The image was surprisingly cute. "I see you took the lessons to heart. I think many people in Laitha would be surprised to learn their feared air pirate is a learned man."

Rivas chuckled softly, a movement that quickly turned into a wince. "It's easier to make someone a demon if you keep from seeing any similarity to yourself. Also, Laitha has become more intolerant over the years since I first visited it." Rivas shivered a bit, the movement almost lost in the growing dark of the room.

Antoine stood up, moving to light the various gas lamps in the two rooms. After that, he gathered up the tray that contained the food that had been brought in earlier. It looked to be a very simple meal, some dried meat, bread, and cheese. Antoine carried the tray over to the bed and set it on the edge.

The meal passed quietly, with little talk. Toward the end Rivas began to show some increased discomfort, his face taking on a paler cast. Antoine quickly moved the tray back into the cabin, snatching up the bowl that contained the tincture to help deaden pain and ease sleep. He mixed it into the cup of water as instructed and carried it back into the room. Rivas gave no resistance to the elixir, which caused Antoine to bite his lip in concern.

After drinking only half the cup, Rivas pushed it away, shaking his head. "No more. You should save some for yourself," he said, attempting to shift himself to a lying position.

"I don't need it really, I'll be fine," Antoine assured him, moving to help Rivas settle on the bed. "I'm just going to settle you and lower the lamps before resting myself."

Rivas was frowning, the expression making his face look haggard. "You're not sleeping in the hammock," he said firmly, slowly moving over on the bed. "There is plenty of space with me. Trying to sleep in the hammock will be painful for you with your bruises. Don't think I haven't noticed the way you favor them."

Antoine swallowed, looking down at his boots. He had tried to hide the aches that flared along his sternum every time he breathed. Evidently he wasn't a very good actor. "You're more hurt than I am. I don't need to impose on you. I'll be fine in the hammock, or I can sleep in the main cabin."

"Antoine." Rivas's voice was stern, green eyes seeming to glow in the light of the dimmed lamps. "I'm not so injured that having you nearby will damage me further. In fact, it would ease my mind to know you are nearby and safe, not harming yourself further."

Guilt spiked in Antoine, effectively putting an end to his resistance. After drinking the remaining mixture, he carefully climbed onto the bed. Antoine stayed as close to the edge, and as far from Rivas, as he could be. Rivas gave a heavy sigh behind him, but Antoine refused to turn to check. He had given in to Rivas's request to stay on the bed, but he would not risk making the air pirate captain's injuries worse by getting too close. That's what Antoine firmly told himself as he began to drift off to sleep.

CHAPTER TWENTY-SIX

THE STREETS on the upper terraces of Laitha were wide and well-lit boulevards where the rich and noble of the city strolled, safe in the idea that they were protected from the rabble that lived beneath them. The area was commonly called Sharpsbury, not as prestigious as living in the Spire, but the Spire was only open to the highest nobles and the Archduke and Duchess. Yet even in the most well-lit streets, there were shadows that could overhear all manner of things. In a city that ran on secrets, information was the ultimate power. The people on the upper terraces pretended not to notice those that lurked in the shadows.

Certainly the last thing on Adrian Suvalese's mind was the lurkers in the shadows. Much more important things weighed on him as he strode down the boulevard. In his hand he clutched a large black case containing what he hoped would bring him the safety of his youngest son.

His destination was a gentleman's club that catered to a select clientele. It was a refuge for well-to-do men, a place to mingle, strike deals, drink, and gamble. Normally a visit to the club was something Adrian would enjoy, spending hours there in comfort. This visit, though, was not for the pleasure of like-minded company. Adrian was here to meet someone in particular, which made it a business transaction. Business transactions were not things that were meant to be enjoyed, that was Adrian's belief—they also weren't meant to be personal either.

Upon reaching the club, he received a respectful bow from the doorman, something that he barely noticed. He strode into one of the private parlors, giving the space a sharp glance before pushing the door shut behind him. There was only one other person in the room, sitting in front of the fireplace in one of the large wingback chairs, knees crossed. The relaxed posture made him seem younger than the thirty or so years Adrian guessed him to be. He was dressed in the uniform of a naval officer with a high-collared dark coat and stark white breeches tucked into a pair of high, polished boots. Gold epaulets bearing the stripes of a captain gleamed in the firelight.

After striding over to the other chair, Adrian sat down heavily in it, settling the case by his feet. The other man hadn't turned away from his contemplation of the fire. They sat in silence for several minutes, Adrian quietly taking the measure of the man. It had taken a great deal of persuading and more than a few bribes to get to this moment, but if it brought Antoine back safely, then it was worth it.

After several minutes had passed, Adrian spoke up. "So you are the one that is going after the air pirates that have my son. Because of that, I would like to know what kind of man you are."

"What kind of man I am, Mr. Suvalese?" Turning away from the fire, the young captain's face was revealed. He had strong features framed by well-groomed muttonchops that gave him a severe look. "I am Captain Randalf Hildebard, captain of an aero of the line for the Archduke's Navy. I have been entrusted by the Archduchess to track down the filthy air pirates that have been plaguing the aerolines. That they have the gall to take the son of a good citizen hostage is beyond the pale. My duty to my city and my lord is to hunt down these monsters and bring them to justice." Dark eyes burned with a purpose, reflecting the steel in his spine.

Adrian approved of a man with a purpose, so long as the purpose coincided with his own. Whether the captain's purpose would work with his, he was about to find out. "I care less for the safety of the aerolines. They are not what concerns me. What concerns me is the safety of my son."

"I understand and appreciate your concern, sir, but surely you must see the larger picture."

"Tell me, captain, do you have children? Are you a married man?"

"I have yet to find the right woman to settle down with. It takes a special woman who can put up with a man in the navy."

"Well, one day you will have children of your own, and you will understand that when they are in danger, there is no picture bigger than their well-being." Adrian stared down at his hand, which was clenched around the ornate cane that had been a present from Nigel. "And punishment for those who have put them in danger."

"I promise you, Mr. Suvalese, we are going to do all we can to get your son back safe and unharmed." Hildebard leaned forward, eyes straying for the first time to the black case resting by the older man's feet. "Is that the ransom?"

Adrian nodded, reaching down and wrapping his fingers around the handle for a minute. "Yes, this is the ransom. I am going to entrust it to you so that it can be exchanged for my Antoine's safety." He picked it up, holding it out to Captain Hildebard.

As Hildebard reached for it, Adrian pulled it back slightly, leaning forward so that their eyes locked. "If you can get my son back safe you are welcome to punish the pirates for their crimes against Laitha. If you manage to do so, then you are welcome to keep the ransom for yourself. A reward for bringing my son safely back to me." It was also an incentive to be sure that those that had taken Antoine were dealt with.

No one stole from Adrian Suvalese without consequences, and absolutely no one threatened his family. Adrian was a vengeful man. It was something he was well aware of. He had cultivated that trait a great deal in his youth, and it was what had allowed him to make Suva Coal Company the power it was now. Even though any true competition had long since fallen under the wheels of his company, that did not mean he had grown any less ruthless. Now these scum of air pirates, who had not only stolen from his ships but had taken his son, would learn just how ruthless he could be.

Looking into the hard eyes of Captain Hildebard, Adrian was confident he had found someone of a similar bent to himself. The captain was ruthless, dedicated to his cause like all good officers, yet there was a hint of mercenary understanding beneath it all. After all, the ransom money was quite substantial, the equivalent of several years' salary even for a distinguished captain.

"You needn't concern yourself any further, Mr. Suvalese." Hildebard took the case calmly, bringing it to rest by his side. "The Archduchy's aero navy is one of the best on the whole continent. We shan't let these air pirates escape us."

Adrian nodded, standing up then. "Very good. I shall rest easier knowing you are in charge of this matter. I will await the news of your successful return." Adrian buttoned his coat, nodding to the officer before he turned and walked out, confident now that the matter would be dealt with to his satisfaction.

AFTER MR. Suvalese left, Randalf stayed on in the parlor, lazily waving over one of the servants that always hovered discreetly at the edges. "Give me a glass of brandy, some of the best." Once his drink arrived, he dismissed the servant swiftly, turning back to the fireplace. In the silence, he contemplated all the things that had happened in the course of his day.

It had started when he had been summoned to see the Archduchess. It had been a private audience in one of the small gardens that made up the fortress at the top of the Spire. It was her private garden, and she was waiting for him, seated on a carved stone bench. Randalf had to admit that the Archduchess was still an incredibly fetching woman, her dark hair gleaming with faint highlights in the mountain sun, held back in the latest style.

She sat him down, offered him tea, and then informed him that his aero would be leaving the following day to hunt down a band of air pirates and retrieve the kidnapped son of a prominent businessman. Of course, Randalf saw it as no hardship to go and dispose of the air pirates who had dared to commit this heinous act. It was his duty as a naval officer to see to the protection of his city, and to follow the orders of those who ruled it.

What had been interesting, though, was that the Archduchess had made it clear that while stopping the air pirates and retrieving Mr. Suvalese's son was important, it was not to be his primary mission. There was another person on the ship that the Archduchess particularly wished to be rid of. She had made it clear that if he managed to do that, Randalf could expect not only a bonus, but a promotion as well.

Randalf allowed a smirk to flit over his features as he took a long sip of his brandy. How his fortunes had increased in but a single day. This was going to be a turning point in his life, he could see it already. From here on his prospects would surely only increase, leading him right to the very top levels of society. Perhaps even all the way up to the high admiralty.

AS MUCH as Mr. Suvalese, Captain Hildebard and the other inhabitants of Sharpsbury and the Spire terraces liked to think they were alone when they were scheming and planning, they never actually were. They took for granted the people always around them. Their servants and the shadow dwellers were always present and listening—even inside the most prestigious of gentleman's clubs—and what they learned was available, for a price.

"The aero leaves tomorrow, a full ship of the line. Commanded by a Captain Randalf Hildebard. Suvalese gave him the ransom money, told him that if he could take out the air pirates he could keep it for himself. I think there was something else, because the captain seemed far too smug. Also, he mentioned the Archduchess specifically."

Beznik sat back in his chair, staring at the man across from him. He was glad now that he had rushed back to the city from Tyrnium—Shandor would need this information. They were meeting in a small pub on a lower terrace that was just shady enough for them not to stand out. He was a good informant; his access to the congregating places of the upper class was invaluable. Especially now when he was able to provide information on something as big as this. With a gesture, Beznik ordered another tankard of ale for his informant.

"Drink up, it's on me. As part of your payment."

"That better not be all of my payment, Beznik. I know you've been looking for information on the navy's movements for a while now."

"Of course that's not all of it, just the first part. It's a damned sight better ale than you would normally be able to get." Beznik reached into one of the inner pockets of his coat, before tossing a few coins onto the table. "You should find that sufficient."

The coins disappeared quickly, a brief raising of the tankard the only acknowledgment of the money having passed hands. With the transaction completed, Beznik felt no need to stay around in the smoky pub. He strode out and swiftly made his way through the darkened alleyways up to the aerodocks.

Even late into the night, the docks were a bustle of activity. Granted, it was of a much seedier nature than took place in the daylight, but activity nonetheless. Beznik made his way silently to a rather shabbier pub than the one he had left, but it offered cheap lodgings. He kept a room there both for the convenience and the owner's forgetful ways. It was a place he could go to regroup where his appearance would not be remarked on.

Once in the room, he quickly moved over to the ramshackle table, and pulled out a sheaf of paper and a pencil. The message he scrawled on it was brief—no time for anything more detailed. Rolling it up, he secured it with a bit of twine then walked over to the corner where a large metal birdcage stood.

"Now, my sweet, you'll get to stretch your wings. I have a job for you." Unhooking the door, Beznik reached in, carefully scooping the bird up. It was not a normal bird, though, in the dim light it resembled a brightly colored parrot. Beznik knew that if anyone bothered to look closely they would realize the colors to be too flat to be anything other than paint. There was a faint clicking noise from inside of it, gears moving in unison. It was still now, but once Beznik wound the key in the back, it moved exactly as a normal bird would. It was a piece of beautifully intricate work that any mechanist would appreciate.

Beznik inserted the note into a small compartment in the leg before carrying it over to the window. "Take the message directly to Shandor. Deliver it to him only. Then await his instructions." With that he held out his hand, watching as the bird spread its wings, before leaping off and taking flight.

CHAPTER TWENTY-SEVEN

ANTOINE AWOKE slowly the next morning, light cutting across his face. He was incredibly warm and comfortable, and he had no desire to wake at all. Turning away from the bright light, Antoine attempted to burrow further into his warm pillow. What he wasn't expecting was for his pillow to let out a grunt, followed by a slightly more pained groan. Forcing his eyes open, Antoine was met with an expanse of white. After a few additional seconds, the white transformed into bandages.

With a start, Antoine realized his pillow wasn't actually a pillow. Stiff hairs tickled his cheek when he moved slowly, his ribs giving a twinge as he pushed up to a sitting position. The pain was no longer sharp, more of a dull throb that Antoine took as a good sign. Hesitantly he peered down at Rivas from under his mussed hair obscuring his eyes. He was greeted by the sight of Rivas smirking sleepily up at him. Antoine felt his face heat with embarrassment.

"Good morning, Antoine." Rivas's voice was hoarse and scratchy as he spoke. He seemed rather amused by Antoine's embarrassment.

"Good... good morning." Antoine stuttered over the greeting, the remnants of sleep and embarrassment making his tongue stick.

"If it's all the same to you, I could use some help getting up off this bed." Rivas, it seemed, was taking pity on Antoine's befuddled state.

"Are you sure you should move around? Sawbones didn't say anything about that."

"Well, unless you want to clean up the bed after I make a mess of it, he had better be alright with me at least going to the head."

Antoine's blush returned in full force as he shifted closer to the captain. Placing an arm under Rivas's shoulders, Antoine helped move him to the edge of the bed. It took a great deal more maneuvering to get Rivas up off the bed and standing. The broken leg and the splint to keep it in place meant Rivas couldn't put any weight on it. Antoine watched as he attempted to put pressure on it, only to let out a shout of pain once he did so. Antoine felt Rivas shift all of his weight onto him, and he nearly collapsed from the larger man's unexpected bulk.

Getting to the toilet, though, was only the first step. The next proved both difficult and endlessly embarrassing. Antoine couldn't leave Rivas alone. With only one leg to balance on, there was no way the older man could relieve himself and stay upright. Which meant Antoine had to stay in the privy with him, either to hold Rivas up or hold his cock as he pissed. In the end, Antoine opted for holding up Rivas, as it seemed the least embarrassing option.

He tried to keep his eyes focused on the far wall throughout, respecting Rivas's privacy. However, curiosity eventually won out over good manners, and he glanced down. Antoine swallowed as he watched Rivas handle his cock. Even limp it was impressive, or so it seemed to Antoine because truthfully he didn't have much to use for comparison. In his own pants, Antoine's own cock stirred, growing harder the longer he watched.

It took a large effort to look away, more than Antoine wanted to admit. Glancing up, he met Rivas's smirking expression in the small mirror that hung on the wall. Warmth flooded Antoine, completely different from his previous embarrassment. He forced himself to look away, clearing his throat uncomfortably. "Did you need to wash up as well?"

A warm, hard hand cupped Antoine's cheek, turning his head so he had to meet Rivas's eyes. "No need to be so embarrassed, Antoine. Can't be the first time you've seen a man's prick." Rivas's voice dropped an octave, the smirk changing slightly. "Unless there's something else causing you discomfort."

The hand painted a slow path down from Antoine's cheek, to his neck then his throat. Rivas paused there, his fingers resting on Antoine's wildly fluttering pulse. Antoine swallowed reflexively—the feel of Rivas's rough fingers scraping over his skin sent bolts of heat through his entire body. After resting there for another moment, Rivas's fingers continued to trek downward.

Rivas's fingers traced his collarbone and then slowly moved farther down. Antoine was suddenly, rather painfully, aware that he wasn't wearing anything above his waist. Rivas braced his free hand by Antoine's head, the first continuing to wander down Antoine's chest. A shudder racked Antoine's body when he felt Rivas circle his nipple before tweaking it gently. Heat raced through Antoine, making him gasp and arch into the pleasuring touch.

Antoine's cock was hard now, throbbing in time with his racing pulse. Rivas looked as though he wanted to devour Antoine whole. His hand continued to move down Antoine's body, over his chest until it encountered the bandages covering his sternum. Rivas only hesitated a moment before letting his hand continue its downward descent. The heat from that hand soaked into Antoine, even though the touch itself was much lighter now, as if Rivas was afraid of hurting him.

Antoine opened his eyes, not even aware that he had closed them until then, to find Rivas's face directly in front of him. The desire burning in those green eyes stole his breath away. Antoine watched as Rivas leaned forward, their lips brushing against each other in a faint kiss. It was followed by another and another, each kiss growing more heated as Rivas met no resistance. Antoine let out a moan, his eyes closing again as he opened to Rivas's insistent tongue. Rivas took complete control of Antoine's mouth, tasting him thoroughly until he grew dizzy from lack of air.

It was impossible to tell how much further things might have gone, except that the main door of the cabin flew open with a bang. It was enough to startle them apart and to upset the delicate balancing act that had been keeping Rivas upright. Antoine desperately grabbed for the older man in an effort to keep him from falling and hurting himself anew.

The lack of coordination between them did nothing to help this endeavor. In the confusion and flailing Rivas subconsciously put his other leg down to keep upright. The howl of pain he let out made Antoine wince and scramble to take the entirety of Rivas's weight.

In doing so, Antoine nearly fell over himself since he hadn't managed to entirely regain his own footing.

The sound of laughter did not help in the slightest. After getting his footing back, Antoine shifted himself so he could better support Rivas. Once he'd settled the weight, Antoine looked up to see just who had interrupted them. He was greeted by the sight of Shandor's mismatched eyes dancing with mirth. Antoine glared back, slowly leading Rivas back to the bed.

"I hope I didn't interrupt anything important, Captain." Shandor didn't even try to keep the mirth out of his voice.

"Now Shandor, what could possibly give you that idea?" Rivas's words came out through gritted teeth, green eyes glaring daggers at the other air pirate.

The dual glares he received didn't seem enough to prevent Shandor's continued amusement. He did come over and take some of the weight, supporting Rivas's other side. Between the two of them, they managed to get Rivas back to the bed without further incident.

"Antoine, after that event Rivas could do with some of the powder that Sawbones left."

It was a rather unsubtle order for Antoine to leave the room for a few minutes. However, there was also obvious pain in Rivas's face, even as he reclined on the bed. So Antoine left and began to prepare the powdered medicine that would help to deaden Rivas's pain.

As he was waiting for the water to heat, Antoine pulled his coveralls back up, fumbling with the buttons. Once that was finished, he took a deep breath, trying to calm down his body, which still felt flushed with heat. Voices trickled out from the bedroom, nothing understandable, just a wash of noise. The water gave a hiss, prompting Antoine to go through the motions of mixing the concoction. There was also a tray of food on the desk for them, and Antoine added the cup to the tray and carried it all back to the bedroom.

"Oh good, you found the food. It's what I came for originally, but then I interrupted the fun." Shandor still sounded amused. However, he readily got off the bed to make room for the tray.

"Thanks for your great consideration," Antoine said, setting the tray across Rivas's lap. "Your medicine is in the mug."

Rivas picked up the mug, taking a healthy drink before making a face. "There has got to be a way to make this taste better."

"I doubt it. My mother always said that the bitterness of the tonic is a sign of its strength. Besides, no one has anything sweet on board, except perhaps Yi, and I don't think anyone is going to try and cross our fair master gunner." Shandor ran a hand through his hair as he turned toward the door. "Best to get back to work, have to keep on the crew after all. Make sure they don't decide to test my authority."

"Be careful, Shan. And keep me in the loop. That's an order."

"Since when do you give me orders?"

"Get on out of here. Leave me to my breakfast in peace with Antoine. He's better company and better looking than you." Rivas took another drink from his mug.

Shandor snorted as he walked out. "Don't strain yourself. You're still injured."

Antoine felt himself start to flush again. He wasn't sure he would ever get used to the innuendo and crude behavior of the *Aria*'s crew. Antoine grabbed one of the bowls of porridge off the tray, focusing on shoveling the food into his mouth. Rivas chuckled softly as he turned to his own meal, and Antoine pretended the sound didn't make him feel warm inside.

CHAPTER TWENTY-EIGHT

THE MEAL, such as it was, passed mostly in silence. Once it was over, Antoine gathered the dishes together and removed the tray. As he walked back into the bedroom, Antoine was confronted with the fact there was a whole day spreading in front of him with just Rivas for company and no idea how to fill the time.

Well, that wasn't quite correct. His mind conjured up activities they could do, all of them threatening to bring a new blush to his face. Even if he wanted to, Antoine would never be able to ask about them without choking on his tongue. Shandor's words about not straining themselves still rang in his ears.

"Chess."

The sound of Rivas's voice jolted Antoine out of his thoughts. He blinked stupidly at Rivas for a full minute. "Chess?"

Rivas gave a small chuckle. "Yes, chess. Do you play it? I thought we could use it to pass the time." He pointed to a chest in the corner.

"Oh, right. Yes, I've played the game before, but I must confess to not being exceptionally talented." Antoine moved over to the chest, lifting the top. There was a jumble of items inside, a tangled clutter that Antoine sifted through to find the game.

"Can't say I'm the best at it either. However, I think there are few other ways we can pass the time that will not result in greater injury for the both of us. The chess set should be on the left side, can't miss it."

After shifting some items, Antoine found it. The set was made of polished metal, brass and tin squares bolted together. The pieces themselves were of a similar craftsmanship. They were metal as well, with small wind-up keys in the back so they could make motions while sitting on their squares. Antoine was thoroughly entranced as he set up the board.

"This is wonderful, Rivas. Where did you come across such a thing?" Antoine stroked the king, which was done up like an aero captain.

"It was a custom job. Got it in Laitha at a little shop on one of the market terraces. The man who ran it, one of the best mechanists I've ever seen. A real talent he has, probably still in the city if you ever want to look it up." Rivas studied the board, and then moved one of the pawns forward.

"Perhaps I'll have him make one for me. It's quite enchanting." Antoine moved his own piece, smiling a bit. "Strange, though, when I think of Laitha and everything back there it seems like a dream."

"A dream, guess that's one way to look at it. When you get back there, though, maybe this life will look like a dream. Or perhaps a nightmare."

Antoine frowned, thinking about that as he contemplated his next move. "I should. This is a kidnapping. I should consider it to be a nightmare. Instead it's been almost an adventure. An educational adventure perhaps, definitely an eye-opening one."

Rivas was quiet for the next few moves, seeming to focus entirely on the board. When he did speak, his voice was muted. "I must admit, part of what I wanted was to open your eyes to the world outside of Laitha, outside of Sharpsbury and the life they live at the top." Rivas carefully moved his bishop, capturing one of Antoine's pawns. "Probably sounds a bit pretentious, but the times are changing. There's a darkness spreading through Laitha, poisoning the city."

Antoine frowned, studying the board intently. "A poison, you say? I guess it's another thing I haven't noticed."

"It's a selective thing. Not many people in Laitha are aware of it, no matter their station. That's the nature of poisons. You don't realize what's going on until it's reached a toxic level."

Antoine chewed his lip before moving his knight and waiting. "Shandor asked me about the city. About whether I had ever met the Archduke, or even seen him about. Honestly, even now, I can't remember the last time that I saw or heard of him being in public."

Rivas tilted his head to the side, scratching his chin. The dark blond stubble made a rasping sound against his fingers. "Shandor's

147

complicated. He has some kind of connection high up in Laitha, and a keen interest in what is going on there. Plans within plans and all that."

"A ship of vengeance. That's what Shiv'ren called the *Aria*."

"Not too far off in that. Then again, I don't know of anyone who becomes a pirate just for the lark of it." Rivas moved another piece, leaning back with a sigh and a slight wince. "Certainly not something you do to live a long life."

Antoine looked up, catching the wince. "Do you need more medicine? Is it very bad?"

Rivas waved it off, closing his eyes. "Not so bad, just starting to get a bit tired." He smiled softly. "Consider your next move and we'll pick up again after some rest."

Antoine nodded, carefully standing up so he didn't disturb the board. He pretended to study the board, but really he was watching Rivas. The conversation had been enjoyable. It had given him more of an insight into the man that had completely upended his life. Antoine wanted to know even more about Rivas, about what had made him into the person he was now. He kept receiving little pieces and glimpses of it, yet he couldn't seem to get them to align properly.

Unwittingly his mind drifted back to the touches from this morning. His body tingled and his cock stirred in his pants. Antoine turned away, stepping out of the cabin and into the main room. Restlessly he paced over to the small porthole, staring out at the circle of sky and clouds. He tried to ignore the arousal curling in his stomach, yet it proved impossible. The attraction he felt to the captain was another part of the puzzle that was Rivas. If he were completely honest, the attraction had been there almost from the beginning, and Antoine could no longer ignore it. Of course, Antoine rather wished he could have continued to ignore it. Life certainly would have been easier without it. Denial was nice—however, Antoine was coming to the distressing realization that he was past that point. So that meant he had to face the facts of his attraction to Rivas.

Accepting that fact did not make it any easier for Antoine to deal with. He shouldn't be attracted to his kidnapper. That was what his logical mind kept telling him, but Antoine's body, though, had no trouble with it, and neither did his heart really. Antoine's emotions had been in such tumult of late, he'd hardly had a chance to sort through it all. Now that he was faced with a large block of time and nothing to fill it with, it seemed the perfect time to work through everything.

Turning away from the porthole, Antoine walked over to one of the chairs and flopped down with a sigh. For once, Antoine just let himself sprawl out like he had always wanted to. Good manners had been drilled into him since his childhood. His mother would not have allowed him to sprawl out on one of her elaborate chaises. No one was around to care about it at the moment, and Antoine found it invigorating. He allowed himself to get good and comfortable for once before settling down to some serious contemplation.

THE SHUDDERING of the ship woke Antoine from the rather unexpected nap. Another shudder knocked him out of the chair and onto his ass. It sent a jolt of pain all the way to his bruised sternum. Letting out a groan, Antoine stumbled to his feet.

"Rivas? Are you alright?" Antoine stumbled into the bedroom, rubbing the sleep out of his eyes. When he cleared them, he saw the pirate captain was sitting up in the bed, looking more alert than he had before. The chess set hadn't fared as well. It had fallen onto the ground, tilted on one side. Due to the magnets on the bottom of the pieces, none of them had dislodged from the board.

Antoine bent over, picking up the set and placing it back on the bed. "What made the ship shudder like that, Rivas?"

"We pulled up anchor. The *Aria* is leaving Black Rocks, not sure what the destination is that they've chosen, though. Hopefully somewhere safe. It's not time for the ransom exchange yet. Wouldn't do to be caught by a patrol ship before we're supposed to meet them."

"I guess not. I just never felt the ship actually lift anchor before." He thought of when they had left Tyrnium. "Well, that I was conscious for."

"It can be a bit rough. You get used to it, though, and soon enough you don't even notice anymore. When you don't notice the engine, or the roughness of docking and the change of elevation, you've become a true aeronaught."

"I'm not sure I'll ever get that far along." Antoine sat down on the edge of the bed, staring at the chess set. "Feel ready to finish our game?"

"Of course. Whenever you're ready to make your move."

The evening passed with them playing chess, only breaking when food was brought to them. They talked the entire time, the conversation varied but carefully avoided any serious topics. Rivas, it turned out, was well read even though he had no formal schooling. Antoine found he had a fondness for philosophy and the natural sciences. It gave Antoine more pieces for the puzzle he was trying to assemble of Rivas.

Eventually, as the night grew later, Antoine's yawns became more numerous. Rivas also was looking tired, and his expression had gradually taken on a more pained cast as the hours wore on. When it was obvious the pain was becoming too much, Antoine got up to fix another mug of the pain tonic. Then came the matter of sleeping arrangements. The idea of another night in the same bed with Rivas left Antoine feeling uneasy. Even though he had accepted that he felt a very strong physical attraction to the captain, Antoine wasn't sure what exactly he should do with that knowledge. He definitely knew he wouldn't be brave enough to start anything on his own, yet sleeping in the same bed seemed to be asking for something to happen. Antoine told himself to stop being ridiculous. They had managed to share a bed last night without any incident. There was absolutely no reason to think tonight would be any different. Resolutely Antoine kept telling himself that as he walked back out and over to the bed.

Before they could retire for sleep, Rivas needed to make another visit to the privy. Which required that Antoine again assist him in getting out of the bed and over to the small toilet with only the one leg for balance. This time, Antoine swore to himself he was not going to be caught looking at Rivas's cock. Which was all well and good to say to himself, but the reality was much harder for Antoine to deal with.

Without his eyes to supply the images, Antoine's brain was more than happy to fill in the blanks. New jolts of heat went through Antoine at the pictures his brain conjured. Images of Rivas's cock from this morning as he had relieved himself. On the heels of that image was the remembrance of the touches this morning and the kiss they had shared.

Antoine's own cock was hard now, causing him to shift carefully as he was still supporting Rivas. He was glad that Rivas hadn't noticed the state he was in, or at least hadn't felt the need to comment on it.

The slow walk back to the bed was torture for Antoine. He was grateful for the distraction, even if it wasn't exactly comfortable. It gave him time to get his body under control before Rivas noticed what had been going on. At least he hoped Rivas hadn't noticed his current state.

"So, are you going to argue about sharing the bed with me tonight, Antoine? Because I won't allow you to sleep in the hammock." Rivas's words were soft, but there was an obvious order in them.

"I won't argue, Rivas. I figured you wouldn't let me sleep in the hammock." Antoine focused on getting him settled into the bed, steadfastly ignoring his still half-hard cock.

"Good. I'm glad we won't have to argue about it. Though, trying to convince you might have ended up being fun." Rivas leered at the flush spreading up Antoine's cheeks.

"You enjoy making sport of me, don't you?" Antoine shot back, carefully climbing onto the bed. It took a minute to get into a comfortable position before pulling the blanket up to cover them.

Rivas gave a quiet laugh. "You take to it so well, I simply can't help it."

Antoine let out a huff, reaching over and turning the gas down on the lamp. In the newly formed darkness, he allowed himself to smile.

Chapter Twenty-Nine

Out on the deck, Shandor was standing on the bow, looking out at the clouds streaming by the ship. A few lamps were lit to give the crew light to see, but not enough that they would be easily noticed by passing aeros. They had various lookouts who kept a watch for other aeros in order to avoid a collision.

Sleep was evading him this night—too many thoughts clamoring in his head. He'd had the ship pull anchor without a specific direction in mind. Instead he had them heading in a general direction so they would avoid being caught by a wandering patrol.

It also helped to keep the crew occupied and prevented them from gossiping too much about their captain and their captive. Leaning on the railing, Shandor felt that he could curse both Rivas and Antoine for their foolishness back in Black Rocks. The earthquake had destabilized everything on the ship, and they wouldn't have been injured if they hadn't been running all over the place like lovesick fools.

Shandor exhaled, shaking his head until his dark curls were caught by the wind. The last two days had been stressful, and he was taking his frustration out on other people. Even if the cause of his stress was their fault, it hadn't been maliciously done. Which actually made it even more frustrating for him.

The whole plan for this ransom had been cooked up by Rivas. There were parts of it Shandor wasn't aware of, which therefore made it hard to continue on in his place. Not just continue, but hold together a sometimes fractious crew so they didn't decide to replace the captain before it was all over.

Shandor reached up, pushing his hair back from his face. He had finally decided to go back inside and see if he could find some rest when he caught sight of a glimmer in the distance. Frowning, Shandor had his mechanical eye zoom in a bit, a smile spreading as he made out the shape of a bird. Only normal birds did not shine in the moonlight, at least not like this one did.

As it got closer, Shandor straightened up, taking a step back from the railing. The mechanical bird settled lightly on the rail. The whine of the gears was masked by the general din from the *Bloody Aria*, but he could imagine them quite clearly.

"Well, good to see you again. What message do you have for me this time?" Shandor murmured, holding his arm out. The bird hopped onto his forearm, settling down easily once it was there. Shandor reached out, prying open the compartment in the leg and pulling out the rolled up message. After the message was removed, the mechanical bird hopped up onto Shandor's shoulder, settling down to wait. Shandor paid it little mind, instead focusing on the slip of paper.

> *Aeronaught Diomede under command of Captain Randalf Hildebard being sent with ransom. Suvalese promised him the ransom as reward if he takes down the pirates. Additional orders to target with extreme prejudice. Departing on morning wind, be prepared.*

There was no signature, but one was hardly needed as only one man would have sent this message. Shandor sighed, putting the slip of paper into his pocket. "Well, certainly nothing good, then. One of these days, you're going to bring me news of a more positive nature, my friend. Then I might just keel over of surprise." The bird let out a hollow squawk before settling down more firmly on his shoulder. Shandor smirked, turning to head below deck. New players had been added to the game. It was time to go and update the strategies.

WHEN ANTOINE woke up that morning, he found himself in a rather interesting situation. He was resting on and curled around something very warm and firm. Opening his eyes revealed an expanse of muscled chest with blond hairs peeking through the white bandages. As consciousness continued to return, Antoine became acutely aware that he was sporting a morning erection, which was pressed firmly against Rivas's hip.

Swallowing heavily, Antoine slowly forced himself to glance up, checking to see if Rivas was awake yet or not. He prayed that the older man was still asleep and hadn't noticed. Antoine wasn't embarrassed about his erection—it was a natural thing after all—it was more the fact that he was practically rubbing against Rivas in his sleep that was embarrassing. That, and Antoine knew Rivas would be insufferably smug about the entire incident. Thankfully, though, his eyes were closed and his breathing was steady.

Antoine slowly pulled back, carefully working himself free from the bed. After that, he left the room as quietly as possible. Food was already waiting for them on the table, the same rather bland fare that had been delivered yesterday. Antoine supposed that was one thing he did miss about his life in Laitha: decent food. Food with flavor and variety instead of just the same tasteless fare.

There was a small note propped up on the tray that contained the food. It had Rivas's name written on it in strong, slanted handwriting. Antoine was tempted to read the letter, running a finger over the piece of paper. Something must have happened in the night that Rivas needed to know about. As tempting as it was to snoop, a part of Antoine was afraid of what might be written on it—that it would be about him.

Antoine left the main room in an effort to control his curiosity. Instead he went to wash up for the day. When stripping off his clothes, Antoine was reminded of a problem he had managed to push out of his mind earlier. He was still half-hard, and thinking about how he had woken brought him back to full hardness very quickly.

He tried to ignore it, he really did. But every part of his body seemed to be connected to his cock. It quickly became obvious that ignoring it wasn't an option. So Antoine decided to take the problem in hand, as it were. Antoine reached down and wrapped his fist around his aching cock. He gasped through his teeth, firmly stroking himself. The pleasure radiated out from his cock with each stroke. Closing his eyes, Antoine's mind immediately conjured Rivas.

Antoine bit his lower lip, stroking faster. In his mind Rivas grinned, pressing Antoine back against the wall.

Trapped with nowhere to go, Antoine arched up into the large warm body as Rivas kissed him fiercely. His hands scrambled for purchase, looping around Rivas's waist, dragging him closer. Antoine ground himself against Rivas, moaning into the kiss when he felt the answering hardness in the larger man's pants. Rivas pressed Antoine more firmly against the wall, holding him so he could grind his sizable erection against Antoine's hip. They both grew more frantic, the kiss breaking so they both could gulp in much-needed oxygen.

Antoine came with a small whimper, his body arching into the sensation. When he opened his eyes, the fantasy faded away with the return of reality. He let out another whimper as he milked the last bit of sensation from his spent cock.

Antoine was left with a strange, hollow feeling in his gut. The orgasm had taken away the edge, but he didn't feel satisfied. As he cleaned up, Antoine looked at himself in the small, cloudy bit of mirror. He looked different. The man—no longer the boy—staring back at him, and it was a man now, had dirt smudged on his face. The shoulder-length brown hair that was normally neatly groomed was loose and wild. His normally flat brown eyes were livelier than Antoine could ever remember. Staring at this new man, Antoine found he couldn't lie to himself. He felt empty because he wanted the fantasy to be real.

Antoine sighed, shaking his head. No sense in dwelling on it or getting himself into knots. Rivas had made it very clear on several occasions that he wanted Antoine for more than just the money his father could pay. Which meant the next move would realistically be Antoine's. That meant he would have to pluck up the courage to make that move.

Stepping out, Antoine saw Rivas slowly sitting up. He had his arm wrapped around his bandaged chest, reminding Antoine of the other stumbling block. Rivas was injured and would probably not be in any kind of state for anything for at least a few more days.

"Good morning. They've already dropped off our breakfast. Are you hungry?" Antoine said, glad his voice came out steady.

"Bring it in, then. By any chance did the wretches leave any coffee?"

Antoine grinned a bit. "I don't remember seeing any, but I'll check."

Exiting the bedroom, Antoine went to gather up the tray with the food on it. Glancing over at the fireplace, he grinned when he saw a pot hanging on a hook over the fire. Antoine grabbed the tray, carrying it into the bedroom and setting it on the bed. "You're in luck. It seems they did leave coffee for you."

Rivas grinned, relaxing back against the pillows. "Thank heavens. I wasn't sure I'd be able to go without for two days."

Antoine laughed, shaking his head. "Eat your breakfast and I'll get your coffee." Antoine returned within a couple of minutes, carefully carrying over the steaming beverage. After smelling the strength of the coffee, Antoine declined to have one himself.

As he was setting it down, Antoine noticed the frown creasing Rivas's face. The folded up slip of paper from the tray was in his hand. Obviously it was not anything good, or Rivas wouldn't have had that look on his face. Antoine was glad now he hadn't given in to his curiosity to read it. He was sure he wouldn't have liked what it contained.

Breakfast was a quiet affair after that. Whatever had been in that note had dampened the good mood Rivas had had upon waking. Antoine wanted to ask, yet there was a small part of him that said he wouldn't like the answers. It might be related to his ransom, which was a subject Antoine didn't wish to think about.

After the meal, Antoine retrieved the chess set so they could begin a new game. Almost immediately, Antoine noticed Rivas's distraction. But Rivas's distraction continued even then: the previous day Antoine had never managed to win a game. He had come close twice, but he had still lost in the end. Now, though, Antoine could tell he was not only close to winning, Rivas was missing obvious moves. Finally Antoine couldn't take it anymore. He studied the way the captain stared blankly at the board without blinking. Antoine slowly pulled the board away, setting it at the far end of the bed.

"What's wrong, Rivas? Something is distracting you, I can tell." Antoine did his best to summon the stern look his mother always gave when she was trying to guilt him into something.

Rivas gave a short laugh, which sounded more like a sigh. "Just reminiscing, I suppose. Tell me, Antoine, are you and your father very close?"

Antoine blinked at the unexpected question. "Well, I suppose we're close. He always spends time with me. He's been teaching me the business recently. Father, he can be a bit hard to understand, but he's always there if I need him. I know he has a lot of expectations for me. He's made it clear he wants me to take over the business, even though Nigel is the older one."

Rivas shifted a bit, leaning back with a pained groan. Antoine moved to go and get the medication, but Rivas quickly shook his head.

"I'll be fine for a bit. Just hurt from shifting. You worry too much, Antoine."

Antoine flushed, looking down and fiddling with the strap of his coverall. "I suppose I've always been like that. I've been told that I'm far too caring."

"They make it sound like a bad thing. It's not really. More people should be as caring as you." Rivas stretched out his arm, grasping Antoine's hand.

Antoine drew a breath as the warmth seeped into his body. "Thank you. Though, Father and Mother tell me I'm too sensitive. Father's always searching for ways to toughen me up and Mother supports him on that. I'm usually not given much of a choice in the matters."

Rivas smiled a bit, green eyes taking on a faraway look. "I never really knew my mother. The fever took her when I was a baby. It was just me and my father really. He'd tell me the same thing, said that the life of a miner was a hard one and you had to be just as hard. There was never enough time to properly shore the tunnels, so any time there was a tremor they would collapse. The miners would say it was better to have a quick death than to linger on."

Antoine shivered, staring down at his hands, trying to get his thoughts into a coherent order. More of the pieces clicked together in his head, finally giving Antoine a feeling that he was getting an idea of the picture that the puzzle was forming. The man that was Rivas the Ramshot, a man that was very different from the newspaper's stories.

"Why would you wish for him to be crushed?" Antoine wasn't sure that was the best question for him to start with, but it was the one stuck in his mind.

"Being crushed at least would be a quick death. Better than a slow death of suffocation as the air ran out."

Antoine nodded a bit at that. "I suppose I can see that. A quick death is better than a slow and lingering one. At least then they didn't suffer." He stared at the board, picking up one of the pieces. He ran a finger over the intricate workings before setting it back down. "It seems... sad and pointless, that they died from something that might have been prevented."

Rivas smiled, eyes turning to focus on Antoine finally. "I'm glad that you think that it was pointless." Rivas sighed, rubbing a hand lightly over his side. "I was hoping that would be one of the things I could explain to you in the time you were my guest."

Antoine let out a long sigh, some of the feelings from the earlier days coming back. The sense of disappointment and anger returned in a surge, making him turn away. "I know, you've made that clear already. Besides the money, you wanted me to learn what it's like for those that work for the Suva Coal Company."

Antoine glanced over long enough to see the wince that crossed Rivas's face. He wondered briefly if there was something else going on, but he didn't quite have the courage to ask. Instead Antoine studied his hands, trying to work up the guts to speak. He couldn't find his voice, though, as fear of the answer to the question kept him from speaking. Before he could manage to reply, the door to the main cabin opened with a clang.

Antoine stood, rubbing his hands over the thighs of his pants in an effort to calm his suddenly racing heart. He glanced over at Rivas, who was frowning as he stared at the closed bedroom door, like he could see through the walls if he concentrated hard enough. Antoine decided not to try to peer through the walls. Instead he opened the door, poking his head out cautiously. He was greeted by the sight of Sawbones standing in the middle of the room, hands on his hips. When he saw Antoine poke his head out, he flashed him a bright grin, teeth gleaming.

"G'morning to you, Antoine. See you've already eaten the food I left."

Antoine blinked, straightening up. "Yes, thank you." He shifted, pushing the door open wider so Rivas could see out. "Is there something you needed?"

Sawbones walked closer, pulling a satchel off his back. "Yeah, I got to check on the cap'n's injuries. Need t'check, make sure the bones be settlin' right."

"Can you really tell so soon after the injury?" Antoine shuffled back, letting the large man into the bedroom. He pulled the chair he had been using out of the way, perching on the edge so he could watch.

"Sawbones knows more about things like this than a dozen doctors in Laitha," Rivas said, sitting up a little bit straighter. "He's also less prone to quack theories and medicine than the doctors you find in the cities."

There came a deep, rumbling chuckle from the darker-skinned man as he perched on the bed. "Now, Cap'n, flattery won't get you out of this. It don' take much to be better than those fools."

Sawbones was efficient in his work, unwrapping the bandages that covered Rivas's chest. The bruises on his skin were diminished greatly, some already faded to an ugly yellow color. Antoine couldn't help wincing when he saw that, yet Sawbones seemed pleased with it.

"Color is good, less tender." Sawbones poked at the bruises, ignoring how Rivas hissed and flinched each time. After the examination, Sawbones pulled out a jar of balm, setting it on the small table. "Need to apply that to the bruises, make dem heal better. Your ribs still need wrapping, though. Now, for de leg."

Rivas visibly braced himself for that, gripping the edges of the bed so hard his fingers turned white. Antoine watched as Sawbones pressed gently on the leg, taking in the hiss of breath Rivas gave through his teeth. Eventually Antoine had to glance away, unable to watch the pain carving itself onto Rivas's face.

"Leg doing good too, but got to be careful. Need a couple days, then you might be able to use a crutch." Sawbones stood up, pulling a flask out of his satchel. "Here, take it all. After that, you want t'sleep for a while."

Rivas let out a weak chuckle, his hand shaking as he took the flask. "My gratitude for your consideration," he said, uncorking it and taking a healthy swallow of it. "Still as awful-tasting as ever."

Sawbones just laughed, straightening up. He met Antoine's gaze, gesturing to the jar. "Apply that to the bruises after he wakes up. I be back later to bandage it again." With that he gathered the last of his supplies and left the room.

Rivas continued to chug the tonic, his eyes getting heavier as he neared the end. "Is there anything you need?" Antoine walked over, sitting down on the edge of the bed. He fidgeted with the covers, smoothing them out over Rivas's body.

"Stay with me." Rivas looked tired and worn lying there, suddenly no longer the larger than life air pirate that was the scourge of the skies. Instead, he looked like just a man, tired, in pain, and looking for comfort. Antoine was helpless before that, so he carefully lay down on the bed next to Rivas.

"You know...." Rivas's voice was slurred, whether from sleep or Sawbones's tonic was hard to tell. "It wasn't.... this wasn't what you think it was." He frowned, licking his lips before trying again. "Bringing you here... it wasn't entirely about... about what you think."

"What do you mean?" Antoine's heart skipped a bit. The green eyes were cloudy, lids drooping closed. Antoine wanted to press for an answer, a better explanation, yet the sight of Rivas's exhaustion stopped him. Rivas needed rest more than Antoine needed an explanation. That could wait until later. He woke up hours later, mostly because his stomach was cramping with hunger. Sometime as they slept, the two of them had shifted. Antoine's head was pillowed on Rivas's shoulder, his arm draped across the older man's shoulders. In turn, Rivas had his arm wrapped around Antoine, his chin resting on top of Antoine's head. It was warm and safe, a place Antoine didn't want to leave at all.

Staying wasn't an option, though. Antoine's stomach was making its hunger known. He tried to detangle himself gently, so he wouldn't disturb Rivas. It was difficult, and when he did, there was a sense of emptiness that had nothing to do with hunger.

Turning away, Antoine left the room quickly, barely stopping himself from looking back. After he took care of the gnawing hunger, he returned to the bedroom. Just in time, it seemed, to witness Rivas wakening from his own nap. His face was still pinched, but the cloudiness was gone from earlier, leaving the green eyes bright and alert. Those eyes focused intently on Antoine, making his newly full stomach twist.

"Now, this is a sight I'm glad to wake up to." Rivas growled softly, reaching up and rubbing his face. "Could use a proper drink, though. Had enough of those bloody tonics for a while."

Antoine couldn't help but laugh at that, shaking his head. "I'm not sure they've given us any proper drink, if that's what you'd call that rotgut you drink on this ship. However, there's some water, which is probably better for you."

There was a quick scoff at that. "Water's horrible unless it's got some rum in it. Ends up tasting of the barrels soon enough. I'll have to tell them to bring me some proper drink when they come again. Something to wash the bloody taste away."

That caused Antoine to chuckle as he brought some water over. Rivas drank the water, grumbling about the lack of rum as Antoine watched in amusement. As they sat there, Antoine remembered what Rivas had started to tell him before he fell asleep.

"What were you saying? Before you fell asleep."

There was a pause, Rivas looking over at him and tilting his head to the side. "What was I saying? I'm not sure. It's a little fuzzy after I started drinking that tonic."

"You… you were saying…." Antoine felt nervous, his heart pounding. He sat down heavily on the bed, afraid the weakness in his voice would spread to all of his limbs. "You were saying that my coming here, it wasn't entirely for what I thought it was."

Rivas blinked, and then set the cup of water on the side table carefully. "Now, I truly would like something stronger."

He rubbed his hands over his face, and several days' worth of beard made a rasping sound as he did so. Rivas leaned back, staring at the ceiling for a minute before he spoke.

"The transport ship was the first time we met, but it wasn't the first time I had seen you. I didn't choose you at random or blind luck. If it had been merely a case of wanting some ransom money, there were any number of other targets that we could have taken. Quite a few which would have been far less trouble and given even more money for a safe return."

"I know. You've already said that it was about more than the money." Antoine turned away, using his annoyance to hide the other emotions moving through him. "I thought you said there was another reason you chose me."

"That's what I'm trying to get to. I just, I guess I'm not going about it very well." Rivas let out a long sigh, slumping a bit. "I'm horrid at things like this, putting words to things." Another sigh. "Maybe starting from the beginning would be good?"

"That tends to help."

"I guess the beginning goes back a while. Well, a couple of years at the least. I saw you back then, in Laitha. It was at a distance. I think there was some sort of celebration going on. I was with the revelers, and there was a lot of drinking that night, but through it all, I saw you. I saw you there with your family." Rivas paused, a small smile crossing his face. "You were beautiful, do you know that? I'm not sure what was going on, but you were in a fancy suit just standing there. Then, you laughed. You laughed and it felt like the whole city was suddenly full of light, and you were beautiful."

Antoine felt like the world had started spinning wildly around him. He'd never been called beautiful before; he'd never considered his looks to be very extraordinary. In fact, ordinary was how he heard himself most often described. There wasn't anything remarkable about him, just plain brown hair, brown eyes, with a thin frame. Even his features were plain. "You can't be serious."

"Very serious." Rivas leaned forward, grabbing Antoine's hand. "You are beautiful. You were beautiful then when you were laughing, and you're beautiful now." He squeezed Antoine's hand. "That is the other reason I picked you, Antoine. Because you were beautiful, and I was completely captivated from that first sighting to now."

"Captivated by me?" Antoine shook his head, but he gripped Rivas's hand tightly. He felt… giddy. The idea that someone found him captivating, let alone someone like Rivas, who was handsome, strong, and alluring in his own right, was unbelievable. Yet Rivas had been entranced enough to kidnap him so they could meet. He was also getting money for it, but still it was a boost to the ego. "What could possibly be captivating about me?"

"That, for instance." Rivas leaned over, poking Antoine lightly before he began to gently pull him down so he was lying on the bed next to Rivas. "You're not arrogant like many would be, and you have no idea of your own strengths." Rivas took a long breath, nervously glancing away. "I studied you after that. At first, I wasn't sure who you were, so I asked around. When I learned your name I became even more captivated."

Antoine's astonishment grew as he continued to listen to Rivas.

"I studied you, tried to learn what I could when we were actually in Laitha. Pirates, though, can't make frequent stops at major cities, tends to get us noticed. So it wasn't easy."

Antoine swallowed, nodding a bit. "I imagine it would be difficult. The navy, though, would have a field day if they knew you had waltzed right by them several times to make it to the city."

Rivas laughed, and then winced as his ribs obviously hurt from the movement. "No doubt, but they're not nearly as good as they like to think they are. They miss the small things, especially if you know how to slip by unnoticed. Of course, we can't very well pull the *Aria* into an aeroport, so we have to be stealthier. Not always easy, you know."

Antoine laughed a bit, looking down at Rivas in amazement. The things the air pirate had said to him were incredible. That someone could see him that way, to want to actually learn about *him* instead of letting his family name define everything. It was not what he had ever expected from an infamous air pirate who was supposed to be uncouth, a bloody barbarian who had no higher purpose than pillaging. Instead he was faced with a man that was smart, had brought himself up from the dismal circumstances he had been raised in. That, more than anything, captured Antoine's admiration.

"I can't... I can't really believe it." Antoine whispered the words, staring down into Rivas's green eyes. He ran a hand over Rivas's cheek, tracing the scar and feeling the scrape of stubble. Without giving himself time to think, Antoine leaned down and pressed a kiss to Rivas's lips. He pulled back quickly, a smile stretching across his face as he took in the surprised look on the captain's face. "I never really thought I was anything special."

"Ah, but you are, Antoine," Rivas said, bringing a hand up to smooth Antoine's hair back, before gently tugging him down onto the bed. "Getting to know you over the past few days has proven that. If anything, I've gotten more entranced by you. Do you realize how remarkable you've been about this whole affair? We've had a couple of other small ransoms before, and they were all terrified of us. Spent the whole time cowering in a corner, certain that we were going to do horrible things to them at the drop of a hat." Rivas let out a long sigh. "Quite frustrating, to be honest."

Then Rivas grinned, guiding Antoine into a quick kiss. "You, though, you were afraid but you moved beyond it. You actually took an interest in doing something around the ship. You tried to be helpful and quickly you weren't frightened of us at all." Rivas smirked, stroking his fingers over Antoine's cheek. "I think you've even started treating it like an adventure, and that makes you so unique."

Antoine laughed, not even trying to hide his grin. "You really do make me sound more extraordinary than I am. It is an adventure if you think about it. When else will I have an experience like this again?" Antoine frowned a bit. "Never, that's the hopeful part. I have to make the most out of it." The thought that his time here was limited started to depress him, but Antoine pushed it back. There would be time for that later. Right now was for other things. Like the smile he couldn't keep off his face.

Antoine pressed the smile against Rivas in another kiss, letting this one draw out. From there it was easy to transition to another kiss, this one lingering a bit more than the other one. Soon, the kisses between them grew more intense and heated. Antoine tangled his fingers in the fine blond hair fanned out over the pillows.

Eventually the need for air made Antoine draw back, gulping in air. His cock was hard and straining inside his pants, and he could feel a matching hardness pressing back against him. Unconsciously Antoine gave a small thrust, moaning as the friction raced up his spine. He wanted to continue, his body moving to do so until strong hands came to rest on his hips. Rivas reluctantly pulled him back, panting softly.

"Can't, not like this." Rivas's voice was hoarse, the lust easily discernible there. However, there was also a hint of pain, serving as a reminder of the serious injuries that Rivas still had. Including the leg, which prevented him from moving easily.

"How?" Antoine asked, gulping in air as he tried to control himself. There had to be a way, because Antoine didn't think he would be able to stay sane if there wasn't.

"Help me to sit up properly." Rivas's voice was almost as desperate as Antoine's was. Antoine immediately moved to help Rivas sit up, propping him against pillows at the head of the bed. Afterward, he allowed his hands to explore the bared skin, mapping the texture with his fingers. It was very warm, coarse hair tickling the pads of his fingers. There were shiny patches, lighter than the rest of his skin, scars from the life Rivas had lived for so long. Antoine wondered what that skin would taste like, and he wanted to explore it so thoroughly it would be burned into his memory.

Before Antoine got a chance to do much more, Rivas grabbed him in a strong hold, dragging him forward until Antoine was straddling Rivas's lap. Antoine immediately realized the advantages of this position when he felt his erection pressing against an answering hardness. Instinctively Antoine tried to move, his hips arching forward to try to get greater friction. Only Rivas's tight hold on his hips kept Antoine firmly in place.

"Stay still." The words were stern, and Antoine could feel them pinning him in place. "I want to see you properly."

Rivas let go of Antoine's hips, moving up and quickly undoing the buttons that ran down the front of Antoine's coveralls. The rough clothing was pushed down off his shoulders and further until Antoine was bare from the hips up, cock standing in the cool air. Rivas's green eyes ran over all of the bared skin, burning with barely checked desire. The intensity of those eyes caused shivers to race down Antoine's spine. "Beautiful…," Rivas murmured, his hands coming to rest on Antoine's hips and then moving up his stomach, lightly ghosting the still tender bruises over his ribs.

All of Antoine's nerves were on fire, and every single one of them seemed connected directly to his cock. When Rivas reached his nipples, there was no way Antoine could keep quiet any longer. As Rivas teased and twisted his nipples, Antoine let out a keening moan, arching up into the touches. His cock brushed against the air pirate's stomach, the tip dragging through the coarse hair on Rivas's stomach.

Antoine leaned forward, kissing Rivas hungrily. He felt like he was going to go crazy, his own hands moving clumsily down to Rivas's pants wanting to get to feel Rivas's cock. It was difficult to do while engaged in a heated kiss, but Antoine was loath to break it. Slowly he managed to undo the lacings of Rivas's pants, pushing them down enough to free the older man's erection.

Without hesitation Antoine wrapped his hand around Rivas's erection. A distant part of his mind noted again Rivas's rather impressive girth, even more noticeable now that he was completely erect. Antoine stroked up and down the length, breaking from the kiss to let out a low moan. Antoine gripped Rivas's shoulder, gulping in as much air as he could. He needed more, more *something*. He just didn't know what exactly he needed yet.

"Rivas… please…." He gasped, arching so his own erection brushed against Rivas's. It sent a jolt of hot pleasure through his whole body. Antoine whimpered, seeking more of the wonderful friction.

Fortunately Rivas seemed to know exactly what to do. He began to shift Antoine to a new position that would be more advantageous for them. Rivas wasn't in any shape for a more energetic exchange, but at this point Antoine was too keyed up to care. It wouldn't take much to push him over the edge, especially once he realized what Rivas was planning. Rivas lined them up so that their cocks were brushing against each other. He wrapped his hand around both of their erections, calloused hand moving firmly over them.

Antoine lost himself to the pleasure racing through his body. His eyes had long since fallen closed, head falling forward to rest on Rivas's shoulder. Distantly Antoine heard a keening noise that he eventually realized was coming from himself. All too soon, his orgasm ripped through him, every muscle in his body tensing as he spurted over Rivas's hand and their stomachs. He felt an answering warmth as well, the soft groaning grunt of Rivas's own orgasm.

Once the aftershocks had died down, Antoine felt completely wrung out, sated and weak. It was hard to move, but Antoine knew he had to. While Rivas was managing to hold him up for now, it wouldn't last very long. Slowly he forced his body upright and off Rivas. Antoine kept himself from collapsing mostly through force of will and the knowledge that he needed to clean them up first.

Cleaning up took several minutes. Antoine's brain was not quite functioning yet. When he made it to the privy, he found water in the basin, but finding a clean cloth for wiping up took a bit of time. Eventually Antoine got them both cleaned up, flushing a bit under the tired smirk Rivas gave him. When he finished, Antoine refastened his overalls to just over his belly button.

As Antoine yawned, he heard Rivas give a chuckle. Carefully he shifted on the bed until he was lying down. "Get back into the bed, before you fall over where you stand."

Antoine saw no reason to argue with that, especially when it was both logical and extremely tempting. Climbing into the bed, he grabbed the blankets from where they had gathered at the foot, making sure to cover the two of them. Antoine scooted as close as he dared, letting his head rest on the pillow next to Rivas's. His head had barely hit the pillow before he was asleep.

CHAPTER THIRTY

ANTOINE WASN'T sure how long they slept. It felt like it had only been minutes, but when he woke up the room was dark. Not even the gas lamps were burning, and the only light was the faint amount that spilled in through the open door from the other room. Antoine sat up, rubbing his eyes as he waited for the disorientation to pass. He wasn't sure what exactly had woken him, until he heard it again. There was someone moving in the other room. It was quiet, but it was definitely movement. His heart leaped, racing as he continued to listen. A quick glance at the bed proved that Rivas was still asleep, the soft noises not having disturbed him. Antoine was glad for that, even as Shandor's warnings returned to him. Mustering his courage, Antoine climbed to his feet and moved as quietly as he could toward the door.

The sounds continued. They didn't sound particularly threatening, more like someone was moving things around. Yet just the fact that someone was there made Antoine's pulse quicken with dread. He paused at the doorway, taking a fortifying breath before he stepped out into the main room, bracing himself for anything.

Li looked up from where he was standing, a book open in his hands, dark eyes blinking curiously at Antoine. The sight was so normal and safe that Antoine sagged against the door. His relief was obvious, even from across the room, enough to make Li frown and close the book.

"You alright, Antoine?" Li walked over, setting the book on the desk before moving to stand in front of Antoine.

"Fine, I'm fine." Antoine carefully pulled in a breath, straightening quickly. "I heard you in here, and I didn't know who it was." Now that the mystery was gone, his previous trepidation seemed rather silly.

169

"You were concerned. You thought someone might be here to cause harm to you or the captain."

Antoine had never concealed his feelings, a trait that his mother frequently lamented. Blood rushed to his face, and he ducked his head. He felt foolish for being so concerned, foolish that his paranoia was that obvious.

"Don't be upset." Li patted him on the shoulder lightly before moving away. "It can be a good thing to be a bit wary. It helps to keep the mind sharp and alert." Li was mixing powders on the table now. "I came in to see to redoing Rivas's bandages. Sawbones would have come to do it but he is, how do you say it? Ah, tied up at the moment." There was a strange twist of Li's lips as he said those words, almost a smirk really.

Antoine blinked, not sure how he should react. Ultimately he decided to ignore them until later. "Rivas is still asleep." With those words, Antoine was suddenly aware of the state he was in. His coverall was still half off him, leaving his chest bare. Without his arms in it, the whole thing was starting to sag on his hips. Self-consciously he pulled it up a bit. However, the action only seemed to draw Li's attention to his undressed state.

"I see…. Well, I can wait if you think he needs the rest more." There was that slight smirk again. "I do hope you didn't tire him out too much, or cause any stress to his injuries."

Heat rushed to Antoine's face making it feel like it glowed. "Uhm… I'll… I'll check… perhaps he's awake…." He stumbled backward into the bedroom, slamming the door behind him. Antoine took a couple of measured breaths, attempting to calm himself down after what had happened.

"Fool, I'm a complete fool." He muttered the words quietly, finally turning away from the door. As he did so, he was greeted by the sight of Rivas propped up on an elbow, smiling at him. "You're awake! That's… that's good." Antoine felt flustered and knew he was doing a poor job of hiding it. "Li is in the other room. He came to wrap your ribs again."

Rivas nodded, carefully settling back onto the bed. "I see. That explains why you were so red when you came in. He doesn't look it really, you can't tell by his face or anything, but there is a streak of pure wickedness within that man. It's one of the few things I know for certain he shares with his sister."

"I gathered that…" Antoine muttered, pulling up his coverall. He fumbled with the buttons a bit, still flustered from earlier. "I seem to make good sport for your crew."

"Only those I trust would come in, those that have my complete faith. So don't worry if they tease you. It's all in good fun. They'll take their turn at me no doubt, just wait and see." Rivas smirked. "But why is Li here, instead of Sawbones?"

Antoine had finally finished fastening the buttons, feeling calmer and more secure. "He, ah, said that Sawbones was tied up at the moment." Antoine looked up sharply when Rivas broke out into guffaws of laughter. He couldn't imagine what was so amusing to Rivas to make him laugh that hard. Especially when it obviously began to cause him pain. Yet even as he winced and wrapped an arm around himself, he was still chuckling.

Antoine's surprise swiftly changed to annoyance, though. The longer Rivas laughed, the greater Antoine's annoyance grew. "Stop it! What's so amusing about what he said?"

The door opened, Li poking his head in at the noise. "I see you haven't completely ruined him yet. I would say you were slipping, Captain, but you've been indisposed." He stepped in, his boots silent on the metal flooring as he went. "Let's get you up so I can tend to this, then. I will need your help with it, Antoine."

Antoine scowled, wanting to tell them to stop making fun of him. Only his concern for Rivas overrode that urge, for the moment at least. It took several minutes, but between the two of them they managed to get Rivas sitting up straight in the bed. Antoine was left to brace Rivas upright while Li tended to the bruises. More cream was applied, and then fresh bandages were wrapped around him. By the end of it Rivas's amusement had definitely faded, his face having gone slightly gray with discomfort.

"There, you are done for now." Li stood up, stretching slowly. "I will go and make some of your medicine to ease your pain."

Antoine watched Li exit the room, pulling the door closed behind him. He turned to look at Rivas, who had closed his eyes, his body slumping over in exhaustion. Carefully Antoine shifted his position on the bed so that Rivas was not supported by him so much as the larger man was lying against him. In this new position, Antoine was able to bring his hand up, gently carding it through the sweaty blond hair.

If he had been asked, Antoine wouldn't have been able to say if he was doing it to comfort Rivas or himself. Ultimately he supposed it didn't truly matter who it was for if they both benefited from it. Lightly Antoine pressed a kiss to Rivas's forehead, tasting the salty sweat that had gathered there.

Li returned soon with a mug holding a familiar-smelling beverage. He pressed it into Rivas's hand, holding on to help stabilize it when the captain's hand shook too much to keep it steady. When he finished the drink, Rivas collapsed back against Antoine, all the strength seeming to have left his body. Antoine was entirely focused on supporting Rivas, not even acknowledging Li as he left them alone. They had napped for quite a while, but Rivas dropped off to sleep quickly. Antoine suspected there was something in the tonic to help Rivas sleep even when he might not wish to. With Rivas asleep, though, Antoine was left completely alone in the cabin. Normally it wouldn't be so bad, but tonight the silence felt too heavy, too oppressive for him to handle. Quite suddenly Antoine wanted nothing more than to get out, feel the wind on his face, and let the coolness clear his head.

With great care, Antoine extracted himself from the bed, making sure Rivas was settled comfortably before he left. He knew that Shandor said he shouldn't leave the room, but judging from the sky out the porthole window, it was dark outside. Since it was so late, there should only be the nighttime skeleton crew on the deck. A small enough group that Antoine thought he would be safe as long as he kept it brief.

Keeping that thought at the forefront, Antoine climbed the steps leading up to the deck. When he stepped out, the cold wind hit him with shocking force, instantly clearing cobwebs from his head.

It gave him a feeling of clarity that he had been missing before. Opening his eyes, Antoine strode over to the railing on the deck, looking out at the few wisps of clouds that decorated the sky.

Staring at the vast sky above him, and then the peaks of the mountains in the distance, gave Antoine a sense of perspective he'd been missing. When held against the vastness in front of him, the cluttered thoughts that had been in his head of late seemed insignificant. Antoine had a slow revelation as he stared up at the darkened sky filled with thousands and thousands of stars.

His pulse started to race as he faced all of the consequences of the recent revelations in his head. Antoine was happy here. He shouldn't be, but he was. Even though parts of it had been trying, greatly confusing, and initially terrifying. Antoine had met incredible people on the *Bloody Aria*, and he knew his experiences here would shape him for the rest of his life. Then there was Rivas, Rivas the Ramshot, who made his pulse race in a very pleasant way. It was more than physical, yet the emotions Antoine felt toward Rivas were an impenetrable tangle. Even so, the truth of them seemed simple enough, a simple truth with the power to completely destroy Antoine. Perhaps his musings would have continued all night, or at least until Antoine was brave enough to own up to the full extent of his emotions, except there was an interruption. A figure stepped up beside him, footsteps heavy and unfamiliar.

"Are you sure you should be out here? What if the captain needs you?" The voice was blandly curious, no inflection to give anything away. The person speaking appeared equally unremarkable.

"The captain is resting right now. I just needed to get some air," Antoine said, taking a careful step back. Not so far that it would seem like he was frightened or intimidated by the newcomer, just enough to provide some space.

"I see. It is a lovely night to be out." The stranger gave a small smile, glancing up at the sky, which from his angle could only be seen in the gaps between the balloons. "I imagine having to take care of an invalid would make one require space after a while."

Antoine's stomach dropped a little as he listened to those words. "It's no trouble at all. I'm glad to help Captain Rivas if he needs me," Antoine said, picking his words carefully. Shandor's warnings suddenly came back in force.

There came a snort of laughter, gray eyes watching him carefully. "Well, you certainly are dedicated to someone who is holding you here against your will."

That brought a frown to Antoine's face, which he quickly worked to wipe away. "Things are how they are. I'm not sure it's really any of your concern." The words were carefully chosen.

"You're probably right." The pirate shoved his hands into the pockets of his trousers, slowly strolling away. "Oh, I forgot to introduce myself." He paused at the edge of the door leading below deck. "M'name's Ciel, pleasure to meet you, Antoine Suvalese." Ciel threw the introduction out casually before disappearing below deck.

There were a few frantic moments when Antoine tried to place the name. He went through all the people he knew on the crew, but none matched up with Ciel. The air pirate was so average-looking it would be hard to remember him unless he drew attention to himself. They could have met anytime that Antoine was on the ship, which did nothing to settle the unease he was feeling.

Antoine didn't realize how lost in his thoughts he was until the moonlight was suddenly blocked. Blinking slowly, he saw Shandor standing in front of him. The scowl on the taller man's face had Antoine instinctively shrinking back against the railing. He had hoped to get back to the cabin without Shandor knowing he had left.

The dark-haired pirate didn't say anything. He simply grabbed Antoine's arm and dragged him back below deck. Antoine didn't struggle. Not only would it be useless, given that Shandor was stronger than he was, but also because he had planned to go back soon anyway. No words passed between them until they had made it back to the cabin. Only then did Shandor let go of Antoine and pace away from him.

"Well, if you had to pick any time and place to decide you needed to wander out on deck without permission, you at least picked a good time to do it," Shandor said, rubbing his face. "Minimal exposure, probably no one noticed you wandering around on deck." Antoine couldn't tell if Shandor was talking to himself or not.

"Sorry. I just, I needed to get some air. I needed to get out for a bit, you know?" Antoine sat down heavily on one of the chairs, rubbing his arms. "Going a bit stir crazy with Rivas sleeping. Wanted to get some perspective."

Shandor gave a soft laugh. "I can understand that, always helps to have some perspective. Except when it potentially puts you in danger."

"I was hoping to get back before you could find out."

"Good plan, hard to follow through on, but a good plan overall." Shandor paused at the grate that heated the room. "Just please don't do it again. Or if you have to, let someone know first. Someone we trust who can watch you."

Antoine nodded, leaning back into the chair. He understood Shandor's paranoia, yet part of him thought maybe it was a bit overblown. As he thought that, his mind flashed back to the sailor who had been talking to him up on deck. The strange way he talked, the things he had said, and Antoine thought maybe the paranoia wasn't as unwarranted as he thought.

"Shandor, can I ask something?"

Shandor glanced up, a few curls falling across his face. "Of course. I may not give you an answer, though."

"You're the quartermaster on the ship, right? So you know all of the sailors that serve on the *Aria,* don't you?"

Shandor nodded easily enough. "'Course I do, part of being the quartermaster. Have to know everyone, know what they can do. What makes them tick and who they work best with."

Antoine nodded, chewing on his lip for a minute before he spoke. "Is there a sailor on board named Ciel?"

Whatever reaction Antoine thought he might get, it was definitely not the one Shandor gave. The larger man went completely still before slowly turning to look at Antoine intently. Antoine could almost see the multitude of thoughts chasing themselves around inside of Shandor's head. "You met Ciel? Did you run into him on deck? Was he already there?"

Antoine shook his head, because when he thought about it, he didn't remember seeing Ciel on deck when he first arrived. "No. I don't remember seeing him initially when I went up. I tried to avoid the crew if I could. I remember thinking the deck looked completely abandoned." He frowned slightly, looking up at Shandor. "It was… almost like he was seeking me out."

Shandor spat something unintelligible, striding across the room. He paced for several moments, his mismatched eyes flashing brilliantly in the lamplight. Eventually he seemed to settle down, or at least come to a decision. He strode over to Antoine, staring intently at him. "No matter what, Antoine, stay away from Ciel if you can. There is something not to be trusted about him."

"What do you mean? Not to be trusted? Is he dangerous?"

"He's an air pirate, Antoine. We're all dangerous," Shandor said quickly. "There is something about him that I can't bring myself to trust. He was the one that Rivas sent to Laitha with the ransom demands. Reason enough to be wary of him right there. That he has taken the motive to look for an opportune time to speak with you only increases the suspicion."

Antoine tried to reconcile Shandor's words with the man he had met on deck. There had indeed been something disturbing about Ciel, something that had set Antoine on edge despite the man's plainness. Yet even with his own intuition as well as the trust he had in Shandor's opinion, Antoine's mind just couldn't come to grip with the implications of it all. It seemed ridiculously grandiose for all of this to be focused on him.

Shandor ran a hand over his wild hair, absently smoothing it down before releasing it to run riot again. "There is something else here, something that I can't see. It makes no sense for Ciel to seek you out now. What does it gain him?" Antoine opened his mouth to respond, only for Shandor to turn away as he continued his pacing. At that moment, Antoine realized the man was not talking to him so much as thinking out loud to himself. "Unless he's trying to get you used to him? But again, why?"

"Are you sure this isn't being exaggerated? I mean he just spoke to me. Yes, I admit he was a little unsettling, but that doesn't mean he's planning something devious."

"Doesn't mean he isn't, either," Shandor responded, finally halting his pacing. "Just be extra cautious from now on. And get some rest, will you? It's late."

Antoine snorted, standing up slowly, his body heavy, like he was moving through molasses. The restless energy that had driven him up on deck and the adrenaline that had followed his departure had faded now, leaving exhaustion to crash upon him like a wave. As quickly as he could, Antoine stumbled into the bedroom, his eyelids drooping as soon as he caught sight of the bed. Even with all of his tiredness, he still had to stop and admire the sight of Rivas sprawled out on the bed. Quietly he pulled off his boots and climbed into the bed. Antoine had barely enough time to get comfortable before he dropped off to sleep.

CHAPTER THIRTY-ONE

THE NEXT several days were peaceful for Antoine and for Rivas. Well, peaceful in a relative way. They played chess to pass the time, and when that lost appeal, Rivas taught Antoine a different strategy game, the one from the east. Antoine admired Rivas's quick wit and was continuously surprised by how well read he was. The nights were filled with a mutual exploration of each other's bodies. However, due to both of their injuries it could never go as far as they both wanted.

Now that Antoine understood some of the reasoning behind his kidnapping—at least Rivas's motives—a lot of the uncertainty left him. As strange as it might seem, Antoine was happy, or at least contented in a way he never had been before. The nexus of all these emotions seemed to be Rivas. A logical part of Antoine's mind liked to whisper to him, in the dark of the night when he was trying to sleep wrapped in Rivas's arms, that it couldn't last. By its very design, it had to end, and soon. Antoine was doing his best to ignore that voice for as long as he could.

Unfortunately he couldn't ignore it nearly as long as he would have liked. A week and a half after the accident, Shandor made another visit to the room. This time he came while Rivas was awake and sitting up in bed. The two of them were in the middle of another game, Antoine intently focused on his next move, determined to finally win a round. Rivas's bemused affection was a distraction, though, as was the hand running teasingly over his thigh.

Shandor knocked quickly, not bothering to wait for any kind of response before stepping in. His lips twitched up into a smirk before it dropped. "I need to speak with you for a minute, Rivas." He glanced over at Antoine pointedly. "In private if you don't mind, Antoine."

It was a peculiar feeling, to know people were going to be talking about him while he wasn't there. There was a chance that the topic of conversation was not going to be related to him, but Antoine had a hard time imagining what else it could be. Antoine stood up with a small sigh, stepping out of the room and pulling the door closed behind him. He knew he should walk away, should give them privacy for their conversation. Perhaps he would have before, but now he was rather tired of being the focus of so much without knowing what exactly was happening.

Carefully Antoine pressed his ear to the metal of the door, trying to catch their conversation. Fortunately they weren't trying to keep their voices down, so he didn't have to strain too hard. Antoine focused on making sure his breathing didn't get too loud and reveal him.

"The exchange date is coming up soon. We're heading to the agreed rendezvous point now, should be there within about a day or so." Those words caused an uncomfortable churning in Antoine's gut.

There was a pause before Rivas spoke up. "Seems like it came quickly, I thought there was more time before that. Though perhaps it's just my own wishful thoughts."

There was a small snort of laughter. "It's amusing to see you being the lovesick one for a change. Rather nice retribution, I think." Antoine tried to ignore the lurch his heart gave at Shandor's words. "Maybe now you'll have a better understanding of my position in these affairs."

"No, because I'm fortunate enough to have at least some returned affection. Unlike you, who can't even get them to acknowledge your interest."

"Who says he doesn't acknowledge my interest? Maybe he does it in private," Shandor shot back, a slightly defensive tone to his voice.

"He's just shy, is that it? Nothing to do with not being at all interested or bothered by your pursuit?"

"See, that's where you're wrong, Rivas. It's not that he has no interest, he simply doesn't know how to handle it."

Antoine grinned as he listened to their banter. This was so obviously a conversation they'd had on numerous occasions. Though he did wonder how truthful the whole conversation was. The next words wrenched Antoine from his contemplation.

"There's something else I came to inform you of. I received a message a week ago from one of my contacts in the city. The ship that is to meet us for the exchange is an aeronaught, top of the line ship."

"We planned for this, Shandor, remember? We knew that Suvalese would insist on the best possible ship to do the exchange. We stick to the plan. Do we know who the captain is?"

"Randalf Hildebard. He's young, most likely very ambitious to already be in control of an aeronaught. We need to be prepared for what might come of that." There was the faint sound of boots on the floor. When Shandor spoke again, his voice was fainter and more muffled. "I have a bad feeling about this, Rivas."

There came a slight scoff before Rivas spoke, his voice lower than normal. The words were too muffled to make out much more than the tone of them. Antoine pulled back, his mind racing over what he'd heard.

Antoine walked over to the window, staring out at the sky as it streamed behind the *Aria*. His gut churned as he stood there, parts of the conversation jumping around in his mind. Taking a deep breath, Antoine decided to sort through his emotions instead of letting them ride over him. So that meant he had to focus on the largest part of it.

As he focused, Antoine realized something important. He was sad—incredibly, deeply saddened by the thought that soon he would have to head back to a life that seemed more like a dream than a reality he had lived. Antoine thought of the things he would miss about the *Aria*. He knew he would miss the freedom, the lack of expectations placed upon him; that was something he had enjoyed immensely. However, that was not what caused his pulse to race at the thought of leaving.

The thought of leaving Rivas, of not seeing the pirate again, caused an ache in his chest. Antoine leaned forward to rest his head on the cool glass and force himself to breathe deeply. His heart was still hammering as his brain went over and over the thought of leaving Rivas. The meaning of what he felt made his heart speed up again. It was an uncomfortable revelation, one Antoine didn't want to face up to at that moment, or any moment honestly.

Except it was rapidly getting past the point where he could ignore it. He had only a few more days here, a few more days with Rivas before it would all be over. Every time he thought that, it felt like all the air was sucked out of his lungs. Antoine didn't want this feeling, yet there was no escape from it. Somehow, he had fallen in love with an air pirate. An air pirate that saw so much more in him than anyone else ever had. A man who had been stunned by him at a distance. In a situation like that, how could he not have fallen in love? The realization that he loved Rivas was followed by the knowledge that he would lose him. Next to that, everything else seemed insignificant in comparison. Antoine had to decide what he would do with his new revelation. Antoine turned from the window, dropping down into one of the chairs. There was only a short amount of time left to act, and also to find out what Rivas felt. Antoine turned to look at the door. It was surprising to realize that they were still talking in there. It felt like a long time had passed, but maybe not as long as he had thought. After standing back up, Antoine carefully walked over to the door and pressed his ear back against it. The sounds of the voices were hushed now, the tone of the words quieter so that he had to strain to make out any of them.

"Keep what I said in mind, Rivas. I'm going to go and work on preparations. Also, rest as much as possible. You'll need to be up for the exchange. It'll be a good sign to the crew and the navy."

"I'll be ready. Just tell Sawbones to give me a good crutch and bandage my leg better."

Antoine quickly moved away from the door and back to the window. He tried hard not to tense when the door opened. He listened to the sound of the boots echoing across the room, glancing over when they came to a stop behind him. Antoine turned to face Shandor, hoping that he didn't look guilty.

Shandor still looked moody as he stood there, his entire body radiating tension. Whether Shandor knew that Antoine had overheard the conversation or not, he didn't let on. Instead he just stared at him, his mechanical eye seeming to glow brighter than before. "Remember what I said before, Antoine. Especially when it comes time for the rendezvous."

Reflexively Antoine nodded, straightening up a bit. "I will...." He'd taken heed of Shandor's earlier warnings to be careful. He hadn't left the room, and he hadn't spoken to anyone other than the people who brought their food. Only the senior officers were trusted enough by Rivas and Shandor to bring in supplies.

He nodded quickly before turning away, striding out without another word passing his lips. Antoine watched Shandor go, wondering just what had gone on in there. That thought was followed by the more pertinent question of whether he really wanted to know. Taking a long breath, Antoine turned and headed back into the sleeping cabin.

SHANDOR WAITED outside the room for a minute, trying to organize his thoughts so he could figure out what to do next. Rivas had a point when he said they couldn't change the plans based on Shandor's bad feelings. Still, that didn't mean he couldn't take extra precautions to ensure they were all safe.

Especially if there was a young officer coming toward them that could be fishing for both glory and a large payout. The ransom money was enough to set himself up for a good life and a smooth ride into the upper echelons of society. Beznik's warning had contained a hidden meaning for him. Shandor couldn't verify anything more than a name and rank, so he was going to be exceedingly careful.

He turned to the task of rounding up the others. If there was a chance of the whole thing going south, everyone needed to know. It took a quarter of an hour to gather them all together, forcing them all into Sawbones's quarters because it was the most private location. Of course, by the time they all got inside it was a bit cramped. Especially once Shiv'ren made his way inside, wings tucked as tight against his body as possible.

Shandor was quiet at first, leaning against the rear wall with his head bowed. None of those assembled were in a hurry to force him to speak. In fact, the only one giving him specific, direct attention was Shiv'ren, who was staring at him intently. Yi stood by the door, her arms folded within her wide sleeves. Li stood at the opposite end of the room, perched lightly on the end of Sawbones's bed, next to the man himself.

Shan waited for another minute before he spoke up. "The switch takes place in a few days. I don't trust the setup for it. Mostly I don't trust the officer that is being put in charge of this exchange. As much as possible, make extra precautions when we change over. Be sure you're all armed as much as possible, just in case."

"You fear us being attacked while we do the ransom exchange." Yi straightened, tilting her head to the side. "You think there is going to be some kind of double cross."

Shandor let out a long breath. "Yes. I can't explain it. I just have a feeling about the whole affair. It would be better if we were all prepared before it goes down. It would be a rather large feather in the cap of any naval officer to capture the crew of the infamous *Bloody Aria*. I would rather not end my life on a hangman's rope that an officer uses to climb up to a position in the Spire."

"So, we shall prepare as best we can when the time arrives," Li said, nodding firmly. "I too have no desire to be on the end of a noose. A feeling I think is shared by the whole crew. There will be great caution taken, Shan."

"That's all I'm asking for, caution. Along with preparedness." Shandor straightened, signaling the end of their brief meeting. As they all went their separate ways, Shandor followed after Shiv'ren.

They didn't get very far before Shiv'ren stopped and whirled around, golden eyes flashing in annoyance. Shandor loved it when there was emotion heating up those eyes, turning them into molten pools, even when they weren't the emotions he wanted to see. "Is there a reason you're following me, Shandor? Or is it just your normal reasons?"

"I always have a reason, Shiv'ren. However, this time it is a bit different than normal." Shandor walked over, purposefully invading Shiv'ren's space. "That thing we were discussing before, I would like it to be ready by the time we do the switch. As a backup."

Shiv'ren stared up at him for a minute before nodding. "Aye, aye."

CHAPTER THIRTY-TWO

ANTOINE SETTLED down on the edge of the bed, watching as Rivas slept. It was one of the few times he got to see Rivas at rest with his guard down. No clever wit or calculating mind running behind his green eyes. Years fell off his face, and even the scar on his cheek was softened, becoming just a white line instead of a mark of his status.

Antoine gave in to the desire to run his fingers over the scar. He had thought it might be rough, but instead it was very smooth. He wondered exactly how Rivas had gotten the scar. Perhaps it was during some great battle against the navy or another ship. It would be more poetic if he had received it in that way.

Antoine smiled, leaning over to ghost a kiss over the mark. He trailed kisses from the scar over to Rivas's ear, brushing his lips over the shell. Beneath him Rivas shifted, causing Antoine's smile to widen a little. He nipped at the lobe, smothering the urge to laugh when Rivas pulled away. Sitting up, Antoine watched as Rivas opened his eyes, giving him a feigned glare before bringing his hands up to grip Antoine's arms.

"You were taking liberties, weren't you?" He growled the words out, tugging Antoine closer.

"A few perhaps, but you were simply too tempting to resist, Captain," Antoine responded, unable to pull away but not really wanting to. "It was a rare opportunity to observe and explore uninterrupted."

Rivas let out a husky chuckle, tipping his head back. "Then if it helps, I can pretend to sleep longer."

Antoine laughed, running a hand lightly over Rivas's chest, marveling again at the contrasting textures he found. Smooth skin, coarse chest hair, and the rough cloth of the bandages. "Well, it's not entirely bad that you're awake. Still lots of things that can be done."

"World enough and time I suppose." Rivas said the words idly, his fingers lacing into Antoine's hair. The words might have sounded light, but they brought back the specter of the coming meeting. There wasn't world enough and time, and there never would be. There was only these few stolen moments, which Antoine had no desire to waste.

"This moment is enough," Antoine murmured, pressing a kiss to Rivas's chin. "I want to make it last as long as possible. Every moment counts, especially when they might not last."

So far all of their activities had been light, not exactly gentle but nothing too energetic. Mostly it had involved a lot of touching, and Antoine wanted to change that. His stomach was clenched in nervousness, but he refused to let it stop him. Antoine clung to the thought that it would all be over soon because if he didn't, he would get too nervous.

"Such sobering thoughts to be having," Rivas murmured, cupping Antoine's face gently. "Surely there is something better that your mind could be focusing on?" A rough hand smoothed over Antoine's cheek, making him shiver. "Or shall I distract you?"

Antoine forced a grin, pressing a kiss to Rivas's lips. He let it linger there, drawing it out slowly. This time there was no need to force the smile as Antoine took in the new heat in Rivas's gaze. The next kiss was much more heated, tongues tangling together. When they finally broke apart, both of them were panting heavily.

There was much fumbling and tearing at Antoine's clothes, both struggling to get the material off. Of course, it was made more difficult by the fact that they couldn't seem to stop kissing each other. Once the top of Antoine's coveralls had been pushed down, their lips clashed in another fervent kiss.

This time when they broke apart, Antoine made certain to seize the initiative. He pushed Rivas onto his back, leaning over the older man. He flashed a quick grin at him before lowering himself further. Pressing a kiss to the hollow of Rivas's throat, Antoine began a thorough exploration of Rivas. Antoine ran his hands over the skin, learning the feel before following it with lips and tongue. As he came to the old scars, Antoine made sure to press a kiss to each one. When he came to the stark whiteness of the remaining bandages, instead of shying away as he normally would, Antoine gently ran his hands over the length and breadth of them, hyper aware of any sign of discomfort he might cause.

Antoine kissed all over the bandages and the fading bruises that peeked out from the edges. He wished that just kissing the injuries would be enough to heal them. Even now, Antoine could still feel a swell of guilt for the myriad injuries Rivas had that were still healing. He shook his head quickly, refocusing on the moment at hand. Recrimination would only get in the way, and when he had a handsome pirate captain spread beneath him, panting in arousal, that was an even worse affront.

Glancing down, Antoine could clearly see the outline of Rivas's erection against his breeches, the heat and hardness pressing against Antoine's thigh. Smirking to himself, Antoine slithered down further, hands fumbling with the closure on the breeches. He knew from experience that there was no way to get the breeches entirely off, so instead he worked them down as far as he could, exposing Rivas to the air of the cabin. He had to admit that the sight of the hard organ jumping in the cool air made his pulse race even faster. Staring at it, what Antoine wanted to do no longer seemed as intimidating.

Gently Antoine stroked a finger down the divide of Rivas's abdominal muscles and then slowly traced the definition of them. Leaning forward, he pressed kisses along the muscled abdomen, following the trail of dark golden hair that led ever downward. He only paused for a moment when he felt strong hands grip his shoulders. Rivas didn't push him. Instead he seemed to be just trying to hold on to Antoine. As Antoine continued his journey south, the hands loosened from his shoulders, migrating up to his hair, tightening suddenly as Antoine's cheek brushed against Rivas's erection. Antoine turned his head, running his fingers over the hot flesh, taking a moment to enjoy the feel of it. His own cock was hard and throbbing in his coveralls, but he wasn't ready to be distracted from his ultimate goal.

Wrapping his hand around the base, Antoine leaned forward and pressed a kiss to the head. His tongue darted out to get a taste of the clear liquid leaking from the tip. He took a minute to catalog the flavor before taking the entire head into his mouth. Antoine had no idea what exactly he was doing, so he decided to just follow his instincts. Antoine ran his tongue over the head before sucking on the tip. Slowly he worked his way down the length, taking in as much as he could before he began to choke. Above him, he heard Rivas gasp, the hands tightening in his hair. Antoine took that as a sign that he was doing something right, so he decided to continue what he had been doing.

Suddenly there was a sharp tug on his head that forced him up. Antoine let out a low moan, feeling his still confined erection rubbing over Rivas's side. "Stop…. Antoine…." Rivas was panting, his skin shimmering with sweat. "Too close, don't want to end it yet."

Antoine whimpered, looking down at Rivas. The sight of the older man almost completely undone, knowing that he was the cause, made fire race through Antoine's veins. Suddenly he couldn't take the constriction of his erection any longer. Sitting up, Antoine quickly worked at the clasps on his coveralls, pushing it down until it fell loose around his hips. His own cock was leaking heavily at this point, begging for attention.

A strangled gasp escaped Antoine's throat when Rivas clasped his hand around it, jerking it roughly several times. He whimpered at the assault, leaning against Rivas in an attempt to catch his breath. His mind was fuzzy with desire and pleasure, yet he still managed to remember there was something else he wanted to do. It was something he had heard mentioned on the coal transport, in very crude terms. He just wasn't sure how to go about it. Instead of repeating the words he had heard, Antoine tried to find a way to show it.

As these thoughts raced through his muddy head, Rivas gripped him firmly, shifting their positions until Antoine straddled the older man. The new position brought their faces closer, allowing them to see each other's eyes, making the entire act more intimate. Antoine leaned forward, lifting himself up to kiss Rivas, hands fisting in the thick blond waves. When the kiss finally broke, he leaned back, letting out a gasp as he felt Rivas's thick erection brushing against his ass. Without out any direct thought, Antoine rocked back, rubbing against the thick column of flesh.

Antoine's eyes had fallen closed at some point, but they flew open when strong fingers dug into the flesh of his ass. He was met with the positively burning gaze of Rivas, green eyes glowing in the dim light. Rivas was panting hard, hands spreading the fleshy globes so calloused fingers could run over the crease. Any remaining thoughts in Antoine's head were burned away by a wave of pleasure so intense he lost his breath.

"You tread on dangerous territory." Rivas's voice came out as a low growl. He pressed a finger against the puckered opening that he found. "Keep it up and I may not be able to stop myself. Are you prepared to deal with that?"

Antoine could only nod, his body burning up with the intense pleasure Rivas was wringing out of him. All Antoine could focus on was breathing and not being entirely consumed by the feelings raging through him. Every new sensation burned through him with greater intensity.

From somewhere Rivas produced a small vial of oil, pouring a stream down the crevasse of Antoine's ass. The oil was followed by thick, calloused fingers that gathered it up and pressed against the puckered opening. When one of the fingers penetrated him, Antoine let out a harsh whimper, rocking back against the digit. Soon the finger went deeper and was slowly joined by another one, and then a third. Antoine kept rocking back to meet each new penetration, constantly seeking more.

"Please...." It came out as a broken whimper, Antoine not entirely aware of what he was asking, only that there was something else he desperately needed, something more than the fingers.

The next thing Antoine was aware of was the feeling of the fingers withdrawing. He gave a keening whimper, eyes opening to look around him in a daze. He was caught by Rivas's burning green gaze and the hungry smirk that stretched across his face.

Soon Antoine felt something hot and much larger than fingers press against him. Antoine whimpered at the feeling, trying to lean back into it. Rivas's hands settled like iron on his hips to keep him in place.

"Not until I am ready." There was a definite growl of command in his voice that sent a shiver through Antoine's body. He wondered if Rivas sounded this sexy when he gave orders during a pirate raid.

Slowly Rivas lowered Antoine down, pausing at times to let him adjust. Antoine was glad for the slowness, because even with the preparation, it was the first time he had done anything like this. The feeling was not something Antoine could describe, yet he knew he would never forget it.

Once Rivas was completely sheathed inside of him, there was a long pause as Antoine's body adjusted to the feeling. Soon, though, the urge, the need to move was too great, and he started to lift himself up, letting gravity do the rest. Rivas seemed content at the moment to let Antoine control the pace and speed.

Eventually Antoine felt fingers tighten on his hips, taking control away from him. Rivas couldn't move a lot himself, so instead he demonstrated his great strength by moving Antoine. He felt himself being lifted up then slammed down, the movement sending bolts of pleasure through him and stealing his breath away. Antoine gripped Rivas's shoulder with one hand, holding on as much as he could. He brought his other hand to his own cock, stroking it quickly.

Soon Antoine felt his orgasm rushing through him, sweeping away all thought. Rivas held him down, his cock pulsing and sending a wave of liquid heat into him. Afterward, Antoine collapsed against Rivas, completely boneless.

As he slowly came back to himself, Antoine could feel words welling up inside him. Words that he didn't want to say, because they would make the feelings too real and permanent. Antoine bit his lip hard, closing his eyes against it all. He wanted to hold on to the moment he had, not ruin it with unneeded words.

When Rivas's hand came up and began to stroke his hair, Antoine held on even tighter, squeezing back tears. Neither of them said anything, simply staying wrapped around each other. Antoine felt sleep tugging at his mind, yet he struggled to stay awake, not wanting to lose the closeness that existed right now.

The next day ended up being dedicated to resting themselves. Both were sore, though in markedly different ways. Antoine found he could barely walk when he got up that morning. For Rivas, the excitement of yesterday had strained some of his injuries, leaving him aching and tired. Through mutual decision, they stayed in bed unless necessity required they leave it.

For all that it would seem to be a lazy day, there was a sense of urgency, of impending loss that made it anything but. This was one of the last days, perhaps the last day itself, that they could be together. So, for a little longer, they both tried to block out the world that would take away their precious time.

No one came to bother them except to bring food, which was left quietly with no disturbance. It was as if someone had instructed the crew to leave the captain alone. Antoine thought that perhaps it was Shandor's doing, but regardless of who, he was deeply grateful for the discretion. He soaked up the time and the memories, storing them all away for the future.

In the evening, the vibration of the engines changed. The sense of movement had become so constant that it was only the absence of it that brought it to Antoine's attention. He lifted his head from where he had been dozing, rubbing his eyes tiredly.

"What is it? What's going on?" Antoine yawned in the middle, trying to make his eyes focus in the dim gaslight.

"Don't worry about it," Rivas said, gently pulling Antoine back down. "We reached our destination. We're idling now. Go back to sleep."

Antoine's stomach dropped, an ill feeling sweeping through him. "I'm not sure I can sleep now, knowing we're here. I suppose the exchange will be soon, then."

"Soon enough," Rivas said, running his fingers through Antoine's hair, tilting his head back enough that he could lean down and kiss him. "But that is still the future. Focus on the present before fretting over the future."

Antoine smiled, leaning up and kissing him back. It was good advice, so he resolved to follow it. The future was fast approaching, but it was not yet there. Antoine wasn't going to let it steal his time with Rivas. There would be time for that later. For now he wanted to fill his mind with memories that he could take with him.

CHAPTER THIRTY-THREE

POUNDING WOKE Antoine the next day, making his head ache. There had been little sleep to be had for him the night before, something Antoine couldn't bring himself to regret. The pounding came again, this time accompanied by words that Antoine's tired brain failed to interpret. Soon, though, the words and the voice became clearer.

"Get up! Both of you, get up now!" Shandor's voice boomed through the door. "The aeronaught has been spotted on the horizon! You both need to get up as soon as you can." Shandor beat on the door several more times before pausing.

Antoine grunted, climbing stiffly to his feet before heading over to the door. He paused to pull up his coveralls and fumble with some of the buttons. He opened the door to see Shandor standing there with his arm raised to pound on the door again. Shandor grunted when he saw him, eyes flicking over Antoine's very disheveled state then back up to his face. "Good, you're awake. Get Rivas up too." Shandor's voice was stiff and controlled, his entire body radiating tension.

"I'm awake, Shan, no need to shout quite so much." Rivas had pushed himself into an upright position on the bed. He scrubbed a hand over his face, making a halfhearted attempt to smooth out his hair. "You said something about the aeronaught?"

"It's been spotted on the horizon, closing in quickly. You and Antoine need to get up on the deck as soon as possible. Preferably before they get here. The crew needs to see you present and in control. Which means you need to get moving, now." Shandor's voice was brusque as he spoke, lacking its normal warmth. He moved into the room, pushing Antoine aside and setting a large crutch by the bed.

"Very well, we'll be up as soon as I'm dressed." Rivas drew the crutch to him, looking it over before setting it aside and slowly moving to the edge of the bed. Using the crutch, he pushed himself to his feet, settling his weight on the length of wood. It held under his weight, and slowly he began to make his way to the washroom under his own power.

Getting dressed proved to be a bit of a process. Antoine had to help Rivas, and the most difficult part was getting his trousers over the splint and bandages wrapped around his leg. In the end, Rivas took a knife to the leg and split it up to his knee so it would fit.

As Rivas dressed, it was like watching a veil being lowered over him. His mannerisms, posture, and even the feel of the air around took on a different quality. Suddenly in front of Antoine was not the man he had gotten to know over the past weeks, the one who spoke with an educated mind about subjects and held Antoine tightly in the night. Antoine was now seeing the fearsome air pirate who had earned the name of Ramshot. For a brief moment, Antoine wondered if the man he had come to love was just an illusion. Then Rivas flashed him a grin, his scar pulling up with the motion, and Antoine felt his heart ease.

"Come on, it's time to head up to the deck. It can't start without us, and it wouldn't be good manners to be late." Rivas limped to the door, laboriously lifting himself over the edge of the door and out into the corridor. It was a slow advance through the ship, Antoine always being alert to any sign that his help would be needed. He pretended not to see the way that pain creased Rivas's face as they moved.

Once they hit the deck, though, any sign of pain or discomfort vanished. Rivas straightened up as much as he could with his injured leg, projecting an air of authority. He pulled ahead of Antoine, head held high. Antoine was forced to fall back, shoving his hands into his pockets.

It was a change from what they had shared in the privacy of the cabin. It made Antoine wish they could turn around, go back and shut everything else out. The sight of the naval aeronaught off in the distance brought only dread to his heart. The wind whipped through his clothes, making him shiver and hunch over against the chill. Shouted orders and commands rang over the deck, and Antoine quickly followed Rivas to the wheelhouse, attempting to stay out of the way.

The *Bloody Aria* was in the high mountains, near a collection of jagged rocks and peaks that the sailors referred to as the Shark's Jaws. It made for a good place to meet, Antoine supposed—lots of places for aeros to hide. A good strategic place to do a prisoner exchange.

The approaching aeronaught had already hoisted the white flag of truce, showing their peaceable intentions. A shout went across the deck. "Raise the flag!" Soon the *Aria* was flying its own white flag as the pirates waited. For all that there was a flag of peace, every sailor Antoine looked at was armed in some way, several fingering the weapons nervously.

"Antoine." He jumped at the sound of his name. Evidently he had been lost in his thoughts because he hadn't noticed Rivas coming to stand in front of him. "Listen, when we start the handover, stay to the back or the side until the exchange has been made. The last thing I want is someone getting nervous and doing something that might get you injured. Or worse." The last part was soft, and for a moment Antoine saw a brief glimpse of the other Rivas, his Rivas. Then he pulled away, and it was gone, replaced with the air pirate captain who went back to barking out instructions.

Antoine took a deep breath, shuffling back from the door. Glancing around, he was surprised to see so many people gathered in one place. He even caught a glimpse of Ciel in the background with some of the other air pirates. It seemed almost everyone he knew on the crew was there. Everyone, it seemed, except for Shiv'ren. Antoine's heart sank a little bit at the fact that there would be no chance to say farewell. After Rivas, Shiv'ren was the one Antoine had been closest to.

"They're here."

Antoine looked up, taking in the sight of the gleaming metal hull of the aeronaught. It was larger than the *Bloody Aria*, cannons mounted bristling along the sides. Grappling hooks were launched at the aeronaught, lashing the two of them together and letting them pull parallel. A plank was stretched out between the two ships, allowing for Captain Hildebard and his entourage of armed sailors to cross onto the *Aria*. There were quite a few, more than Antoine would have expected.

The pirates parted for the other sailors, but Antoine could see that none of them showed their backs to the sailors. Likewise, the sailors never took their wary eyes off the pirates and had come fully armed themselves. Even if they both flew the flag of peace, neither of them trusted the other.

Captain Hildebard strode at the head of his party, his uniform gleaming in the sunlight. He had a hand on his saber and the other held a large case that presumably held the ransom. He swept the whole deck with his gaze, taking in the pirates with a look that seemed both assessing and dismissive. Shandor had walked out of the wheelhouse and was the one who greeted Hildebard.

No words were exchanged, just a look, and then Shandor led the officer into the wheelhouse. Again Hildebard's gaze swept over the assembled people in the wheelhouse critically. He was followed by at least six other men, all of whom were heavily armed. Antoine wondered at so many people accompanying the captain, with even more outside.

"I am Captain Randalf Hildebard of the ADS *Diomede*. I have been tasked to take custody of Antoine Suvalese in exchange for the demanded ransom. Where is Captain Rivas?"

Rivas limped forward, holding himself completely upright, his gaze giving no quarter. "Here," he said shortly. "Put the ransom there, that we might inspect it," he said, gesturing to a spot in front of the wheel, directly in the center between the two groups.

Hildebard shook his head quickly. "Not yet. First I want confirmation that Mr. Suvalese is alive and unharmed. Where is he?"

Rivas snorted, shaking his head. "Come over here, Antoine, show the honorable captain that you are hale and hearty." Antoine swallowed, slowly walking forward into the light. He paused before he got too far, though, hesitating between Rivas and Shandor.

195

"Are you well, sir? These wretches haven't treated you too poorly, have they?" Hildebard's voice was stern, his eyes fixing on Antoine and seeming to hold him in place where he stood. The young captain's presence was imposing enough that Antoine's voice completely left him. "Mr. Suvalese? Have they cut your tongue or in some other manner deprived you of your speech?" Hildebard was frowning now, his muttonchops quivering slightly as he glared at those behind Antoine.

"No, no such thing." Antoine croaked the words out, desperately trying to get his equilibrium back. "I am as well as might be given the circumstances, Captain."

Hildebard nodded brusquely, walking forward and setting the case down on the ground. He quickly retreated, moving back to stand in front of his sailors. Rivas limped over to it, his crutch making a loud thumping sound on the metal plates as he walked. Leaning over, he opened the case, inspecting the contents of it. He moved the contents around, making sure it was filled with currency. As he did this, a shout came from outside, followed by the faint popping sound of rifles being fired.

All eyes turned to the windows, which showed more sailors coming over the planks, firing on the pirates as they went. Antoine turned to look at the sailors in the wheelhouse, all of whom had pulled their weapons, including Captain Hildebard. Each one was pointed at one of the assembled pirates. Outside the fighting ended quickly, with the sailors soon overpowering the pirates, holding each one at gunpoint.

Silence stretched out for a long uncomfortable moment as the sailors and the air pirates stared each other down. It was only broken when a commotion started outside. Antoine could see that one of the sailors had grabbed Yi about the waist, pulling her close. He couldn't make out the words, but their meaning was all too clear. Yi held an open fan up to her face, as if to hide, when suddenly the sailor jerked. A small cloud of smoke curled around Yi's face before she pulled away, the sailor slumping down to the ground with blood running down his face. She wasted no time in running down the length of the deck even as shots were fired at her retreating figure.

196

Yi reached into her hair, pulled out one of the long strings of ornaments that had decorated it, and threw it behind her. A series of pops, bright flashes, and heavy smoke followed it.

Antoine held his breath when the smoke cleared, revealing Yi as she leapt off the side of the boat. Instinctively Antoine jerked forward, stopping when one of the guns swung around and focused on him. No one else had moved, a deathly silence hanging over the whole room. Antoine swallowed, carefully straightening up.

"I would be careful, Mr. Suvalese, I would hate to have to explain to your father that you got shot by my own men," Captain Hildebard said sternly, moving forward. Antoine nodded, carefully backing away from both the sailors and Captain Hildebard. "Finally, I've captured the infamous crew of the *Bloody Aria*. Bringing you and your cursed ship back to Laitha will no doubt be the pinnacle of my career."

"Let's not be too hasty here, Captain." Shandor's voice spoke up from behind Antoine, his voice carrying a commanding edge that was completely new to Antoine. Turning slightly, Antoine saw Shandor slowly reaching up to his neck, pulling out a medallion strung on a chain. It looked like some kind of seal, and Shandor was holding it forward for Hildebard to see.

Captain Hildebard took a step forward, squinting at the medallion before he let out a dismissive snort. He turned away, taking several steps. "That means nothing now. I have higher orders, direct from the Archduchess herself."

Shandor snorted slightly, lowering his hands. "I see, you're one of hers. Her puppets. Then there is no use attempting to dissuade you." There was something in Shandor's voice as he spoke, but Antoine didn't have the faculties or mind to decipher what it was.

Silence hung thick in the air, until suddenly there came an echoing bang up one of the speaking tubes. It was followed quickly by another, and then another, four in total ringing out. When it was over, Antoine felt himself being pulled back roughly. Shandor's hand fisted in his hair, holding his head back, and pressing a knife against his throat. "Stay back, all of you. I would hate to see what having to explain how you killed the hostage would do to your career." Shandor spat the words out, slowly backing the both of them away from the armed sailors.

"You won't get to see what it would do to my career, you'll be dead," Hildebard spat, eyes blazing. Yet he held the men back, causing Antoine to gratefully realize that he wasn't quite ready to sacrifice Antoine to bring the *Aria*'s crew in.

"I'm sorry about this, but it's the only way." Shandor's words were soft, little more than a breath against Antoine's ear. Carefully Antoine tried to look around, noting that they were by the wheel now. His main focus was Rivas, who looked both frustrated and hurt by the recent turn of events. Antoine wanted to tell Rivas it would be all right, that obviously Shandor had a plan of some kind, but the knife was pressed too firmly against his skin for him to even move. Behind him, he felt Shandor shift, lifting a foot and setting it on something and pushing. There came a long, sharp grinding noise, followed by a loud click. After that came just one command. "Now!"

The *Aria* shuddered beneath their feet, throwing everyone off balance. Shandor let go of Antoine, throwing him onto the ground and grabbing onto the wheel to keep his feet under him. The shudder was followed immediately by a loud staccato popping sound from on deck. Antoine managed to lift his head up enough to see each of the balloons released from the clamp that had tethered it to the deck. More shudders shook the aero, accompanied by sharp grinding noises, almost as if parts of the ship were moving.

"Control transfer completed, auxiliary controls live and active." Shiv'ren's voice echoed up the tube, answering the question of where the elf had been. "Coal feed increased and engines at full strength." The *Aria* gave a final shudder before lurching forward, heedless of the fact that the aeronaught was still tethered to it.

Everyone had been thrown off balance by the sudden movement of the aero. By the time Antoine managed to regain his feet, the air pirates had already recovered and proceeded to retaliate. Three of the sailors were already lying dead on the floor, one nearly cut in half from the large machete Sawbones was wielding. Antoine decided it would be in his best interest to stay on the ground for the time being. The last thing he wanted to do was get caught in the crossfire.

It was chaos, both in the wheelhouse and outside of it. The pirates had begun their counterattack in earnest. Yi appeared back on deck, throwing small bombs at the sailors— evidently she had not fallen to her death earlier. Through it all, there was the sensation of the ship moving at a fast clip. Antoine was surprised that the smaller aero could generate so much speed while dragging a larger craft. The admiration faded when he saw that Shiv'ren was flying the aero straight into the jagged peaks of the Shark's Jaws.

"I'm going to thread the needle, Shan." Shiv'ren's voice echoed up through the speaking tube. It sounded cold and hollow to Antoine, instantly filling him with dread. He looked over at Shandor, whose face had hardened at the news and immediately searched the area for something. He quickly moved out of the wheelhouse, onto the deck and into the thick of the fighting.

Antoine glanced around, trying to find Rivas in the midst of the mayhem. Most of the fighting had left the wheelhouse now, the sailors having been killed or injured so greatly they could no longer fight. Hildebard had retreated out onto the open deck and most of the pirates had moved on to other areas as well. Rivas, though, hadn't been able to leave because of his leg. Thus he was stuck standing by the doorway, taking shots with a revolver whenever he could.

Antoine ran over to Rivas, scrambling over the debris on the deck. He glanced out at the chaos, growing dizzy as he tried to follow the fighting. He watched as Rivas aimed his pistol, firing at a navy sailor. He let out a curse of frustration as the shot went wide, turning away to reload his pistol.

"Let me help," Antoine said, grabbing the pistol to reload it. This at least he could do, something other than lying around. He hoped it would help to ease some of the frustration that he could feel coming off Rivas like a wave. It didn't matter to him that he was aiding his kidnappers instead of his rescuers.

Rivas didn't respond. He simply released the pistol and grabbed a fallen rifle. Antoine focused on reloading the pistol as quick as he could. He'd just finished reloading and was handing the revolver back when he heard a scuffing noise from the back of the wheelhouse. Turning to look over his shoulder, Antoine caught sight of Ciel getting to his feet, slowly limping over toward them.

Antoine let out a sigh of relief at the thought of someone else being with them, someone who could better support Rivas as he fought. He opened his mouth to speak when suddenly a shot rang out. The bullet impacted the wall scant inches from his head. Slowly Antoine turned around, wide frightened eyes focusing on the pirate.

"Dammit. Ship shakin' so much I can't aim." Ciel's voice was cold and tight, the hand that held the gun shaking. "Don't worry, though, I won't miss this time. I promise."

Rivas spun around, firing the pistol rapidly, each bullet hitting Ciel. Ciel fell to the ground, his eyes glassy and blank. The sight of Ciel falling back as the life drained from him, that was not something Antoine would ever forget.

"Betraying bastard," Rivas ground out, collapsing back against the wall. "He was trying to kill you." He spat the words out, green eyes flashing with anger. "Wish I could kill him again for that."

Antoine blinked in surprise, heat flashing through him. He leaned over and kissed Rivas long and hard, pulling back only when there was no more breath. "I love you." He whispered the words gently, stroking the long scar on Rivas's cheek. "I want you to know that."

Rivas blinked, smiling in return. "And I you, ever since that first time I saw you."

CHAPTER THIRTY-FOUR

"DECIDE, HILDEBARD!" Shandor's voice cracked out, louder than a gunshot. Silence fell over the ship. "At this very moment, we are heading right into the heart of the Shark's Jaws. I have men ready to slit the lines connecting our aeros at my command. I know we can make it through without harm. I sincerely doubt your ship is as maneuverable." Shandor's voice was hard. "Decide, Hildebard! Because soon it will be too late!"

Peeking around the doorway, Antoine saw Shandor standing in the middle of the deck with Captain Hildebard. Both men had weapons drawn and aimed at the other. Shandor was completely calm in his manner while the young navy captain seemed angry and anxious. He kept looking around as the scenery flew by, jagged peaks growing ever larger, like it would soon eat them completely.

There was a long, tense moment when no one moved; then slowly Hildebard lowered his gun before tossing it down. It seemed to be a sign to everyone because all of the remaining navy sailors threw down their weapons as well. Immediately two pirates appeared, holding guns on the navy captain while the rest of the pirates rounded up the sailors. Shandor nodded, turning and walking quickly into the wheelhouse.

He strode over to the speaking tube, calling down, "V'ren, Bank! Bank now!"

The *Bloody Aria* gave another lurch, turning quickly and climbing. One jagged peak passed extremely close to the side before fading into the distance. The speed noticeably decreased as the ships slowly leveled out.

"Cruising point reached, will continue on a… north, northwest heading for the moment." Shiv'ren's voice echoed up from the engine room. "Take care of business up there."

Shandor turned away from the speaking tubes, his mismatched eyes sweeping over the room. He took in all of the details, stopping to rest on Ciel's corpse for a second before moving on. "Come on, Rivas, you need to come out while we end this."

Rivas nodded, even as his face settled into a scowl. Slowly the injured captain straightened up, gripping onto the crutch to support his broken leg. Antoine held himself back from trying to help Rivas even though part of him desperately wanted to reach out. From the set of the larger man's shoulders, Antoine knew his help would not be appreciated.

"Stay here, Antoine, until we've finished our new negotiations. I'll have someone come and stand guard." The words were cold and impartial, but those green eyes that had so enchanted Antoine were alive with some kind of emotion Antoine was afraid to decipher. So he stayed back as requested, hovering in the doorway.

He was left to watch as the three men negotiated heatedly in the middle of the deck. Antoine didn't know the precise words, but it was obvious who was in the better bargaining position now. Hildebard's gambit had failed, so now he was having to bargain with men he disliked and considered grossly inferior to himself. Yet negotiate he did, because he had been given no choice in the matter.

As the negotiations went on, Li and several other pirates entered the wheelhouse. They moved the injured and dead out to clear the way. Li went over to the wheel, speaking down into the tube. There was a small shudder through the ship, followed by Li pulling the lever back up. Once that was done, he placed his hands on the wheel and began to steer the aero.

Antoine knew a bargain had finally been struck when Rivas and Hildebard shook hands. With that, Antoine knew he would be going back to Laitha with the navy captain. As Rivas limped back over to him, Antoine's stomach twisted sickeningly. Putting on the strongest face he could come up with, Antoine stepped forward to meet him.

"I release you here, to the care of Captain Hildebard. You will be returned to your family and your father as promised." Rivas said the words loudly, but his entire focus was on Antoine. Carefully he reached into the pocket of his jacket, pulling out an envelope and handing it over. "For you, when you have reached the city." Those words were whispered, meant only for Antoine's ears.

Antoine gave a quick nod, slipping the letter into his pocket. He was afraid to look up at Rivas because then the tears he was struggling to hide would become obvious. As he started walking toward Captain Hildebard, a flash of gold caught his eye. Turning, he saw Shiv'ren standing in the doorway, having come up from the engine room. Their eyes caught for a minute, and Shiv'ren brought a hand up in a farewell salute. Antoine inclined his head slightly before turning away. He hurried after Captain Hildebard, knowing he couldn't afford to linger any longer.

Once they were on the *Diomede*, the connecting cables between the two ships were cut. The *Aria* pulled away quickly, speeding back toward the Shark's Jaws, disappearing into a thick cloudbank. Antoine stayed on deck, watching until it had completely disappeared from sight.

"Follow me, Mr. Suvalese. We'll get you settled in the guest quarters." A young man had come up beside Antoine, bowing politely to him. Glancing at the rank on his collar, Antoine put him down as a lieutenant.

He followed the young lieutenant into the depths of the ship, letting himself be led to a large reasonably comfortably appointed room. After stepping inside the door was shut, and Antoine heard the sound of a lock being turned. A small smile twisted his lips. Here he seemed more of a prisoner than on the pirate ship.

Antoine spent the rest of the trip back to Laitha in that cabin. He didn't try to leave, nor was he really allowed to either. Meals were brought, better meals than he'd had in a while, yet it was still hard to adjust. The days alone gave him a chance to try to figure out how he was going to go back to being the person he had been before.

When the ship sailed back into Laitha, Antoine was greeted at the aeroport by his parents. His mother swiftly broke down into tears at the sight of him, but his father was less demonstrative. They bundled him up into a carriage and quickly whisked him up through the terraces to their home. Once back home, he spotted his brother in the side parlor. Antoine nodded to him, and he thought a flash of surprise crossed Nigel's face. Antoine decided to think about it at a later time, when everything seemed more real to him.

He put up with the fussing for as long as he could, knowing it was more for his family's sake than for his. Eventually, though, it became too suffocating, and the overwhelming concern felt like it was going to choke him. With great difficulty, Antoine managed to excuse himself to go to his room.

Once there, he turned up the gaslights, taking in his room. It was pristine, exactly as he had left it. The space felt both familiar and alien at the same time. In a way, it mirrored how Antoine felt himself. He hadn't changed on the outside, but on the inside he felt completely alien to this world.

Antoine pulled off his jacket, carefully extracting the letter Rivas had given him. He set it gently on the table by his bed before changing out of the clothes he had been given. Sitting there, completely naked, Antoine felt more at ease than he had in the fine clothes he had been wearing.

He picked up the letter, staring at it for a long minute, tracing fingers over where his name was written. The writing was bold and self-assured, everything he had come to associate with Rivas. It sent a stab of grief and longing through Antoine so intense that he felt almost sick. The fact that he most likely would never get to see Rivas again made him feel like there was a giant hole in his chest and his life. It was several minutes before Antoine got himself under control enough to open the letter. Unfolding the letter and bringing himself to read it took even longer.

> *Dearest Antoine,*
>
> *I suppose by the time you read this you'll be back in Laitha with your family and your normal life. I've often wondered what kind of lasting impact your time with me will have. I know that I may not have told you, or made it properly clear, but my heart is full of a*

great love for you. Strangely it's easier to write it out than it is to say it out loud.

I wanted to show you a wider world, to open your eyes to the truths that might have been hidden from you, that you might have been innocently unaware of. My hope was that it will be a positive change for you, that it will lead to greater changes. I hope that those will also be positive.

I have seen so much of you come alive over these days we have been together. It has been like watching spring blossom into vibrancy after the cold harshness of winter. I fear the parting from you, even as I know it must come.

I will miss you greatly, and a part of my vanity hopes that you will miss me too. Having been with you these past couple of weeks, the idea of being separated makes me sick at heart. I hope and wish that it might be the same for you.

I think, once we are parted, I will begin to look for a way to return to you. Air pirates have short lives as a general rule, but I find I have always enjoyed breaking rules. I will find a way to break this one too.

Yours,
Rivas the Ramshot

Antoine read the letter half a dozen times, caught between an urge to cry and a desire to laugh at what had been written. Best of all, he felt the tight knot of tension in his stomach ease. It might not be much in the end, but it was enough. Enough to ease the uncomfortable emptiness he had felt since he had left the *Bloody Aria*. Antoine folded the letter and slipped it under his pillow. As he stretched out, the bed felt softer and warmer than anything he had slept in for weeks, but it was infinitely lonelier. Under his pillow, though, Antoine had a letter and a spark of hope that gave him the imperative to keep going.

CHAPTER THIRTY-FIVE

RIVAS SAT in his cabin, a glass of strong rum cradled in one hand as he looked out of the port window. He was waiting, and he knew exactly what he was waiting for. It was a conversation several days in the making. Probably even longer than that if he were honest. It had been put off several times, but now there was no stopping it.

When the door opened, he took a hearty drink, closing his eyes and feeling the burn of the alcohol going down his throat. When he finished, Rivas opened his eyes, turning to meet Shandor's gaze. Another beat of silence hung between them, stretching past the point of ease and sanity until finally Rivas snapped.

"Just say it already, Shandor, and get it over with," Rivas snapped, setting aside his mug.

"Never one for a good buildup, were you?" Shandor said, moving over to the chair opposite Rivas. Shandor rubbed his face, pushing his wild, dark hair back. "You can't stay an air pirate anymore, Rivas. I know you're aware of it, but the handover was the final straw. The crew isn't going to see you as being in command anymore. They'll call for a vote after we get back from Tyrnium. On top of that, your injury is going to be too much. Even after you finish recovering, you're going to have a limp for the rest of your life. Hardly a good thing of a man on an aero."

Rivas snorted, leaning back in his chair. "I'm aware of that, Shandor. I've been aware of it for a while. Especially after everything that happened." Rivas sighed. "I always kind of thought this might be the last raid I ever went on as part of the *Aria*."

Shandor let out a slow breath, some of the tenseness bleeding out of his body now. He sat up straighter, leaning forward with his elbows on his knees. "I was afraid I was going to have to convince you of it. I'm glad it didn't come to that."

"I'm not that far gone, Shandor. I know I lost a lot of the crew's respect after that fight. You were the real hero of that encounter." Rivas smirked a bit, leaning back against his chair and taking another drink. "I have to admit, I was surprised by the entire chain of events."

Shandor shrugged slightly. "I told you, I had a bad feeling about it. I simply took extra precautions to ensure we would all make it out." Shandor tapped out a slow beat on the arm of the chair. "What are you going to do? Are you going to find him?"

Rivas let out a long sigh, looking out the porthole. "I'm going to miss being in the sky, you know. I think that's going to be the hardest part to let go of. I think, though, for him, I could let it all go gladly. I had an escape plan in place. I just have to go and take it over. Always have an escape plan in place. I've always wondered what yours is," he said, looking at his old friend.

Shandor let out a small snort. "I don't have one, don't need it. Got bigger plans that I'm cooking up, and they don't have room for a safety net."

"I know. I just hope you don't cook yourself while you're doing it." Rivas leaned forward, holding out his hand. "If you ever have need of me, you know you will always have my support, my friend."

"Thank you for that." Shandor clasped his hand, shaking it firmly. "I fear that someday I may have to take you up on it. And may you have good luck and fair winds on your own journey."

IT HAD been over two months since Antoine had been returned home from the *Bloody Aria* to Laitha. It still felt strange to be back, and the world around him sometimes seemed more like a dream than reality. He had returned to his everyday life, helping his father with the business and attending the endless social functions his mother wished him to go to.

After his encounter with the air pirates, Antoine found himself something of a darling on the social scene of Laitha's upper echelons. Every time he attended a party or a ball, he was called on to retell the tales of his imprisonment and ransom. It made him uncomfortable to be the center of so much attention, and undeserved attention as well. He tried to tell them there wasn't much to the story—not that anyone truly believed him. The stories seemed to be embellished by people, so each story they asked him to tell was more fantastical than the last.

As a result of this, Antoine had taken to avoiding the outings as much as possible. He would only go when his mother absolutely insisted. He was aware this was causing concern for his parents, but he couldn't bring himself to care. It was simply too trying for Antoine to go out and be asked to talk, to interact with people who were only looking for some new piece of gossip to float amongst themselves. On top of that, he saw more now when he went to these events than he wanted to. He saw the winged elves that were paraded around, and he wondered how many were like Shiv'ren or Lesh'ra. The fact that there was nothing Antoine could do to help was greatly upsetting.

He felt much more at home when he was in the office with his father. There, he had a purpose and a way to utilize all the things he had seen. Antoine began work to improve upon the things that Rivas had pointed out to him. To start with, he started researching the condition of the mines and the miners. He also began looking into other ways to mine the coal and minerals his family had built their fortune upon.

Antoine was studying just such a thing when his father returned to the house. The sound of two voices coming from the entry hall surprised Antoine enough to make him look up from his reading. One he recognized as his father, and the other voice made Antoine's heart trip over itself. Carefully setting aside his papers, Antoine stood up, nervously wiping his hands on his breeches as his father walked in.

"Antoine! My son, I'm glad I was able to find you. I made a new acquaintance today and I have invited him over to join us for supper. He's a merchant who recently shifted his trade here from farther east." Antoine smiled at his father's excitement as he spoke.

Growing the business was his father's passion, and someone with an eastern connection would be considered a great opportunity.

"By all means, bring him in, Father. I look forward to meeting with him," Antoine said, glad his voice held steady, conveying little of the anxiety he felt.

A tall man stepped into the study behind Adrian. He was dressed in a fine suit, the fit impeccably showing off the muscles that bulged under the garment. The man had a finely crafted cane in one hand, which he leaned on as he stood there. Antoine slowly looked up, taking in the shining blond hair pulled back in an orderly queue that revealed a ruggedly handsome face containing piercing green eyes and a long jagged scar over his jaw.

"Travis Chandler, allow me to introduce my younger son, Antoine. Antoine, this is Mr. Travis Chandler, recently moved to Laitha," Adrian said, making the formal introductions.

"It's a pleasure to meet you, Antoine," he said, stepping forward and holding out his hand.

Antoine swallowed, unable to stop the small smile that crossed his face. "A pleasure to meet you as well," he said, taking the hand and shaking it.

"Excellent! Now that the introductions are done, I must go and inform my wife that you will be staying for dinner, Mr. Chandler. I leave you in the hands of my son. Please keep our guest entertained while I speak with your mother, Antoine."

"Of course, Father," Antoine mumbled, not daring to take his eyes off the man in front of him until the door closed. Then he couldn't hold himself back any longer. "Rivas? Is it… really you?"

Antoine had a brief glimpse of a smirk before he was pulled against the other man's chest. Instead of speaking, he leaned down to press a hard kiss to Antoine's lips. When he finally pulled back, Antoine was weak in the knees, gripping Rivas's arms to stay upright.

"I do hope that answers your question, Antoine. Because unfortunately there isn't quite enough time for me to prove it any other way."

The words made Antoine shiver and grin to himself. He felt like he was floating, excitement thrumming through his veins like quicksilver. On top of all of this was just one question. "Travis?"

There came a low laugh, a calloused hand gently smoothing over Antoine's hair. "It's my name, my true name. When I first left Black Rocks and joined up with the pirate crew, the captain couldn't say my name properly. He kept saying it as Rivas, instead of Travis, and the name stuck with me. I'm glad for it now as it provides me with a new identity now that my other life is over."

Antoine swallowed slightly at that. "Over? You're no longer captain of the… the aero?" Antoine didn't want to name the ship, in case one of the servants happened to be listening. The last thing he wanted was to see Rivas—Travis, he reminded himself—taken away to be hung for his crimes.

"No, after the unfortunate accident that caused my injury, I was no longer able to conduct my business onboard an aero," he said, tapping his cane lightly on the floor. "So now I have moved my shipping business here, in the hopes of building it further. As well as perhaps finding something for myself here of a more… personal nature."

Antoine let out a chuckle, leaning up and kissing Travis lightly. "I do think I can be of some assistance with that."

As a child LORRAINE ULRICH had lots of imaginary friends. As she grew older, they started to tell her stories about themselves that she tried to write down. High school led to the discovery of yaoi and M/M relationships, a love that has never left. It quickly found a home in her writing and has gotten very comfortable there.

Currently she lives in St. Louis, Missouri, surrounded by family, friends (both real and imaginary), and far, far too many cats.

She can be reached at lorraine.ulrich0@gmail.com or her blog, http://www.lorraineulrich.wordpress.com.

Mechanical Magic

By Lorraine Ulrich

When Aster Genisov, a creator of mechanical novelties, is asked to help a wounded elf, his special talents and painful past could be the key to the elf's survival.

Y'rean was born to touch the sky, but when his wings are destroyed by a cruel master, not even the life he begins to build with Aster can assuage his despair. Aster has the means to help him—it's written in his gypsy blood—but is love enough for Aster to face his past and embrace his talent for mechanical magic?

http://www.dreamspinnerpress.com

BOOTS FOR THE GENTLEMAN

AUGUST LI AND EON DE BEAUMONT

http://www.dreamspinnerpress.com

www.ingramcontent.com/pod-product-compliance
Lightning Source LLC
Chambersburg PA
CBHW070114260626
47160CB00004B/1457